EVERYDAY MONSTERS

THE ANIMUS CHRONICLES BOOK I

Copyright © 2020 Christian Francis.
All Rights Reserved.

The characters and events in this book are fictitious. Any similarity to real persons, living or dead is coincidental and not intended by the author.

No part of this book may be reproduced in any form or by any electronic or mechanical means, including information storage and retrieval systems, without permission in writing from the publisher, except by a reviewer who may quote brief passages in a review.

ECHO ON
PUBLISHING

ISBN - 978-1-916582-09-5

Always for you, Vicky...
xxx

CONTENTS

Title Page   i

Dedication   1

PART I
THE ORDER

The Offer	7
Mikko and The Moogle	21
Getting a Head	31
The Sicarian	45
The Changeling	75

PART II
BETRAYAL AND PUNISHMENT

Deacon and the Darkness	83
Meares and the End	88
The Sicarian and the Fury	101
Jaden and the Escape	111
The Capture of the Dead	116
Barbara's Bad Day	119

PART III
A VIOLENT PATH

A Head for Interrogation	123
The Stitching of Deacon Sorbic	135
Destroy, Discover, Rebuild	145
A Timely Demise and a Leap of Faith	161

PART IV
THE FACE OF GOD

The Leech	173
A New Regime	183
Lifting The Veil of Death	194
And They All Fell Down	212

PART V
RED SANDS

The Banishment	229
The Fields of Blood	236
Brought Before The Creator	241
In The Presence of Divinity	251
The Lie of Life and Death	254

PART VI
THE SINS OF THE FATHER

The Eternal Darkness	261
The Anger of The Insects	277
And With The Flies Came Death	295
The Coming Dawn	307

PART I

THE ORDER

THE OFFER

"Sorry for what?" replied Jaden, as he stared at Deacon, the man sitting in the chair opposite him. At this moment, Jaden thought to himself that this day could not get much weirder. First a cryptic letter stuffed under his front door, then meeting the man sitting before him along with his undead henchman, now a barrage of vagaries which added to nothing more than an annoyance.

The undead henchman in question, Johnstone, was a large imposing figure who now stood behind Deacon. As far as Jaden could tell, he was a butler of sorts. A kind of willing slave. But he supposed that was what Golems were supposed to be.

Jaden was about to stand up and leave. Sure, he had the advance payment in his pocket, but he was not that broke that he needed to take this job. They all seemed pleasant enough – they were just not telling him everything. And that was what he hated more than most other things.

This Golem leaned in over Deacon's shoulder and grabbed his head in both of his immense and powerful hands. Before another breath could be taken in, or another word uttered,

Johnstone, with a quick and brutal motion, yanked Deacon's head to the side with an insurmountable force, snapping the bones inside his neck with a loud crack. Deacon – still alive at this moment looked to Jaden in agony – but remained silent as he seemed to endure this onslaught with no scream. Blood simply erupted over his lips and dripped down his clean pale shirt.

"What the fuck are you doing?!" Jaden asked Johnstone in horror, as he watched this attack, shock pinning him to his place.

With another show of immense strength, the Golem wrenched Deacon's head around the other way, turning it back as hard as he could. More bones cracked apart with deep and terrifying snaps as Deacon's life was now fluttering away. The skin on his neck tore itself open as Johnstone yanked the head back round yet again, which sent a torrent of blood outwards and onto the wooden floorboards below.

With a large grunt, he then tore Deacon's head clean off from its body. Blood arced into the air from its exposed neck hole, which splashed, nearly landing on Jaden's feet. Deacon's body, now devoid of its recent life, slumped downwards, sliding off from his chair – pushing it backwards as he hit the floor – sending it with speed to the far side of the room, its wheels leaving a trail of blood behind them.

A deep silence filled the room, as Jaden stood wide-eyed.

"Here you go," Johnstone said quietly to Jaden, motioning to the severed head held in his hands, "one head to deliver, as requested." This head – still dripping blood – was lifeless apart from the mouth, which slightly twitched, letting droplets of crimson spill over its bluing lips and into its ginger beard.

Jaden stared back blankly. He remembered the letter. It did say he was to deliver a head. He did agree to the job. He did already have the pay in his pocket. He guessed, with his employer now dead, it might be too late to renege on the deal.

The Golem held the head up higher, insistently.

Of course this would happen to Jaden.

Of course this was the kind of job he was hired for.

Typical.

Fucking Typical.

JADEN HAD NO OTHER NAME, well during his existence he had – but that surname had rotted away within the labyrinth of his brain, many, many years ago – as did quite a few of his other memories.

His employment was as a collector. He hated the term bounty hunter – and his job was moderately simple. Each month he met with, and was given work from, his handler. A man – at least he thought it was a man. It might have been many men who for some reason said they were the same person. Or maybe not a man at all? This was because his handler was a Changeling. Each time they met, it wore a different face. Assigned to a different gender. Met in a different location. Yet the handler always spoke in the same nasally American voice, and called himself by the same name. His handler was the person who gave him his work. All on behalf of The Order. People that Jaden really wanted as little to do with as possible, but as he had no direct contact with them, he justified any paycheck he could get.

The job he had just accepted was unlike any others he had taken recently and was off the books. His handler knew nothing about it. Not that he would mind. But taking extra work seemed a bit shady to Jaden.

He had received a letter from Deacon Sorbic that morning – he was just like Jaden in that he was blessed and cursed in equal measure with being undead. How could he not at least say yes to meeting? It wasn't every day you met another one like you. Though the letter was vague on the pay amount, when they met, Deacon had offered to pay double the going rate, for just collecting and delivering a book and an apparently human head – a simple, though gruesome messenger job. One Jaden would not normally take, but today he was pleased to accept – especially as it was cash up front. And besides, this man seemed to know quite a lot about him. The fact he knew where he lived was impressive enough.

He was a very solitary person, and kept well and truly off-grid. He didn't take jobs like this often. Not for want of trying – but people rarely were able to find him to offer him anything, outside of his handler. This was the first to do so... well, ever.

"How did you find where I lived?" Jaden had asked as he sat in the bar, looking at Deacon – his potential employer.

"Honestly? It was kinda fortuitous. I needed someone, and your name fell into my lap through an old acquaintance. From the Wolf, Gobolt. He said you had an in with the Order. And I need some things anonymously delivered to them."

Jaden had never heard that name before – Gobolt – well, not in the brain he had left. This could have been a name that the rot in his brain had stolen away. Not wanting to appear weak in the face of someone offering work, he just nodded. "Ah," he said as he took a sip of the lukewarm piss this bar tried to call "craft beer", "Gobolt. Okay."

This bar sat on the industrial, rundown side of the town. Normally an area people would not visit for pleasure, but this bar was not really for normal people. It was a place that asked no questions. A place where people like Jaden could go without fear of attack or persecution.

After agreeing to the messenger job – something that would net him five thousand bucks for a day's work – they shook on it, then went back to Deacon's apartment to collect the deliverables.

BEING ONE OF THE UNDEAD, Jaden's skin was hued with a light green tint and his face had a few highlighted signs of decay. His hair was all but gone, as was the skin on his scalp, which exposed his skull in multiple places. The only real hair on his head was a large gray and black-colored beard, as well as some remnants of eyebrows not taken away by the decay. He was the literal walking dead, but, unlike Deacon, he looked more the part. He was what you would expect if you were to think of what a partially rotten zombie would look like. His skin was tight and receding, his bulging eyes were a milky white. Fresh rot had started to eat away at his cheeks. He looked like he might have been in his late 30s. But, with these kinds of inhuman beings, age was irrelevant and not applicable, as their life was as long as they could make it without starving or being lynched.

Deacon, now in his home, sat on a chair opposite Jaden at the mahogany desk. His creased flannel suit looked worse for wear. His skin, though, was almost perfect, and he looked like a healthy human. His undead features were not obvious to anyone who might glance at him, but if anyone looked close, they would see the small signs of death. A slight hue to his skin. A faint smell of decay hiding underneath the aftershave.

"I don't want to be rude... but human skin?" Jaden asked, holding up the large book in his hands, glancing at Deacon, who returned his gaze with a smile.

"Unfortunately, it's too long a story to go into. Don't worry though, the cover and each sheet inside was donated." Deacon spoke with a knowing smirk on his face. A smirk that Jaden knew better than to ask any more questions of.

Without a word, Jaden's attention turned back to the book. He slowly opened its thick front cover and he stared in silence as he confirmed what he had just been informed of. Why he hadn't noticed it before was a mystery to him, but these pages were indeed, sheets of dried human skin. Each page had been inked with collections of strange symbols which he didn't recognize. On closer inspection of these pages, he even could see hair follicles attached to parts of each page, a small detail which somehow turned his dead stomach.

Jaden stared at the inked symbols which had been scrawled on the page front of him.

"You don't speak Catigeux, I take it?" Deacon said, the smirk still on his face. "It's the written language of the Elders of the Order."

"It is?" Jaden asked whilst turning the pages, looking at more of the symbols. By now he was just being polite. He didn't want to look at this book anymore. He just wanted to go and deliver it. But he had to be here to collect the head. Whichever head that was. Then again this was all starting to seem less worth it by the minute.

Jaden looked at his new employer, seemingly in his 60s – with his slicked back red hair, his face hung heavy with thick wrinkles. A man who had many ghosts and lived through many hardships. His voice a gruff bastardized mix of many accents and he looked like he could have possibly been a brawler once upon a time, but now – now he wore suits and played the businessman part to a T. He had a nice city apartment to live in. He was rich enough to get someone else to do his dirty work. Though maybe not on easy street, he was at least on comfortable living avenue.

Behind Deacon stood his assistant, the grim-faced Johnstone. This huge man was a Golem, or so Deacon had told Jaden. Having never met or seen a Golem before, Jaden didn't know if they were even possible. But being undead, he couldn't claim to know every kind of monster in existence.

An hour earlier, in the bar downtown, Deacon had explained to Jaden, "Golems aren't monstrous clay beasts. That's only bullshit legend they try to force feed on you."

"They?" asked Jaden, taking a sip of his beer. Not enjoying a drop of it.

"They. Those in power. The higher-ups. The daddies of the galaxy. The grand fucking poohbahs."

"You mean the Order?"

"Especially them. Anyway, I digress... Golems are more akin to that Frankenstein's monster. They're made up of many bits. Patchwork bodies of deceased human anatomy. Not to mention, they all have a piece of the "master's" own brain. The actual fucking brain, given to these creatures. And cos of this, they're tethered to their master... and before you ask, yes... I took out some of my own gray matter to give him."

Jaden could feel the stare of Johnstone boring into him. He stared from his seat at the table. He had no drink in front of him – instead he just kept refilling Deacon's wine glass each time he took a couple of sips – which was very often. He was drinking heavily, he said, to mask the past, and to prepare for the future.

"Okay... so how long do they... you know..." Jaden asked.

"Live? Well, they can go as long as you take care of them. They're like cars. They need some care now and then. But mainly they run okay. Their bodies have reverted to this living status, so their hearts beat, lungs breathe, dicks get hard, yet they're not built to withstand multiple lifetimes – so... there's some upkeep on the master's end of things. They may need new limbs. Sometimes just a small stitch-up. They can suffer from rot if a limb or two are rejected. In the end though, they can't rejuvenate by ingesting living flesh like our kind can – so more provisions gotta be made to gain access to the parts needed. Arms, legs etc. Friends in low places and such, if you know what I mean. Or just good old-fashioned grave robbery would need to become the order of the day." Jaden listened as Deacon took another large swig of his wine.

"So, despite not understanding any of this... you in? Simple delivery," he continued.

Jaden, of course, said yes, though he had more regrets with each passing moment. He wondered how and why this man would have given some of his own brain to a Golem – but he knew better than to ask such a question of a man offering him money.

"Okay. When do I get the head?"

"I guess now's better than ever, don't you?" Deacon replied. "Let's go to my place."

JOHNSTONE STOOD BEHIND DEACON. He was dressed in a finely pressed black suit, his face showing little emotion – which was de rigueur for this Golem. Though being large and stitched together and blank expression-wise, he still looked somehow friendly.

"Are you ready?" Deacon asked his Golem as he glanced back – Johnstone simply nodded in reply. Deacon then looked forward. "Sorry about this... it will seem a bit mad. But trust me. You wouldn't believe any of it if I told you."

Jaden took a breath in and stood up from the desk, weighing up whether to leave empty-handed or not. But he tried his best to force himself to go along with this job. He picked up the journal, and pushed it into a leather satchel which hung around his waist. Its weight and bulk made it a tight squeeze, but a lucky fit.

Everyday Monsters

"I'll explain more later I'm sure, but for now... sorry for the mess," Deacon said with a half-smile.

"Sorry for what?" was all Jaden managed to say before Johnstone leaned in and grabbed Deacon's head in his hands.

Then the head was ripped from his shoulders.

THE GOLEM STOOD there offering him Deacon's head.

Jaden stared back. Not knowing what he was to do.

"He's the dead body you have to take. Well, not the whole body," the Golem said.

"Yeah..." Jaden managed to say as he stared at the head in the Golem's hands. "I get that." This head whose eyes were half-open – now stared its final stare straight at him.

"You got something to carry him in?" the Golem asked, with his booming accent making the proceedings sound like more of a creepy transaction.

Jaden reached into his pocket and pulled out an empty plastic carrier bag, which he seemed to always have with him in case, but until today had never needed to use it. He then opened it in front of this Golem. He didn't even think twice when the Golem asked. Though in his line of business, he had seen a lot worse than this – a great many times. He wasn't shocked to the level of incapacitation, just surprised that anyone would do this willingly. All he could think was that this was part of an elaborate suicide, maybe he was just a disgruntled employee with a stupid plan. At least at the end of the day, Jaden was getting paid. No matter the stupidity the plan seemed to conceived with.

Johnstone dropped the bleeding head inside the carrier bag. As it fell, the blood smeared down the inside of its clear plastic, sliding its way down, leaving a red trail on the inside.

"Thank you. Nice doing business with you," Johnstone said.

Jaden glanced down at the headless, bleeding body on the floor. "I'm not taking this too, am I?"

"I'll deal with this – you just got the head. All they need," replied the deep voice. "You remember, you have to remember the name to tell them, okay?"

Jaden looked at his hand, where he had the name crudely scrawled on to it, then read it out. "Arius?".

Johnstone nodded, as Jaden then put his hand in the plastic bag carrying Deacon's head and tore off a small chunk of blood-soaked flesh from the wound on its neck. Pulling it out, he glanced this morsel it for a second, then raised it to his forehead – toward Johnstone – and saluted to him with it. He then popped the chunk of flesh into his mouth and turned to leave. Deacon would understand. He was undead as well after all. Ah, well.. he had been... Now he was just... dead.

Johnstone grimaced. "Bloody zombies," he muttered to himself as he looked away. "No goddam respect."

"Have a good day," Jaden said as he walked out of the room, forcing some joviality into his voice. As he swallowed the flesh, the rot on his face started to subside and disappear. His skin slightly loosened from its previous receding tightness. What he just ate had had a modicum of regenerative effect. The small amount of flesh he took from Deacon's head was fixing him. But this regeneration was only slight. From the condition he was in, he would need a lot more flesh to reverse the severe level of necrosis he was currently suffering. Eating a small morsel of a dead man's flesh was barely even a plaster for this large wound.

The door closed as he exited, leaving Johnstone alone in the apartment.

"Disgusting zombies," he uttered again, as he turned his

attention to the body on the floor – the body of his old master. Blood still pumped from the neck wound onto the highly polished wooden floorboards.

He then sighed and walked over to the other side of the room, to where a small double-bladed hand axe lay against the sideboard.

Picking up this weapon – one that had obviously been used many times in the past – he spun it in his hand. This was his old friend. His trusted weapon of choice. One he had used on occasions when the situation required it – and from his life with Deacon, that was required many times. This small axe had previously sent many people the same way as his master.

He slowly walked over to the body, which was now finishing its inevitable self-exsanguination, then gripped the axe in his favored hand. He glanced down and with a slight smile cracking his previously blank expression, he mumbled down to the corpse, "I hope you know what you're doing, boss."

He then swung with brutal force, as the axe flew down and collided with the Deacon's body. Ripping into the small of its back.

OUTSIDE THE APARTMENT, a bloodcurdling scream emanated throughout the streets.

JOHNSTONE TURNED and glanced out of the apartment window, down onto the street below. There, Jaden stood – aghast – with an empty plastic bag in his hand – the decapitated head of Deacon laying on the asphalt in front of him. Looking up at him. Screaming at him. Somehow alive and screaming directly at him.

. . .

Johnstone saw this and smiled. It was no surprise. He turned back, then with a second movement, swung the axe down again, into the Deacon's body

"...The fuck?!" Jaden exclaimed in confusion at Deacon's head – now on its side on the asphalt, still screaming in pain. Still staring at him. His cries were louder from Johnstone's second swing. His eyes locked with Jaden's as it was happening, filling with tears from the agony.

Jaden stared in confusion at this screaming head for what seemed like an eternity, though it was in actuality only a few fleeting moments. This head was – somehow – still alive. This head, which was staring right at him. How was it screaming? But with common sense flooding over his panic, he remembered How was not a question to ask when you, yourself, were a walking impossibility. The major issue he had was that zombies would not normally survive this kind of damage. Ever. This was against everything he knew about his kind – which to be fair was not that exhaustive. But he knew decapitation was one way to kill any of the undead – so How was a question with too many unknown elements to it. Why was it screaming was more apt.

Dropping the confusion, and trying to not falter in that moment, Jaden hurried over to the head, grabbed it by its hair and lifted it off of the street. Without looking any longer at its pained and screaming expression, he pushed Deacon back into the blood-stained plastic bag, the continuous screams were barely being muffled by its thin lining. He had seen weirder, he told himself. Not many things, but this was just another payday. So, no matter how weird, he just had to get

Everyday Monsters

through it. Just another payday, he kept repeating to himself, just another payday.

He turned and looked up at the apartment to where he could see the silhouette of Johnstone – swinging the axe downwards. Jaden could presume that he was cutting up the body and that this must be, somehow, the cause of the screams. He silently prayed for the Golem to stop what he was doing. But no. His prayer fell on deaf ears. THWACK went Johnstone's axe. AARRGHHHH went the head in the bag.

"Shut up!!!" Jaden hissed down to the bag. He then looked around, to ensure that no one was watching. This head would not be quiet and this was a normal human neighborhood.

Reaching into his pocket with one hand, he pulled out the keys to his 1958 Plymouth Fury. He hurriedly walked over the street to where it had been parked up. Time could not hurry up enough for him. He wanted this over. He wanted this easy job done with. But he was too far in it now to forget it.

He quickly unlocked the car door – the head screamed louder from the bag as another axe swung into his separated body in the apartment above.

Reaching his limit for that moment, Jaden slammed the bag onto the body of the car – trying to shut the screams up for a second – anything to stop its noise. But instead of silence, it merely broke up the screams with a yelp, before it continued with more screaming. Jaden then threw the bag into the passenger side of the car. As it hit the passenger seat, it yelped again.

Jaden then turned and for one last time glanced up to the apartment. He saw the silhouette of Johnstone continuing to dismember the body. Each swing of the axe adding more to the cacophony now in his car.

Jaden got into his vehicle as fast as he could, slamming the door behind him. But before he could start the engine to begin his getaway – he noticed something in his peripheral vision. Something out of the passenger side window. Something standing looking right back at him. Something he hadn't noticed before. A small boy sat on a BMX bike. A boy staring in utter horror. Frozen in his place. How long was he there for? Did he see it all? Jaden felt awful for this child. Despite being a rotting being, he still had more empathy than most humans had. And here it was in overdrive.

This boy had just seen a zombie wrestling a severed, screaming head into a plastic bag, then both of them getting into a classic muscle car. None of it could really be explained to someone so young with any degree of kindness or understanding, nor would Jaden even try. It was just best to leave before it got worse.

Turning the car engine on, Jaden could only offer a kindly smile toward the boy as he slowly pulled the car away.

LATER THAT DAY, the boy would tell his mother what he saw. In turn, she would tell his father, who would beat the boy with a belt. As a child who regularly told tall tales, his parents had had enough of the fictions – and this latest one was just too far.

MIKKO AND THE MOOGLE

With a rancid fleshy squelch, the obese foot of the Moogle hit the floor, the sound itself being enough to make anyone's stomach turn. There were a few sounds which could evoke such an emotional reaction: the cries of children, the whimper of an animal, nails down a blackboard. But few could elicit the vomiting reaction that this beast's footstep could – with its grotesque liquidy thud.

His skin was a pale mottled yellow and in a perpetually sweaty state. The smell from his every pore was something that defied traditional description. Imagine a skunk and a mound of rotting flesh had a baby – then that baby had a sweat gland infection – then it was sat in the sun, having never bathed once in its life. If you could imagine this, then you were part of the way to understanding the depth of the stench caused by this monster.

From head to foot, the Moogle was covered in a multitude of inch-long skin tags, all of which were differing shades of brown and yellow from lifelong infections. They nearly covered his entire body, but stopped when they got to the huge belly, two inches or so from a strange wound which ran vertically from his fat hidden groin to his sagging and sporadically hairy gullet. More than a scar, it looked like a closed mouth, which ever-so-slightly opened with each step he took, showing nothing except the darkness that existed within it.

Standing at over 7-foot-tall, the Moogle's stature would impose enough, but his obesity was what anyone would notice first. Virtually all parts of him extruded some sort of dripping balloon – made of greasy stretch-marked skin covering a large portion of blubber, hanging over from wherever it could. Hanging to almost breaking point. His feet would normally have been size 14, but each toe was so engorged with fat, with large areas of fatty skin that dripped off of them, that there were no shoes made which he could wear. This was the case all over his body, there were no clothes that would fit him. Sure, a sheet, or a Muumuu would be able to hide his offensive features, but the Moogle was not an individual who would ever consider masking his body. He was born like that. He would stay like that. Like an animal. Clothing was not an option. It was not even a consideration, whether they existed to fit him or not.

His head was of a relatively normal size, but due to the sheer girth of the rest of him, it looked small and out of proportion. The same went for his genitals – of normal size, but despite him being naked, they were rarely seen, as the fat engulfed any out of proportion sex he had.

His face was masked by the long lank, greasy brown hair which dripped down and stuck to his shoulders, chest and back. Almost reaching his hidden groin, his hair had a sheen, as if it had been bathed in motor oil on a regular basis. Underneath this slicked hair was his face. Monstrous in itself.

Containing multiple rows of rotting teeth in a gargantuan maw which could open to almost 180 degrees.

His eyes were unseen. Sunken so far back, that all that could be viewed were the shadows in which they hid, deep within their sockets. As for a nose, this did not exist. There was just a blank space where you would traditionally assume a nose to be.

There were some aspects of humanity about him, but he was definitely not human. Not by a long shot.

As to why he was called the Moogle? That was the cause of much debate. Even the Moogle didn't know why. It was widely presumed to be a word which had changed over the ages from its original incarnation. Much like words change with Chinese Whispers, as this name did not exist before, in any form, within any language. No one, though, could agree as to what the original word it derived from was. Stranger still, it was a name which was so far removed from being an adequate descriptor of this grotesquery, that it only added to the mystery.

All of his kind shared the same moniker, they had no individual names. They were all called The Moogle. This never got to be an issue, as no more than one of them could live in the same place. They had to be isolated as far apart as possible. You would never get two Moogles in one community. If they met, they would mate upon sight, then rip each other to pieces. The one left alive would be impregnated with a baby which would gestate for years before bursting out of the body of its carrier – destroying their parent in an instant. So, instead, they existed far away from each other and more often than not lived as a human companion. Not with a slave and master relationship, as some people may expect, but more akin to telepathically linked twins, where one was the brains and one was the brawn. The

Moogle could attune to its chosen human's mind and effectively be like a third hand to that person. Fourth or fifth hand for some people, depending on how many hands they natively had.

The Moogle was chaos – plain and simple.

IN AN OLD, dark, stone-lined room, the Moogle grotesquely ambled across to where three male figures were on their knees, bound and gagged. They each looked up at him with consummate terror – and this was the exact emotion which the Moogle wanted from them.

These bound prisoners were not totally human either. Each showcased differing abnormality. One had a beak (which now was cracked and broken from excessive torture), another had a multitude of working eyes all over its body (and all exhibited extreme fear in each one of them), and the third was a scaly creature with its eyes on either side of its head, two slits for a nose, and a tiny round mouth at the front. These beings had endured a wealth of torture against them, which had now abated – yet this was their end, the final painful stop on their life journey.

Behind the Moogle, at an old desk, sat Mikko. A man who looked in his 80s. If you were to guess, you would say he was an accountant or banker. A very powerful one at that. And you would be correct – in a way. Dressed in his tailored, expensive black suit, Mikko sat in his old wooden chair, holding the handset of on an old rotary phone up to his ear. He was in mid-conversation.

He looked in thought, as he listened to the person at the other end of the call. His small round glasses perched at the tip of his large nose.

He took out a small napkin from his breast pocket and dabbed the appearing sweat beads from his bald cranium. A cranium which had a small smattering of white hair, slicked back as tight as he could get it. But this was a losing battle between him and age. His last few wisps of hair were his last vestiges of youth. A youth he longed to return to, and thought this hair style would make him look a bit younger. He thought that shaving these last few strands would signal defeat to the ravages of time.

Mikko was a stern but approachable man. Intelligent yet arrogant along with it. Exactly how you would expect him to be, by the way he looked.

In front of him, on his desk, sat a very large – and very old – ledger. An accountancy ledger of sorts. But instead of numbers, there were multiple strange symbols handwritten into all of the columns.

"Arius?" he said into the telephone in his authoritative tone, as his expression turned to surprise. His accent reflected his Scandinavian origin. "Are you sure you have that name correct? 150% sure? Hmm."

Mikko thought to himself. Getting the head of one of the banished would be quite a useful symbol to deter any possible future unrest.

THE MOOGLE at the other end of the room looked over his shoulder towards Mikko, who noticed him back. He raised a finger to the Moogle, to motion for him to wait, as he continued to talk into the receiver.

"Of course. Can you let me know the time and place of the meeting?" he asked in a matter of fact, but in a mildly panicked tone. "We definitely want this." He listened to the voice on the phone but was getting anxious to end the call. "Yes. You have the authorization, of course."

. . .

Meanwhile, the Moogle had turned back, and looked down at the three bound men. His breathing was like that of a hunting wolf. Low growls under loud slow breaths. The men were attempting to scream at this menace, but their gags prohibited any loud or distinct sound and the chains in which they were bound, held them firmly in place on the floor.

Mikko listened to the voice on the other end of the call and slowly his expression turned wide-eyed.

"Excuse me? A journal made of...? Can you please repeat that?"

He listened to what the person on the other end of the phone was saying – his face fell.

"Yes." His expression turned to shock as much as it could possibly facially, yet he would never allow this shock to be heard in his voice. "Please proceed with utmost urgency... Tell him we will pay whatever he asks. Yes, whatever. We need that book."

Mikko was ready to end the call, he had no intention of elongating a conversation with small talk. He wanted facts only. Small talk was the dialogue of a weak mind – that was why he was so thankful for the Moogle. No words were ever uttered by him. Just thoughts. But now, he HAD to end this call. Not for any personal preference, but this could be a game changer.

"May the light lead you," Mikko said as a goodbye.

Replacing the handset, he picked up a pen from his desk – an old fountain pen – and started to note down a collection of symbols into one of the columns in the ledger.

He was order, plain and simple.

And at this moment, a very surprised, and very worried order.

"They found Arius," he called out to the Moogle as he wrote the symbols down. In the column next to his writing, more symbols were forming of their own accord. Forming on the page as if written by an invisible hand. Words direct from the Elders.

"Yes. I'm telling them now," he said aloud to the Moogle, who was looking back at him. "He may have a forbidden text, it seems."

After hearing his silent reply, Mikko's eyebrow raised slightly as he shrugged. "Yes. I'm afraid it is human skin, allegedly," he answered. Then listening to the next silent reply from the Moogle, Mikko's hidden feeling of dread was reinforced as to how serious this all could be. "I hope none of this is true," Mikko spoke softly, as the Moogle looked back to his prisoners.

Mikko then put the pen down, read the symbols which were appearing in his book – a message from the other realm –to which his eyes widened as he read each one. Quickly standing up, he adjusted his suit. He was not looking forward to the next part of what he had to do. He took a deep breath in, turned and exited the room in a hurry.

THE MOOGLE WAS NOW FOCUSED back towards the tied-up prisoners at his feet. Moving in front of the first prisoner, his skin tags started vibrating in unison, as if they were all excited and trembling with anticipation. His mouth started to open slowly, displaying the multiple rows of jagged, rotting teeth – opening further and further to an unnatural degree.

He expelled a loud guttural growl, as the large wound on his belly started to open up. On the inside of the opening stomach walls sat dozens of sharp small serrated teeth. This "mouth" was opening as well as the one on his face. No internal organs could be seen in his chest – all there was, was a cavernous dark void of bone, teeth and flesh.

As his stomach-mouth opened, thick oozing viscous fluid strung between both sides of its "lips". This would be one of the last things that these prisoners would see.

As Mikko walked down a stone hallway in another part of the building, he could sense the Moogle's pleasure at what he was about to do, and he was pleased his friend had some joy in his work, especially with what was about to happen.

Moving at surprising speed, the Moogle advanced on the first bound man, and engulfed the top half of the man's torso within his opened stomach-mouth. As soon as the man was inside it, its chest-lips slammed shut with extreme force, crunching through this victim's body with a terrifying strength. Blood and gore spewed out of the sides of this now-closed mouth. Like a dinosaur chomping on goat, its mouth sliced through the blood, sinew and bone with incredible and violent ease.

As it was happening, the Moogle's actual mouth remained open wide, making a terrifying high-pitched roar. A roar so high that it sounded almost mechanical in nature. The other prisoners sat screaming into their gags in a maximum state of panic and fear, knowing this was going to come to them in turn.

Little did they know, or be able to see, the Moogle was so excited by all of this that deep within his fat folds, sat his engorged and erect penis. Aroused at the violence in front of him.

As he pulled back from the first victim, with a quick

yanking movement, the remnants of the body crumpled to the floor in a bloody and horrific mush.

The Moogle's closed chest started to undulate as if it were swallowing a meal – but where this "food" went was a question that could never be answered by anyone living. As only those who went on the "journey" would know, a journey he forced upon all of his prisoners.

He took a step to the side, a step now in front of his second prisoner. They tried to back away from the oncoming attack, but the bindings kept them in their intended place, stuck in the very place that they were about to die in – keeping them prepared for the punishment that was about to be meted out upon them. The Moogle had no hesitation in carrying out this same punishment again and again. Over and over. He was more than happy to do this to anyone that he was authorized to do it to.

You would presume that these men's crimes must have been so heinous that no other option for punishment was applicable – but no. Their crimes, like their lives, were insignificant. Doubting the word of the Order was something you could not do. Not just talking against the Order, but questioning any part of it, innocent in intention or not. These men were not rebels. They were not staging a coup. Nor making any wishes to leave. They just asked the simple question "why". They had questioned what was asked of them and because of this, their lives – like their crimes – would be soon forgotten. They knew the laws they had to abide by, but they all had broken them, anyway – claiming a greater good, of wanting to protect the Order from a potential mistake – which was their last mistake.

It may seem strange, but this was not in human normality,

and like every other culture, this one existed with its own system of beliefs and rules. These rules demanded unwavering support and obedience – under pain of death. No exceptions. And it had been like that since the dawn of time. The followers should know better than to ask anything, beyond what they were told.

GETTING A HEAD

The height of summer was unforgiving on the best of days, but for someone like Jaden, it was worse than it was for most others. Heat dehydrated living flesh, and water re-hydrated. But for dead flesh, the heat sped up the decay and shrank the skin at an excessive rate – water had no effect on this process. The consumption of human flesh and blood reversed most of the effects of decay for Jaden and his kind. The more that was eaten, the more the rot was reversed into submission. The difficulty they had was the frequency in which it had to be consumed. To appear alive and well, a zombie must have eaten approximately a pound of living flesh each and every day. By living flesh, it needed to be any flesh where the blood still flowed within it, without congealing of any sort. Of course, this meant they would have little choice but to kill for food. This was not just humans – any mammal would do for those with a less lax morality.

Delving into the science of this would be futile. Nothing about this process remotely resembled science as humanity had known it. When science would develop more over the future centuries, it would discover that science and magic were indeed parts of the same coin – the missing component of this scientific equation would be found to be actual words themselves, whether written or spoken. Words had more of an effect than science had previously assumed or measured. Used in certain ways, words could kill. Literally. The old adage would then be changed to, "Sticks and stones may break my bones, but names can rip me asunder."

Words in their proper use could bend time and space to their will. But in the respect of zombies, the written word had caused this race of people to exist from nowhere. Some might call it a curse, some might call it a saving grace, but after a millennium of evolution, any curse should simply be another word for life. You had what you were given, and you lived with it. Anything you had, cursed or not, would become your normality – so whether a curse or a blessing; it was just – for Jaden at least – normal everyday existence.

Yet, he was never alive to begin with. Not that he remembered anyway, and if he didn't remember, then it did not happen. Simple. To him, he was born as he existed now; as a dead man. But of course, he was not actually dead. His body just suffered from many of the same conditions as any cadaver did.

Death for a zombie was far more difficult than death for a human – who could die from an unlimited amount of consequences. Zombies were more or less unable to die in any traditional sense – as long as they fed, and in doing so, kept the approaching decay far away from their brains, as well as making sure their brains and brain stems stayed in one piece. In the past, he had come close to meeting his death by starvation. He had been deprived of food for 9 long months. His brain had become mostly decayed. Yet, at the moment before the last cell blackened, withered and died, he managed to find sustenance, then as it hit his belly, his body soon began the process of reverting – yet at that late stage, though rebuilt in substance, his brain had been deprived of many memories being rebuilt. Memories of his family, his surname, the long, long past. The different names he once had. His voyages to the hells below. All were gone forever. And he was fine with that. If it's not remembered how could it matter? You could never miss what you cannot know.

Jaden hated killing humans, so instead he normally chose to feed on rats and vermin. Of course, when faced with a human who was had just died, with their final pumps of blood spilling throughout their body, he wouldn't say no. He had morals, but he was not a fool. Which was the reason that his body was in a perpetual state of half-decay. He ate enough to stop the progress, but not enough to reverse it. He knew he was playing Russian Roulette with his own existence, but had been abstaining long enough to be convinced he could do this forever – keeping death at an arm's length away. So, when holding the newly severed head of Deacon Sorbic, he could not help but taste.

Disease didn't affect them. No carotid arteries. No beating heart. No cancer. It is why he was so shocked at Deacon's current state. He should not have been alive. He had his head cut off. Spinal cord severed. How was it even possible? Was he a new kind of zombie? An evolution? He wanted the answers, but was on a deadline.

After calling his handler, telling him of Arius and the journal of human skin, he just had to wait for a callback, to be told if they wanted what he had.

He just focused on the positive, as much as he could. But with all the issues in his life, at this exact moment, his biggest issue was the sun currently baking him from above.

The uncovered ball of sky fire was being exceptionally brutal to him today. He had air-con in his old car, but it was a refurbished unit that he had installed himself, it was too cheap to make much of a difference so was decidedly ineffective in its sole purpose.

From where he was, he could see the head of Deacon Sorbic resting on the dashboard in his car, less than a hundred feet away. His severed head faced outwards, with a face-full of blistering heat. The expression on his somehow alive face was one of insurmountable pain. If he had opened the sliding door to the phone booth which he currently stood in, Jaden would have heard the muffled screams that Deacon was emitting – a sound he was glad to be away from. Yet, he himself was in just as much torment within the glass phone box. He had been there a while now. After making the call to his handler, he had to wait, the heat beating down. Both being sat in a car with broken air-con, being deafened and annoyed by a pissed off and in-pain severed head, as well as waiting in a phone booth under the beating heat were torturous options.

He could feel this heat advancing the shrinking of the skin on his face. His eyelids were slowly tightening, and it was becoming harder and harder for him to blink. He needed to do something. He needed to do something very soon.

When the call-back came, he was relieved it meant he could soon escape the phone booth. Even better that he was told that they wanted what he had. They even seemed very anxious to have it. They offered to pay him handsomely to meet up the next day. They gave him a location and a time. He did, though, forget to ask how handsome the handsome reward would be. He was too relieved that they did exactly what Deacon had told him they would do.

Replacing the handset, he opened the sliding booth door and stepped out onto the dead grass leading from it to the road. This booth was adjacent to a small family-run garage. One which Jaden had passed many times over the last few years, but a place he had never once seen open. There were always different cars in differing states of disrepair outside, resting on the embankment beside the garage itself, but the garage doors were never open. The store never had its lights on. How they earned money, whilst not being open to the public was surprising – almost as surprising as there being a working phone booth anywhere in the country anymore. Especially one this far outside of the city. A sign of the times, he mused, or a front for criminals.

Walking over to his car, he could hear Deacon's screams getting louder and louder the closer he got. It was a good thing that no one else was around to hear this. For someone who knew the truth about the world, knew about the existence of zombies, and other "anomalies", seeing a screaming decapitated head was shocking enough. But, imagine if someone normal saw it. Would Jaden be arrested for a crime? Would he be charged as the latest sick murderer? How could they explain his undead condition, or the head's? This was a question that had surprisingly been answered many times before – not with Jaden, but with others like him, who were not traditionally human, or human at all.

If a being was found to have anything that could not be explained by modern society, they were said to be terrorists. Or on drugs, new scary terrorist drugs. But why was that person eating that other person's face? Scary drugs! Terrorist drugs! That doesn't make sense. Don't do drugs kids! Vote Republican! Vote Democrat! Vote for whomever is paying for this message! Don't think! Just vote!

Humanity had a terrifying way of normalizing the abnormal with scare tactics – and that would never change, no matter what era you existed in. They always found something different to blame the world's latest real and invented horrors on – whether heavy metal, paganism, drugs or sex, black/yellow/brown people, immigrants, the Irish, men with mustaches, liberals... There were always scapegoats. It was why Jaden was terrified of humans in general.

WALKING BACK TOWARDS HIS CAR, he slowed his pace. Up in front, between him and his car, sat a pile of tires. Five black truck tires placed haphazardly on top of one another. Sitting atop of these rings of rubber was a small red squirrel. A squirrel who paid no mind to the screams from the car, or the walking dead man coming towards him. It just focused on the acorn in its tiny hands.

Jaden wondered if he could catch it. He was in need of some renewal after all.

Drinking blood alone worked as well as eating the flesh itself, it was just more palatable to have the blood imbibed with something substantial to go with it. On its own, the taste was not pleasant, even to those beings who regularly fed on it. In the case of squirrels, you had no choice but to drink and not eat. As drinking from it was all you could really do. It was like licking the bowl at the end of a meal. You get little for your efforts, but a taste in your mouth for that effort.

Now sitting in the driver's seat of his Plymouth Fury, Jaden wound down the window of the car. The head of the squirrel was now torn off and still in Jaden's mouth, the body held upright in his other hand, ensuring that little blood could be spilled. He then spat the freshly torn head onto the ground outside.

The screams in the car had ceased. The head was now on the passenger seat. Eyes closed. Jaden had no idea, but presumed the head might finally be dead. He hoped not, as he didn't want to update his handler after informing them that it was alive, but he at least had been paid his initial payment from this man already. So either way, they might not want the head anymore, but they wanted the book, so that was something.

He turned his attention back to the squirrel's body, held upright in his hand. It was relatively easy to catch them when you were, for all intents and purposes, dead. Squirrels were not as twitchy around his kind as they were with humans. They ignored the dead no matter how fast they moved. So, walking up to them and grabbing them was pretty simple – it was the killing of them that was the most difficult task. And was something that Jaden would never get used to, no matter how many decades he had been doing it for. He would, though, ensure – as best he could – that there was no suffering to whatever animal or human he needed to end the life of. This made him a rarity amongst his kind, most did not care at all about the torment of others.

The poor little critter had no idea what happened. It had an acorn. It loved that acorn. Then darkness. It was not uncommon for Jaden, in the dark of his bedroom, to cry about the lives he took. But being dead, there were no tears. Just dry hyperventilating. He may have appeared tough on the outside, but it was in reality merely a façade to get by within an unforgiving world.

He was, behind his bravado, behind him being a blood and flesh-eating being – a lost soul. He had never fit into wherever he was. He was perpetually filled with a constant emptiness, an emptiness he couldn't quite quantify. An emptiness he filled with anything he could. Well, not sex or drugs. Drugs had no effect as he had no beating heart, and sex – well he could not get aroused – but alcohol though... Psychosomatic as it was, he got drunk even though it was an impossibility. It was like his body refused to allow him to have no vices and gave him one which in no way could actually affect him. He just made it affect him by believing with all his might that it could.

Picking up the squirrel's body, he tipped it upside down, dripping its lifeblood out of its neck wound and into his open mouth below.

As the small droplets hit, it felt like tiny bolts of electricity piercing through him. Deacon's blood was not alive, so when Jaden ate the bit of flesh from his head, it only did a tiny amount of rejuvenation, and felt like nothing. It stopped the progress for a second, but a second only. Maybe it would heal a fraction of rot. But it would only take a few minutes to reverse. And as it left, you were back to where you were before. Here, with this squirrel's blood, it was a whole different ballgame. Jaden twitched with each droplet that fell into his mouth. The rot in his face dissipating with each hit at a staggering velocity. As it was only a small amount that he could drink from this small creature, it would only heal a few areas of decay for a day or two. He would need 20 squirrels a day to reverse all of the rot and decay he had over his body. This tiny amount quelled the effects of the burning sun for now, and he was back to the condition that he was in when he had first met Deacon.

Out of the corner of his eye, he could see something. Deacon was not dead, he was alive, and looking straight at him from the passenger seat. His mouth was agape, opening and closing slightly, tongue slightly sticking out. A low, dry exhalation could be heard from his mouth. Animalistic, and what you would expect a starving zombie to sound like.

Jaden returned his glance with a smile.

"Still with us, eh?" he said, noticing that this head was looking at the dead animal in his hands, not at him. "I guess you ain't so special after all, eh? Want some blood like the rest of us?" he continued, moving the squirrel towards Deacon. As it got closer to him, Deacon's eyes widened, his tongue aimed in the animal's direction. He wanted – no – NEEDED that blood. His breathing became heavier the closer the squirrel got to him.

"If I give you some... How about you tell me about what the fuck is going on?" Jaden asked. Deacon suddenly looked at Jaden instead of the squirrel. "Ah, got your attention, I see... I'll give you all the blood in this little guy. IF... If you tell me why the Order want you and that book."

Deacon stared back, his animalistic hunger abating for a moment. He smirked slightly at what was said to him, then glanced urgently at the squirrel. Then back at Jaden again.

"I think we're in agreement here... But to be sure – three blinks for yes," Jaden said.

Deacon without hesitation complied. BLINK, BLINK, BLINK.

Jaden smiled. "Glad we could come to an understanding, aren't you?"

Lifting up the squirrel's body, and turning Deacon's head face-up, he started to pour the remaining blood into his mouth. Like a feral animal, Deacon gnashed his teeth at every drop of blood that hit inside his mouth, each gnash making it obvious he wanted the small carcass nearer to him. Jaden complied by moving the squirrel lower, slowly lower as each moment crept past. As more blood dropped into Deacon's mouth, the decay on him, with surprising speed, started to subside over his face, and his movements got faster and faster.

When the small critter's body was right next to his lips, Deacon opened wide and lunged – as best as a severed head could – grabbing the end of its small body in his mouth and started sucking the rest of the blood out, direct from the source. Jaden looked sickened at what he was doing. It was not something he would dream of. He always hoped that he would never have that much of a ferocious appetite. He hoped that he never became the beast he knew all of his kind could easily give themselves over to. Deacon, though, was sucking and starting to chew on the end of this tiny body. His eyes rolled back into the top of his eyelids, and he made a gurgling and aggressively sexual, moaning noise. Eat bite, each suck was ecstasy for him – each drop of blood gave him more life and more pleasure.

Jaden didn't want to be part of this, but held up the squirrel, anyway. He had a deal after all, he wanted to know what was happening that badly.

With the rest of his life being void of meaning, Jaden obsessed over riddles and puzzles – anything that kept his mind busy – keeping the thoughts far away from the extreme feeling of being lost. The feeling that he would invariably get caught up in, if her were left alone with only his own life to ponder for too long. So, he grasped onto any other topic he could to keep those thoughts at bay. This situation to him, was a puzzle that he needed to obsess over. He wanted the answers. He didn't need satisfactory answers which made logical sense, just answers enough to no longer be an unknown. Anything to keep the silence out.

All of a sudden, Deacon's eyes closed and did not immediately re-open. The sucking on the tiny animal had now ceased, and Deacon's mouth had relaxed his grip on its body. As though he had expired permanently back in his apartment, he seemed to be very much dead – but Jaden knew better; he hoped he knew better. Part of him thought that this might all be an hallucination, that he was in fact deluding himself that the head was alive, part of his rotting brain turning on him. But the other part was less paranoid than that loud voice in his head. He knew full well that when a zombie had had a substantial feed, their body would then switch off while the brain began to repair itself. Like a reboot of a computer. It was a needed event to fix the problems. It would normally take anywhere between an hour and a day to complete, but this was a head on its own, with no body to fix. Who knew what timeframe this would work on? He could guess shorter, as the head was smaller to fix, but as it was just a head, it could also take longer. Nothing was certain. Jaden hoped to all the Gods and Goddesses that it was before the handover was due to happen, so he could get some answers to these questions.

He believed Gods did not exist, but he sure loved the expression of hoping to them. He was a person who regularly exclaimed "Jesus Christ!", "Sweet Lord", and other such religion-based exclamations. Maybe it was a contradiction to hope to other people's fiction. But he liked to believe that no one would mind – this was where his mind took him on occasion. He was there, with a switched-off head, wondering why he would hope anything to a God that wasn't his, or that was even real to begin with.

As he pondered the inconsequential, he started the car. The roar of muscle engines used to excite him when he was a couple of decades younger. He loved it when he heard loud thunderous rumbles erupt from the metal organs of an automobile, just as he loved the sounds of steam trains. Any mechanical roaring as these machines pumped fuel around their systems, alive and yelling to the world about it... But now... he just found it all loud. Too loud. Right now, he wished he could just trade it in for a hybrid, or something else quiet.

He drove his car away from the garage and onto the road, continuing his journey to meet his handler.

The sun, meanwhile, was starting to set and gave the sky a tranquil orange hue. This countryside was beautiful, lush and vibrant. Fields stretched out in yellows and oranges, broken up by the greens of the trees. At this time of the evening, the insects darted throughout the fields, feeding on the barley, wheat or whatever the farmer needed to plant that year. If the car wasn't making so much of a racket, he could probably have heard the vast array of nature at play. Instead, he just drove on, glanced out of the window, and looked at the beauty with little more than a passing thought.

On the passenger seat, Deacon's head was now twitching slightly, as if in the throes of an active dream. Dreaming was a side-effect of any major rejuvenation, and one Jaden was glad he usually avoided by not having enough blood or flesh to cause such unconsciousness. For these were never nice dreams. They were nightmares flooding Deacon's mind. Horrific and vile. Images and feelings of death, destruction and mutilation. As if the victim that you had just feasted on, now passed over some final curse upon you. A curse saying fuck you, thanks for killing me, you asshole!

The last time Jaden fed enough to endure this had been close to a decade ago. Even that long ago, he still remembered that nightmare in every detail. In this awful dream, he had to feed on himself due to starvation. Isolated in the wilderness, with no other forms of food at hand, he slowly cut pieces from his own flesh off and chewed on them in order to sustain himself. A temporary solution to keep himself alive, as it was only dead flesh. But in this dream, he ate too much and then his body shut down. What followed was a dream within the dream he was having – as his body repaired itself in reality – and this second level of his dreaming was a barrage of monstrous imagery. Visions of his own body being ripped apart and reconstituted. Over and Over. Every animal or person he had ever fed on, were now getting their revenge. Maybe it was just him that didn't like these nightmares, but as he never normally dreamed, but it was not something that he could get used to. Sure, he slept on occasion, but the expression "sleep like the dead" meant something real. It directly referred to him and his kind. Whenever they slept, they did not move, live, dream or think. It was only when they woke that they started to breathe again – not for any physical reason – just a subconscious ritual, as they could survive holding their breath indefinitely. And as Deacon proved, with a surprise to Jaden, some – it seemed – did not need lungs to survive, or a body for that matter, or come to think of it, a stomach to take in and digest the blood he'd just drunk. Where the hell did the blood go? It never fell out onto the seat through his open throat tract, he thought to himself. His mind doing what his mind always did – never staying on one thought long enough to finish it.

His thoughts then focused on that question. The curiosity of this quandary intriguing him.

Quickly pulling his car to the side of the empty road, he turned, reached over to Deacon's head and picked it up in his hands. Looking at the seat that this head had rested on, noticing there were no blood stains on the seat's upholstery – nothing apart from the few droplets which fell from the squirrel and had missed Deacon's mouth. He turned the head over and examined its neck hole. He put one finger in the throat tract, then quickly pulled it out, checking for traces of the blood and flesh Deacon had just imbibed as if he were checking the oil in a car. But there was nothing; only the bloody remnants from the decapitation itself. Turning this head towards him and with the same finger, he wiped some blood from off of Deacon's mouth and looked at it. It was so strange. Not something he was scared at, but was intrigued by. If this was a new power, he wanted it too. Anything to stave off the final death. He didn't want that. Ever.

Placing the head back on the passenger seat, he set off in

his car again. So many questions flooded his mind, but as he had experienced already, Deacon was not very forthcoming with information. Maybe that would be different now, with this bargain they'd struck? He did say before he died that he would tell him more later. Maybe he was banished? That wouldn't explain why the Order wanted him. For a book of symbols though? Why would they care? What do they get to gain with it, and who the fuck was Arius? And how did Deacon survive all of this? A head which could magically eat and scream? If Jaden got even one of these questions answered, he would be happy.

The many hours of driving which lay ahead would need be split up with a night's sleep. Jaden had chosen to avoid any motels in favor of sleeping in his car. Not for security reasons, but he had no inclination to spend his hard-earned money whilst on any job. His car was comfortable enough and he would only need to sleep for a few hours. Then tomorrow, it would be over. Deacon and his journal would be handed over. He would get his extra payment, and he would go onto the next job, and it would all start all over again.

THE SICARIAN

Vix woke up with a jolt as the rusty metal door to the cramped cell opened with a predictable metallic screech. Standing only 5-foot-tall with long brown hair – brown hair in which her previous blonde streaks had now grown out and dulled to their original color. Her skin had lost all of its previous rosiness and her clothes were filthy and frayed. Sleeping on this concrete floor, trapped in this cell and kept warm by only a small dirty blanket was the least hellish thing Vix would endure this year.

These were not traditional prison cells as such. They were not meant to lock people away to punish a sin or protect a society. Instead their intent was to keep the occupants safe and under a close and methodical watch as they proved their faith. Yet like a prison, these inhabitants were kept in solitary confinement, trapped alone except for an hour a day where they were free to walk around a courtyard; still alone, though – except for an assigned guard.

Inhabitants were allowed two buckets, one for waste – along with a pile of torn newspaper – and one daily bucket of water. This was for washing or drinking, whatever was deemed necessary. But only one bucket, never more. If it tipped over, you had no refills, and this wasn't spring water either. It was, at Vix's best guess, tap water from plumbing which had not been upgraded or maintained for a century. It tasted stale and metallic, but at least it kept you alive.

This was, despite all the harsh conditions, a holy place. A place where the inhabitants were those people who were deemed worthy. This was not a place of punishment, but a place of reward and prayer. The doors had no locks and everyone who stayed here in the filthy cells, did so voluntarily. They could leave at any time should they so choose – though no one ever had.

This place belonged to the Order, and those who chose to be here did so either out of devotion to the Elders, or for the oldest God of all – wealth. Each and every person in these cubes of dirt and rust, stinking of their own waste, were all ready and willing to do whatever was asked of them.

In exchange for whatever they wished for, a chosen follower would give a year of their lives to the Order. Like military service, but instead they lived in the inhospitable confinement until such time as they might be needed, never knowing what they would be expected to do – if anything at all. And here, in Amorfield, they stayed willingly, waiting for the day they'd be given their duty.

The prison style of accommodation was intentional. Vix knew when she signed up what this place was. It was meant to purify and simplify you for what was needed of you. The Order demanded dedication and devotion – monitoring the inhabitants 24/7 whilst they stayed here, testing their devotion though persecution. Most people would have been here only a few months before being given an assignment handed down by the Elders. Vix, though, was on month 11. She knew it was either because they were keeping her for something big, or because she was simply not worthy. Either way, she just had to wait out the next month and then she could return home, the year done. Part of her wished for the latter, that she was unworthy – then she could while away the rest of the owed time in her own filth and could guarantee that she would walk away with her life intact. She knew the reality of those who became emissaries. First, they were notified of their eligibility, then they were offered a reward for the year's service of "becoming an emissary" as a "gift" – a nice term for a bribe for the desperate. A gift you could choose yourself. Then they were kept in Amorfield, away from the world. When the need was there from the Order, these volunteers were tasked with a job. She never knew what they could be, never knew what they were to be an emissary of, but knew one thing. She had never met anyone who had come back afterward. The persecution part of being trapped in the cell made no logical sense to her. Nothing much with the Order did. Most of what they did seemed like it was decided late at night, after a few drinks, when all other ideas had dissipated. But even though she thought this. She still willingly took part. She had to.

The money she earned from this commitment was not for her, but was intended to buy a life: the life that gave her life; her father's. A dying parent is a powerful motivation to enable something extreme – even something that may be suicidal.

But this sacrifice of dedicating her year and potentially her life to the Order was for nothing. Though she did not know it as she whiled away the days in the cell, her father, whom she paid the Order's money to – that money intended to get him the medical care he needed – had died a few weeks after she was escorted into this very cell. He had died without receiving any of the care that she had paid for. He was a week away from being transferred to the new care facility, one that could treat people who were "different".

With the Order's payment, she had bought the best private care that she could find. The best, though non-refundable under any circumstances, care. Because of this, despite her father never receiving the care – the contracts had been signed, and all transactions were final. For the year of sacrifice, for her being imprisoned and taken away from her father, from missing being able to say goodbye, she had lost all the monetary benefits she had asked for. This was a show of her luck, as she never seemed to be able to get the breaks she wanted. Here, she'd been thinking her luck had changed. A year given up for a life given? It was an easy trade. But with Vix, nothing ever came easy.

Before this, though having to live her life as something different to traditional humanity, Vix actually had nothing different or anomalous about her. Her father had married a normal human and because of this, had fathered a normal baby. He though, was a feathered man, one of a tribe called the Overseers. The ones who, in the past, looked after those humans who deified them. The Native American tribes saw them as God-like Eagle men, beings whom they considered to be the wisest of their Gods' creations. Apart from their bird-like appearance, they had an ability of being able to slow down time around them – which was why the tribes saw them as wise. When they chose to, they could slow down the world around them and analyze everything in their own time. They could be asked a question by a devotee, and could ponder it for hours, days, weeks before actually answering it, yet to the to the questioner it would seem like only a few seconds had passed. Now, they just lived normal lives in hiding. Without any tribes to honor them, they had no real purpose. So-called civilized men saw the Overseers as freaks. They had been – for the last century – vilified, hunted, lynched, maybe at best thrown into a circus freak-show to be gawked at.

Everyday Monsters

The Overseers' abilities and attributes were not passed down to Vix. She did not have a single feather on her body. For this she was glad and grateful as she never suffered the hate her Father had received. As for his power – though spectacular in its potential uses, it had its own drawbacks – as her father found out in his last moments. His life-threatening illness came upon him very quickly. Flesh-eating bacteria took him within 7 months of his diagnosis. An incredibly painful condition caught by happenstance and bad luck – a condition that affected his time-slowing ability. After the bacteria took hold and started to gnaw at him from within, his power became "switched on" permanently, locking him within his own magic. Because of this, he spent the last month of his life, not only in extreme pain, but experiencing it at such a slow pace that in his mind he was in this hell of torment for centuries. Stuck with a searing agony, as he watched the world around him move at a snail's pace, stuck within a terrible torment that his ability had wrought.

The staff at Amorfield knew of what happened to her father, about his untimely death and kept it intentionally from her – not out of any malevolence, or a show of their power – but because it had nothing to do with their business at hand. And this was the Order through and through, concerned with their interests only; anything else was inconsequential and of no importance. Her knowing that her reason for being there had died was deemed a counterproductive piece of information in relation to her purpose here.

"Here you go," the guard stated in monotone, as he brought in her re-filled bucket of water, placing it in the corner of her cell and taking away the old empty bucket. This was what she expected to happen. This was what happened every day; The metal door would screech open at the same time, like clockwork. The same guard. The same phrase. Every single day – but today was not just any day. There was no guard at the door when he was expected. No bucket in hand, full of its metallic tasting liquid. Instead, standing in the doorway, silhouetted by the light behind him, was someone else. A man aged in his 50s, balding with a terrible comb-over of brown, thin, greasy hair. A sweaty little man with a dark olive complexion. As round as he was tall, he was dressed in a light gray, creased, ill-fitting suit – which hung off him, a few sizes too big. The jacket displayed his sweat patches for all the world to see. This disheveled and sweaty man was Albert. Despite working in Amorfield for close to 40 years, he was still not used to the heat within this building, so the fact he was sweating like a tap was quite normal for him. He expected and hated it.

"Madam?" came the small and soft voice from this stout man. "I have been asked to collect you for hosting."

"Hosting?" Vix replied curiously.

"Uh... Yes. Please follow me. I will tell you more along the way."

Mikko was bathed in a blinding light. The room he stood in was nothing except for this light. No furniture or decoration, no walls, no corners. Just a bright whiteness. He stood with his eyes closed as he listened. There was a conversation happening within his mind, just as he conversed with the Moogle, he was conversing here too. That was his ability. He did not need speech to hear what people wanted to say, and this was how he preferred to converse with everyone. As he was taught by his educators: Words lie. The mind cannot. Having this power and with his faith in the Order, it made him perfect for his role as Administrator of Task. Not only the overseer of the Amorfield facility, but as one of the conduits to

Everyday Monsters

the Elders. Amorfield was one of a dozen facilities across the globe, where the holy word of the Elders was put into action by the administrators. All psychics, all devoted to the faith. Each administrator also ran the finances – not just monetary, but in all currencies. Physical, metaphysical and ethereal.

Mikko ran Amorfield like a tight ship, and one which dealt with any opposition swiftly and extremely. Those who went against the will and command of the Elders were terminated with extreme prejudice. Mikko saw no unfairness in this at all. He was unwavering in his dedication to his work. Answerable only to the Elders, he never questioned them, nor would he ever dream to. He insisted that his place in the Order guaranteed that he was incapable of rebelling against them. One could not get to his level without total and complete devotion, faith and obedience to those who were in charge (Though events in the past with previous Administrators proved this theorem not infallible).

The room of light was the place where he communed with the Elders. They spoke to his mind within this conduit room, a room which bridged their worlds. Being otherworldly, not many people could ever claim to have spoken to the Elders, and those that did – like Mikko – claimed it was a holy, purifying experience each and every time he was blessed with their presence.

The Elders had ventured many times into the world before. When the desire or need arose, they would possess a vessel to complete their work, or as they called them; emissaries. This was because their forms could not survive within this realm if they simply stepped over the threshold. Their presence though was never for something as small as a book and a severed head. They usually never concerned themselves with the actual running of the Order nor the transgressions of man. They only ever came to this realm to receive adulation in a ceremony or to gratify their own needs. Now though, there was an Elder who commanded that if the book was what they thought it could be, they would need an emissary to sequester. A soul to tether them to this world. Mikko would never wish to question, but as soon as he heard that an Elder wished to come forth – to personally collect Arius, as well as his book – he knew that it could have negative consequences. Mainly as the Elder in question, the one demanding to break forth into this world in the body of a volunteer, was The Sicarian.

"I will send her to you," Mikko said aloud as he ended the conversation. No response came as he smiled gracefully. "May your light lead us," he then uttered to himself, despite the Elders no longer being linked to him.

Albert glanced awkwardly towards Vix as they walked down a long stone hallway. Not awkward because of any fear or intimidation. It was just because he was the kind of man who had an insurmountable jealous streak. He could not understand why anyone except him would be given the kind of responsibility she was to be handed. He believed that he deserved much more than he had. As warden for the would-be emissary and chosen acolytes in Amorfield, he was second-in-command to Mikko – on a par in seniority with Mikko's enforcer, the Moogle.

From the outside, Albert hid his disdain for the world around him very well. Mikko, though disgusted at Albert's sweaty appearance, saw the truth of his jealousy as he heard his mind. Yet believed despite that, he was a consummate follower – the highest accolade Mikko believed he could bestow on anyone. He also was very much in favor of Albert's hands-on approach to the facility. Albert, though, had managed to mask some of his mind from Mikko. He managed to disguise his true hatred for the Administrator and his Monster. He had become well versed in hiding his darkest thoughts, and only showing false decoy ones. Something that if he hadn't mastered, he would not have survived in his position as long as he had done. His method for hiding his prominent thoughts was simple. He sang songs loudly in his head, then when Mikko heard these songs, he just believed that Albert was a very happy and musical person, not that the mental music blocked the vilest hatred spewing his way.

For the smaller things in the facility, Albert would normally utilize his guards to do them, but for collecting the would-bes who were to be taken toward their divine purpose? He had to do that personally. He had become accustomed to seeing the legions of unworthy swine, bestowed with Elders' purest grace. And he wanted to look them in the eyes and tell them as such. This was not a regular occurrence. Only one or two people a year from the scores in the cells would be chosen to be a host. Despite the low numbers, there were still too many whom he considered "filth" that became one with an Elder. Too many people above him.

Like with Mikko, the Order was his life. He believed in them. But also, believed that they were fallible and mistaken in their choices. He believed people like Mikko were bad for them. But, he still gave it his all. He wanted to be the first choice to carry out their will. For all those chosen above him, he wanted to ensure they knew he was better than them.

Though he would never accept the fact if told, the only reason he had never been given that opportunity he so craved, or any promotion within the order, was that as warden, he excelled more than any others would.

. . .

Mikko walked out of the room of light, rubbing his eyes. Though he was bathed in perpetual light, it was not as blinding as one would expect – him rubbing his eyes was more to adjust to the darkness of where he now stood. His pupils were almost totally contracted from the brightness he was just in, so now in this dimly lit hallway, he could barely see a thing. He waited a few moments for his eyes to focus, allowing him to reassess his surroundings.

When comfortable with the dim light around him, he then adjusted his tie and took in a deep breath. Being in the Elders' presence not only took its toll emotionally but also physically. He walked out feeling like he had just run a mile. His lungs were sore, and he felt like hyperventilating – but, he had been in their presence enough times to be able to keep these side effects under control. Others in the past had immediately vomited after leaving that room, or passed out, or even to the degree where a couple of people had died from the shock.

He glanced over to the part of the hallway where Albert now stood with Vix. She was nervous. She had just been told what would happen, and though knowing she could not back out, the acceptance of this was not easy – especially with this man's words to her as they had walked; You're a whore's filthy cunt, and a blot on the holy order of the Elders. You don't deserve this.

"Ah. Good," Mikko said looking to Vix, then turning his attention to Albert, "You may go, Albert. Thank you," he said through a thin polite smile.

Albert bowed his head in a fake reverence and turned.

"You are undeserving excrement," he said as he passed Vix on his way out. His vicious words were spoken in a soft quiet lilt, out of earshot of Mikko. His mind hid his hatred of Vix very well, as he then turned and sang an old show tune in his head, camouflaging the words he'd just spoken, and repeated in his mind, just as he hid all of his un-Godly thoughts.

Albert walked down, out of the dark hallway, through a doorway to a stairwell. As he walked up the stairs, he daydreamed of the day that would never come; the day he would stand in the light, being part of the great tapestry of the Elder's plan. The day he would be the new Administrator, or even better, as a permanent conduit.

Vix was silent. She knew better than to question anything, or to be anything except quiet around this imposing figure – for she knew what awaited her if she spoke the wrong words. She would face the enforcer, or worse still, her father would be punished for her insolence. If only she knew that her father was now out of harm's way for good.

Mikko motioned to the door to the room of light. "You are expected, my dear," he said.

Vix slowly started her walk towards where he gestured.

After hearing her hidden thoughts, Mikko proffered, "Do not worry. It's a divine duty you're undertaking. You'll be a perfect host for him. And he will in turn protect you from any harm."

Vix smiled, nodding slightly to him as she grabbed the door handle hesitantly.

As Mikko watched her walk inside, he shrugged off her silent comments about him. He had heard a lot worse. Being thought of by a someone as "creepy" was de rigueur in this facility. He recognized that he came across like that. He didn't care, though. It was inconsequential what anyone thought of him – he had important work to do, a divine purpose which he fulfilled without even a moment's hesitation.

. . .

Consciousness slowly seeped back into Vix's mind as the sounds within the room swirled, encompassing her like a cyclone. She could hear some familiar voices wash around her, but they sounded too ethereal to be real, like ghosts in the wind. As she opened her eyes, she instantly got caught up in a wave of dizziness. So much so, she had to close her eyes tight again, to try to regain any equilibrium.

The first voice she heard was Albert's. "Heart rate is... 152."

"I take it that is normal?" Mikko asked.

"I'm actually surprised it's so low, normally his presence runs hearts at the breaking point. 180 and above."

"Is it dropping?"

"Yeah," Albert replied under his breath, curious yet fascinated, "never seen that before."

"Maybe he will avoid burning out of this one as soon as he did the others?"

"Hopefully. There aren't many others left he could inhabit. Well, no one who'd be ready as soon as—" His attention quickly turned back to Vix, cutting himself off in mid-sentence. "Hold on... she's waking up."

As her eyes fluttered open again, the spinning room was slowing down. She heard voices around her again, and although the words themselves were familiar, she was not in her right mind to understand the sentence they were structured in. The spinning now slowing allowed her to begin to focus on the surrounding space. It looked like a cheap room in a roadside fleapit motel, but without the television or vibrating bed function. She looked around her and saw that standing either side of her bed were Mikko and Albert. Upon recognizing these two men, she suddenly understood that she was in the hospital ward of Amorfield, the part of the complex which was barely one step up from the cell that she had been a guest in.

Everyday Monsters

Albert leaned in and lifted up her right eyelid with his finger, checking her dilation with a small hand torch. She was powerless to complain or struggle against this. He then moved over and checked her other eye. The light blinded her for a brief second as his torch moved over and across her eyeline. On any other day, except for the want to push him away, she would have felt his touch upon her. She saw his hand come in, and her eyelid be opened fully – but felt nothing physically. Her mind was too unfocussed to process much of anything. All the thoughts in her head were not concerning this fat man or the Administrator. She only thought of the four things she currently wanted:

to leave this place

to be back with her father

for the room to stop spinning

and for the large creature standing in the doorway – the one staring in at her – to leave. It dripped drool from its half-open mouth as it grinned at her. Though she had never seen it before, she knew that this was the Moogle. She had been told of these creatures by her father – and what he had said about them was the truth; they were the stuff of nightmares. And the smell... even in her delirious state, she could smell its revolting thick odor.

Mikko followed her fearful gaze toward the Moogle and smirked. He loved that people had a primordial fear of his friend. He then turned back to Albert "So, how long?" he asked.

"I would say about an hour? Maybe less."

"Good."

Albert looked at Mikko for a second in curiosity. "You think this is overkill?"

"Above your pay grade to guess, I'm afraid," Mikko answered as he looked down at Vix, who had now turned her blurry gaze to him. She saw his face clearer as the room finally came to a standstill. Her stomach was settled and gave her the nostalgic feeling of a fairground ride finally coming an end. "All I know is that this situation could have far-reaching consequences, and the Elders want this."

Mikko heard Albert's next question, but one that was unspoken. One that Albert did not mean to think. Mikko shot him a stern glance and spoke his warning. "It is not your place to doubt me—"

"I..." Albert interjected, "I didn't mean... I'm not..." His mental wall slipped for a brief moment as his disdain of Mikko crept through the cracks of his mind, for only but a brief second.

Mikko turned, shaking his head, and walked over to the doorway the Moogle was now backing out of. Each backward step the monster took, echoed with a dull squelchy thud.

Albert meanwhile looked relieved, yet still apprehensive as he watched Mikko leave without carrying on any of the conversation. He hoped his insubordinate mental words were not taken to heart – as he could not afford Mikko to know his true opinions.

"Notify me when his full control is attained," Mikko said without looking back. He and the Moogle then walked away from the room, deeper into the complex.

"Yes, of course, Mein Fuhrer," Albert replied under his breath.

Vix's mind had started to flood back in like a tide. She saw Albert now checking the drip that was connected to her arm. In this drip, instead of saline, was a black liquid. *What the hell is that?* she thought to herself.

Do not worry yourself...

She heard these deep and monstrous words clearly, as if whoever or whatever spoke them was standing right next to

Everyday Monsters

her. But she could not see anyone else in the room. It must have been Albert. Her weak and groggy state must have played tricks on her.

"I'm not worried," she managed to whisper with a guttural exhalation.

Albert heard words from her mouth, but not what they were. He leaned in closer to her mouth. "Excuse me?" he asked.

It will all be over soon.

That monstrous voice again.

It was not Albert. His mouth didn't move to those uttered words.

From outside, a buzzer sounded for three short bursts. Albert glanced for a moment to the doorway, before turning back around to Vix and leaning into her – only a few inches from her face, sneering— "You don't deserve a fucking piece of his glory." His vile words to her did not hurt or have any effect on her. He was inconsequential in almost every respect. She didn't care if a man she didn't know didn't like her for some reason. Not now. Not with all that was happening.

She watched as he hurried out of the room.

Still feeling as if her brain had been in a blender, Vix moved one of her legs out of the bed. She still had no feeling in any of her body. It was all numb. She could move these cold limbs slowly but could not even feel as the cold metal frame of the side of the hospital bed rubbed against her exposed thigh. She worried less about that than as to why she was here. Why she could not remember a thing after stepping into that bright room.

Be still, came that awful voice again.

Deep inside her, a force was starting to take a hold. Despite having no physical feeling within her body, she could feel that darkness. That grip of something deep inside of her.

With each individual syllable that was spoken by this voice, she had the unshakeable feeling that this was not a friendly presence. She had the dread feeling that this was not something she would survive. She did not know what a Sicarian was. She was told she was to be its host. Its conduit. But she didn't really know what it entailed.

She had to leave.

She had to find her father.

She had made a mistake.

A dreadful, dreadful mistake.

If she could just get out. Tell her Father she was sorry. It could all be better. Life could be good again.

A person with a rational mind would have been able to see what a mistake it would be to run from this voice, but there was nothing rational about her at the moment. Though she knew that the Order did not suffer any insubordination gladly, it did not stop her. Despite those kinds of criminals very well meeting their fate in the mouth of the Moogle, it was more important to her to find her father. She had to see him and tell him how sorry she was for abandoning him in his time of need. She knew a sorry would have little effect on her fate. The Order would not be compassionate for a familial reason. She would still meet her fate afterwards when caught. Leaving was not a sensible decision at all, but was all Vix could think of. Despite her vision having stopped spinning, she was still confused and sedated. Her thoughts were singular with no rationale. She was running on pure instinct. Her brain was in flight mode.

BE STILL! The voice inside her head shouted at her once more. The voice was so clear, she could hear the malevolence that dripped off of each syllable it enunciated.

Outside of her hospital room, she steadied herself along the wall with one hand. She staggered, one clumsy step at a time down the long bright hallway. She glanced around, panicked, expecting to see guards running to stop her, or the horrible warden. But in her favor, the hallway was empty.

She knew that this was still Amorfield. She had been here long enough to recognize the rooms in this place on sight. This hallway she staggered down, she remembered it to be the same hallway that she was led down every day for her hour in the yard outside. She knew the way out from here. She knew as long as she didn't cross paths with anyone else, she could escape quickly.

GO BACK! the voice screamed.

She tried her best to ignore the screaming in her head. She had to carry on. She knew something was wrong. She knew deep down that something bad was happening to her, something that she would not recover from. She sensed her time running out.

There was a lump in her stomach.

Moving.

Undulating.

Sickening her.

Rising.

Working its way up her throat.

She tried to swallow it down, but she could only cough.

As she did, the first part of the lump was expelled up through her windpipe and out of her mouth. A swarm of flies covered in a black bile erupted from her, swarming around her head. Some briefly landed on her face, before she needed to cough again – at which point they broke off of her, until they felt brave enough to land again. More flies escaped with each cough she hacked. Over them was the same thick black liquid that now seeped from her mouth; a tar-like bile, the taste of which made her feel sicker than anything she had ever tasted. This liquid's stench rose from her mouth and stabbed itself into her nose with it sharp odor. A strong aroma which reminded her of a mix of rotten meat and infected piss.

Staggering, she continued her escape – she knew where she needed to go. Her mind could not focus on the fact that flies were swarming from inside of her – she just focused on her escape. She had to, or she would fail. If she considered the horrors that awaited her, she would lose the will to carry on.

JADEN SAT on the hood of his car with his legs crossed. In front of him, turned to look up at him, was Deacon's severed head. Wide-eyed and awake. The setting sun started to make its temporary retreat far behind them. It cast a dark orange hue over the fields that lay either side of them. This empty stretch of country road broke through the fields like the earth had split in two. This line of dark asphalt cut through the verdant landscape like a scar. The summer night was drawing to a close, as these two dead men spoke.

"Tell me then," Jaden asked.

"What do you wanna know?" the head said. Its voice was almost a whisper. A shadow of its former self but still audible. "This not self-explanatory enough for ya?"

"Why do they want you?"

"Let's just say I did something I shouldn't have. But you can get that from what you know already."

"Anything to do with the skin you used to make that book?"

"No. No. They fear what the book can do. They fear the consequences. Not the materials it's constructed of. The skin is just a Godly requirement. Upon which any language may be written."

Jaden looked at Deacon, "Ok... vague..." he said.

"It's not just a collection of random symbols, you know?"

Deacon smiled weakly at him. "It's written in Catigeux... an ancient language. Their language. The language of the ones who think they are Gods."

"So... What is it... What's it say in their language?" Jaden replied, unhappy about Deacon's last answer.

"I think it's more important to know to why they want it, as opposed to what it actually is? They think it's a roadmap to another reality. And they cannot afford any changes in our lives."

"So, it's about them?"

"I did something a long time ago. I wrote some pages before. They didn't know that I did that until after they banished me. You see? And when they found out, they panicked – and have tried to find me for years – tried to discover what I did. But I knew how to hide from them... And now with these new pages I made, they think I could be doing it again."

"Why would they be afraid of you? What can you do to them? What can writing do to them?"

Beside them an articulated truck passed down this lonesome stretch of road. Slowing down as it travelled past the car, the driver glanced innocently out of the window toward the zombies sitting on the hood. Both looked back at this driver, and Deacon sneered, "I'll swallow your soul, ya cunt!" he shouted loudly above the sound of the rumbling engine – at which, the truck quickly sped up and escaped in a fit of fear.

Deacon looked back at Jaden with a slight smile. His energy was low. "I told you I'd give you answers. But there is a slight issue. I can't really just explain it all well to you yet. You see this requires a lot to be shown, not spoken. So, let me say, the book is what it is, but is not what they think it is." Jaden glanced down unconvinced as Deacon continued. "I promise you, I'm not being vague by accident. You'll know more as we go. I just can't risk that much. You're a variable I chose... But I don't know to what end yet. You are a piece of a puzzle. And besides, you need plausible deniability if any of this goes tits up... So as for that book. You may think it's bollocks, but all you gotta know is they want it. And they'll pay you for it. Doesn't matter what it is. They just have to believe it may be what they are afraid of."

"So, it's a trap, right? You are using me to set them up."

"Not quite, but I like that you can see a bigger picture in all this."

"Uh-huh," Jaden retorted with a patronizing and contempt-filled tone. "Of course. Makes sense."

"If you want a reason. It's quick money. You don't have to know all about it. That's your choice. You just have to go ahead with it. You could just as easily throw me in the trunk and not have any answers. But you chose to speak to me. And you will get your answers. But you won't understand if I just detail it now. You have to be shown."

"So, I go hand you in, and what? All of a sudden I get shown answers?"

"Now that the handover will happen. It's all coming into place... I will have to warn you, though. They may... And I fully expect this... they may send the Sicarian to get me."

Jaden looked down at Deacon, eyes widened. "Why the fuck would you say that? That's not funny."

"I am not trying to amuse you, laddie. It's just an expectation, so you can understand why I am telling you about plausible deniability at this stage. You don't want to face that fucker with a full brain of ammunition against yourself."

Vix was now out of the building, darting amongst the thick woodland that surrounded the facility. She was steadier on her feet than before, yet still staggering – still coughing violently every few steps, her lungs rattling with each expulsion. She hoped that she could make it out of this forest before dark. She had no flashlight or weapon for her protection. The sun was her only shield from the cold, and was also her only ability to see any of the dangers that lurked within these trees. The dangers that would venture out of their woodland hovels as the moon rose.

With each cough, impossibly more flies emerged from her mouth. Their black thick liquid dripped over her lips like blood.

Behind her, in the distance, sat Amorfield. From there a siren could be heard echoing through the sky. She knew that siren was for her. She knew they had found her gone and wanted her back. They were no doubt in a panic and sending people after her.

Staggering at speed, as fast as she could muster, her footing all of a sudden gave way – catching her foot under a raised root, she tripped over – sending her crashing to the ground with a painful thud. Her ankle cracking as she did.

The air expelled from her body upon her impact with the ground. Thankfully her numbness throughout her body kept the pain of her ribs and ankle breaking in this fall, far away from her.

Her energy levels were quickly depleting, as the coughing zapped all remaining strength from her. She wondered if she could ever stand up again. She felt more hopeless and weak than ever before. She looked around in anguish, wondering what to do... and couldn't help but burst into floods of tears.

"Please... let me go," she sobbed though the coughs and wheezes. Her ankle and ribs not felt in her anguish.

Without a second pause, her head wrenched backward as an invisible force grabbed its strong hold of her.

YOU ARE MINE!, it screamed at her, I AM INSIDE OF YOU. INFECTING YOU. I AM YOUR GOD, YOUR DEVIL AND YOUR SOUL!

Gritting her teeth, she screamed as loud as she could. Inside, she could feel her loss of control. She had to escape. She had to run again. Maybe this force was tethered to Amorfield? Maybe she could outrun it?

She got to her feet, using any remaining strength she could find, and tried her best to carry on as fast as she could, her broken ankle giving her no pain as she took each step, painlessly breaking it more and more.

You cannot escape me! You cannot outrun me!

She moved with steely determination, the surrounding flies not dissipating, but getting thicker in the air around her – as if she were a decaying body and they were feasting on her, multiplying from within her.

The woodland got thicker around her as the path came to an abrupt end. Pushing her way through bushes, she swiped branches aside as she moved through the undergrowth. Her footing became more unsteady as, unknown to her, her foot cracked to one side and her weight pressed her ankle into the ground. The skin on her injury now tearing in two. Without the pain, and in her panic, she had no idea this was happening. The branches flailed as she pushed them away, those that she didn't cut and grazed her with their overgrown thorns as she hobbled past. Each slice of her skin as painless as her ankle. She could feel nothing in her body at all

You WILL obey me, the voice screamed.

Getting through the last of the undergrowth, Vix stopped in her tracks as the ground in front of her gave way to a sheer hundred-foot drop, deep into a chalk quarry. The fading sun cast gargantuan shadows beneath her, making most of the rocks hidden within a blanket of darkness. Like a black sea,

Everyday Monsters

she could only see a few cresting rocks over the shadows in the bottom of this quarry.

You really think you will find him? The voice spoke in a calm and malicious manner.

Her mind raced, she did not really hear what the voice had just said to her. She was too consumed with figuring out an escape – but all of her options were running out.

Your father.

She was at a loss of what she could do. Turn back? Could she make it around the quarry?

Your father... Victor. You think he is alive?

She heard that name. She heard her father's name. She now heard and paid attention to what the voice said. The buzz of the flies that swarmed around her, though loud, could not drown out this voice.

"What did you say?" she asked weakly.

You are not worthy of the gift you have been given.

Vix did not care about the threats, she cared only for her father. "How do you know his name?" The fear was steadily building within her, and she sensed that she was about to hear something dreadful.

I know the dead, and he walks amongst them.

Her expression turned more confused and distraught. Was he dead? How would that voice know? No. No, it can't be true. She needed to–

Without another thought being able to be processed, her arm started to twitch. She looked down in shock, as her body was starting to lose total control of its mobility.

Here she noticed her foot. Snapped to one side. The break now open and exposed, the bone touching the dirt of the cliff edge. Screaming, her eyes widened in terror.

They say that in the final moments, the human brain sees the highlights of its life. For Vix, this did not happen. What did happen, was that that has been said and done over the past year at Amorfield, had crystallized into one clear path which she knew she needed to take. All the bullshit in her life dripped away in a fraction of a millisecond. The blinkered reasoning for her escape had now lifted. Though only lasting a couple of seconds, her mind – in a crystalline instant – knew these realities:

This voice did not lie.

Her father was dead.

Her body was being destroyed.

She would not survive this.

She had no choice left. She could only hope that she could end whatever this force wanted, and escape this destruction. Maybe her action would take this malevolent force with her? She did not care about why it was here, or what it wanted to do. It did not matter. The only thing that ever mattered to her was her father. He was the reason she did all of this – and she knew that the voice told the truth about him. She knew this instinctively. The voice was more than a sound. It was a feeling. A dread feeling. And there were no lies within its evil tone. The only things in its words were hate and destruction. She knew that whatever it had planned, her father would have not have approved.

Before the voice could utter another word to her, before it could take control of her in her entirety, she hurled herself from off of the quarry ledge – taking her fate into her own hands with one solitary action.

Her body tumbled downwards, lasting for what felt like an eternity, before she smashed onto the shadow covered rocks below.

After the snapping of bone and meat hitting rock sounded throughout the quarry, a dread silence followed, oppressively blanketing all that lay around.

Broken and draped, Vix lay like a discarded rag doll over a large stone at the base of the quarry. Her bones had shattered upon impact. Her head was cracked wide open. Her eyes half-protruded from their sockets. Blood flowed out from within her – a mix of crimson and black – and coated the shadowed rock beneath. The last of the setting sun was unable to break the darkness to show the thick blood that oozed from her.

The flies were still present, having traveled down in the fall. They crawled over her body, examining every injury they could. Feeding on any available parts of her damage.

The buzz became all that could be heard within in this barren place. The sound of the wild nightlife from high up in the woodland above, as well as the sound of sirens from Amorfield were both absent this far down. All that existed here was the darkness, the silence, and the sound of the flies.

Her lifeless mouth hung agape on the rock face, the jaw now snapped and hung off from one side of her skull.

Her body lay motionless.

The flowing blood now the only movement.

But then, there was something.

Something was still here.

Something was not dead.

Despite hanging off her face by only one side of bone – her mouth suddenly snapped open even wider with a loud crack. A few flies crawled out of from within her throat, over her tongue and scuttled onto her face.

Her dead, broken body arched upwards into a sitting position. Her bones cracked and crunched with the sound of contorted flesh, cracking bones and snapping cartilage.

Her hand – complete with bones breaking through her skin – grabbed one side of her jaw and yanked it back into its normal position, shoving it with force back into her skull.

Though death should have been her only eventuality, she was now conscious, and without any control.

Vix was still there. She had seen the stone below collide and destroy her body on impact. She saw her blood break free from her skin, coating the rocks surrounding her exposed organs. She still felt nothing of the physical pain. She felt only fear from this waking nightmare.

The darkness she jumped towards never came to take her. It just stood by and watched.

He had pushed her death far away from her. Totally out of her reach.

As her body sat up, and the bones snapped back into place, they all started healing at an incredible rate. The flesh on her body very slowly closing over her exposed and healing innards.

This shell of meat and piss is mine! it screamed at her.

Her eyes welled with blood and tears as she heard the voice again. She knew her battle was lost. Her attempt to end her nightmare was futile, and now worse than ever.

YOU WILL LIIIIIIVVVEEE!!!

Her chest expanded with her first breath since leaping off from the rocks above. Her body started filling with the life she tried to take away from her aggressor – she was powerless against it.

As her life started to renew, she felt herself losing her mental grip on her consciousness. As if she was falling backwards into the depths of her own mind. Further and further backwards. Her ability to control any part of her body was now gone. He had control now.

You shall witness my works from the recesses of your own decaying existence, the voice uttered to her with sheer malevolent glee.

As if viewed through a television far away, Vix could see

Everyday Monsters

through her own eyes as they returned back into their sockets. Yet they did not feel like they were her own. She saw her own hands push herself up to her now healed feet. Yet these was not her actions; it was her body, but she was in no control. She was a passenger trapped within her mind. The driver of which now raised its hand and said through her mouth, aloud for the first time, in her voice. "Humanity..." it said. "Such a beautiful damnation."

The flies swarmed around her as she slowly stood. They entered her mouth and ears as if this was now their hive.

If she could make a sound, she would scream. She would cry. She would lament the end of her control. Mourn the death of her father. But where she was, she could only do one thing; she could only watch in fear. And this fear was the only emotion this force allowed her to experience. This sadistic puppet-master fed off of all of her pain – and it relished the anguish she felt from within her mental prison.

This being was the Lord of the Flies.

This being was the The Sicarian.

"LET US SAY, for argument's sake, that the Sicarian was going to show up," Jaden proposed. "Why in fuck's sake aren't you terrified at that prospect?"

"What'd be the point? I'm a severed head resting on a goddamn car hood. My body's bloody miles away getting cut up to pieces. What good would it do, me being afraid of someone? Even that fucker?" Deacon's expression turned to curious. "I do have one question for you, though," he countered.

"Can I answer as bullshit and vague as you've been doing to me?"

"You can answer how you want, laddie."

"Feel free then." Jaden moved off the car bonnet and stood up. Turning to the setting sun. "What you wanna know?"

"I'm guessing that they ordered you not to read the book? Not requested to, but ordered. Despite you telling them you can't understand the language it's written in?"

Jaden turned to look at Deacon. He was indeed ordered by his handler – a direct request from the Order – he was not to read it. "So? What does that matter?" he answered.

"Why do you think that is, that they demanded that? Surely it points to them being afraid of the repercussion of what is written? What possible concern would it be to them if you read an inconsequential collection of scribbles on some poor bastard's skin?"

Jaden didn't reply to him.

"They trust you to deliver me, but don't trust you not to read something you believe is of no consequence."

Jaden still had no answer.

"So, you're faced with the larger question, do they not trust you? Or do they believe what I wrote could have some effect on you, as if what I wrote had more power than they now have?"

"I guess they don't trust me," Jaden smirked, "and I'm fine with that, I don't trust them."

"You don't get any feeling at all that you are written into this story, do you? That you have a larger purpose to play here."

"Why are you saying this?"

"I'm trying to ease your mind, you eejit! You wanted to know what it was. I can't say exactly right now. But I can say that you are part of all this. You were never going to turn down the job, no matter what it was. You are as part of all of this as I am."

Jaden walked over to the trunk, opened it and removed the

leather satchel, bringing it around to the front where Deacon sat. "I'm guessing it's all some type of magic, then?"

"A kind of magic. In a way. Sure."

With the book now taken out of the satchel, he flicked through it. He glanced at the indecipherable writings. There were no English words on any of these pages. There were only scrawled symbols which seemed as alien to him as anything he had ever seen before. He flicked through the rest of the thick leathery pages – there were about 30 in all.

"This is all a joke," Jaden said unimpressed. "At least I'm getting paid," he continued under his breath.

Deacon replied with a smirk "You, m'laddo, as I said, have plausible deniability. That is a most enviable position to be within all of this."

"And what makes you think I won't just tell 'em all you've said."

"Two things. 1 – I know you won't. You were destined for this. It is all predetermined, up until a point. 2 – They wouldn't care, anyway, even if I had a bomb inside my head – ready to explode – they would take me with them and brave the explosion. They are stubborn assholes like that."

"I'm destined for this? Destined to be your postman?"

"This is more than that. You are more than that. I knew that the moment Gobolt spoke your name, and told me who you were... But what and why... I don't know. I never fished that story."

Looking at him for a second, Jaden didn't reply, but put the journal back into the satchel. Walked over to him, picked him up by his hair, then walked around to the trunk.

He lifted up Deacon to look at him in the face and smiled.

"I think that's enough."

He threw both the satchel and Deacon into the trunk, slamming it shut behind them.

He'd had enough of all of this. For the first time, he didn't care about the answers. Being a man who normally needed logic and explanation, he was curiously at peace with just finishing the job. He didn't recall Gobolt, and was too ashamed to ask more about this mystery man. And that was the problem. It was all a mystery, and one that was getting annoying. All this talk of purpose and fate was just tiring.

He just wanted it over with now.

This postman just wanted his post delivered, and wanted to call it a day.

THE CHANGELING

Fate had already determined that Meares would die at the hands of the Sicarian, soon after he assisted a betrayer of the Order. He would never have helped Jaden in any way if he knew that this was to be the case, but circumstances have a way of steering you in the most unexpected and unwanted journeys.

All he wanted was a nice, quiet life. To be able to earn enough money to buy food and pay rent, with a bit extra on the side to afford an occasional trip down the local Armenian karaoke bar to get drunk and sing songs that reminded him of his misspent youth, or down to the vape shop to buy his vaping fluid. These were his small morsels of joy from an otherwise cruel and unforgiving world.

He stayed under the radar as much as he possibly could. Working for the Order was good for him, as they only ever used him as a handler. A position which came with minimal responsibility. No direct management. Good rates of pay. No on the job danger. It was perfect for him.

Unlike the majority of his peers, he was a standard mortal; he could not regenerate like zombies or vampires, and would bleed if cut, and would die if cut too much. He didn't have any superpowers which enabled him to walk through walls or lift up a car above his head. Instead, what made him different was that he could change his appearance to look like other people, though it had to be someone who he was looking at in person. But, this was not as great an ability as it first seemed. The change he undertook could only be of equal size to him, so if he wanted to change into someone in particular who happened to be 6 foot 7 inches tall and was wide with muscles, he would only be able to replicate them at his own height of 5 foot 8, and have his own body mass repositioned to equate the size as much as possible which could result in him being much shorter. So the 6 foot 7 could turn to 4 foot nothing with the huge muscles accounted for. He could not grow more or less mass than he already had – just change its shape, and color.

He was known as the Changeling. And it was this ability which got him into the position he had within the Order. His employment as handler was essentially as a conduit between the Order and those bounty hunters – or collectors – like Jaden. He got the jobs sent to him from an Administrator, and wrote them up into files, arranged the pickup points, and processed payments upon completed jobs. This suited him to the ground. He did not want people to know who he was. Especially when dealing with potentially sensitive materials, and none of his collectors knew what he looked like. It was all very safe. As long as he kept each meeting under an hour.

The danger with this ability was that it was time limited. His body ran hot if in the assumed form for too long. Any more than 30 minutes, and his body would start sweating at an excessive rate. Any more than an hour and the solidity of his body would start to flux.

Yet, despite all of this, Meares was ready to quit his job.

Despite being in his late 30s, he had been doing this for nearly 2 decades. He'd saved up a nice little nest egg. Enough to fund a few decades of meagre living. He wanted to enjoy his tiny fortune and worry about retirement when it came to it. But as fate had already made up his mind, that he would not even reach his next birthday, these were all just pipe dreams – if only he knew it.

If he needed money in the future, he thought, he would get a job at a convenience store, or as a cleaner for some company. He just wanted to stop using his ability. Sure, it was easy, but it was not painless. It felt exactly as you would expect bones bending, breaking and reshaping to feel like. Not to mention there were those people out there that wanted him cut up and examined, picked apart atom by atom to see what made him tick. To see if his gift could be imparted to others with an injection. Historically, his kind were all but wiped out by the Nazis, who gleefully dissected as many changelings as they could find – all in order to replicate their power, and to improve it. To correct its shortcomings. To enable a new changeling Nazi soldier to change into any being no matter the size or shape – which was something they, of course, always failed to do. Ironically, despite believing the Changelings power would end the war in their favor, it did not. Instead it came to a head when there was an assassination attempt on June 20th 1944 – and despite reports, it was indeed successful. And for the 10 months following, one of his kind – a Nazi soldier who previously hid his true self from his peers – acted in public as Adolf Hitler himself. (This of course ended badly after this fake-Hitler was shot by Russian soldiers on 30th April 1945.)

Meares did not know any others like him. His parents abandoned him at birth, and he was not the kind of person to care to hunt out anyone else with his ability. What would he say? So, you can change too, huh? That would be it. He wanted to be left alone, he didn't want the attention. That was when he was happiest. Things like love never concerned him, or more exactly love never gave him a chance to be concerned about it. He was full of wants for missed opportunity, but he never found the one he wanted to be with. No one except those he paid for the privilege.

He gave himself the moniker of the Changeling. It sounded cool and professional. Better than what his real type were called:

Skinwalkers. To him, it made them sound awful. Shapeshifter was just as bad. The Changeling sounded more mysterious. Skinwalker sounded gross, like he wore people's skins.

For this latest job, he was a bit wary. This was not work he was given by the order. He was contacted by one of his hunters, offering something. This was never a normal occurrence. And he turned it down as soon as he was offered. He didn't want to waste the Order's time. They were not people who would be happy with this situation. But his hunter insisted, saying he knew the Order would want this and pay heavily for it. He even gave a name to say to them. Like a special code. Maybe, he thought, if this was indeed something they really wanted, then he would get a bonus for facilitating it? Anything to earn more money in order to bolster his savings. And anything so he could see that particular hunter again.

As soon as he heard the desperation in Mikko's voice after he mentioned the journal of human skin to him – more so than the living head of Arius – he should have known what would happen would go badly. When Mikko had spoken to the Elders, and called him back immediately, he was asked where and when the meeting with his hunter would be, which

Everyday Monsters

was strange as they never normally concerned themselves with details like that. And Meares sensed something else in Mikko's tone, something very unexpected: fear. He should have just driven in the other direction – ditched his phone and just lived his life out on the coast somewhere. But he had already agreed to do this. And he was used to his paranoia screaming at him that he was doing the wrong thing. But in this scenario – his paranoia was justified.

HE NEVER HAD any luck when leaving the city. Even at the best of times the traffic or weather acted as a warning for him to go back. Whenever he had to travel to the suburbs or even further afield, things went wrong. Never the same thing to happen, but somehow, it was never an easy task. He hoped this would be different. He expected large traffic accidents, apocalyptic weather... anything, he thought, could and might happen.

THIS DRIVE he was on now was a long one. What normally should have taken 13 hours, instead took 17. As expected, a 16-car pileup caused the worst kind of chaos. The skies opened and a tropical storm befell those stuck in the accident's aftermath. To all of this, as he expected this kind of bad luck, Meares just rolled his eyes. Of course, what else did he expect? An easy journey?

Never, ever, ever leave this city again. He thought to himself. Not for any reason. Ever. Even if the sky starts to fall on his apartment. Stay at home. At all costs.

None of this really mattered.

He would be dead very, very soon.

PART II

BETRAYAL AND PUNISHMENT

DEACON AND THE DARKNESS

From inside the trunk of the Plymouth Fury, Deacon lay in total blackness.

Ever since his decapitation, his equilibrium had been playing havoc with his sight and was in a state of constant dizziness. Normally, in such situations, blood loss would be the root cause of this, but as his situation was entirely unnatural – and entirely unprecedented – nothing could be presumed to be anything anymore. Presumption demanded logic and there was no logic here. Even though he had some knowledge of the outcome, he had no control of the unknown aspects which he did not plan. He had no idea what this ill feeling he felt was. He had no idea whether his dizziness was normal, or a sign of a larger, insurmountable problem. Something which might result in a problem in the path he saw ahead of him.

None of this was surprising though. Nothing like this had ever happened before – not to his knowledge, anyway. He liked to think he was the first being to still be alive who just existed as a severed head.

He was though, not correct in that thought.

. . .

IN ABYSSINIA, 1283, a farmer named Batu was found crushed underneath a pile of rocks. With only his head being on display, having been severed by the impact of the fallen stone. This accident was caused by both severe weather conditions, as well as quite bad judgement on behalf of this farmer. A man who, before his demise, was so drunk, the world was – to him – a swirling wonderland of hazy beauty. Having – in his 72 years – never tasted any alcohol before, Batu had no memory of what happened that night. He had been gifted a bottle of Rice Mead from a Chinese trader – a thank you for allowing this visitor to use his well. As the moon rose higher in the sky, alone in his home, Batu wondered Why not, what's the worst that could happen? then drank half the bottle in one gulp. This, as the other villagers spoke of after, was a gift from the Gods, as it meant that Batu would have no recollection of the violent end to his life. In this village, they believed your demise was predetermined. That nothing you could do could change it. So even if Batu did not drink the mead, he would have still died the same way. This, though, was not the case. Not the case at all. His death would not have happened if he had drunk slower, or eaten more that day.

After finding his severed head, the villagers quickly concluded that this was an accident, and soon after that, buried him in the desert – within the ground of the same oasis where deceased generations of villagers were also buried. They had no choice but to leave his body where it was, squashed underneath the rock fall, as they had no tools strong enough to move the huge boulders which lay on top of him.

It was a lovely ceremony which was held in Batu's memory. The entire village mourned his passing. Batu was a kindly old man. A man who helped anyone that needed it, at any time

Everyday Monsters

they asked. He never married. He had no children. Yet to everyone in the village, he was called "Abati" (Father).

Little did they know that three days after his burial, Batu, in his decapitated state, awoke with a jolt – deep within his tomb of sand. At first, he tried to scream for attention, to alert the villagers to his situation. But the sand soon poured into his open mouth and muffled any more attempts to yell for assistance. A passing child, playing with some reeds nearby, heard the first scream, but as no more followed, thought it was probably just the wind. So, there Batu stayed, in total darkness, with his airways blocked full of sand.

Over the next few centuries, he wondered many times why he couldn't feel his arms or legs, why he couldn't move his body at all, but, despite the length of time he had been there, with the amount of time he had to think about everything – he had no clue that he was only a head.

And there he remained to this very day.

Silent.

In torment.

Very much alive.

Very much the first person to survive having his head separated from his body.

And somehow, now suffered a hangover for all of eternity.

IT WOULD NEVER BE KNOWN that he was there, nor would it ever been known how it came to be. A silent mystery for no one to solve.

WITHIN THE DARK heat of the trunk of the Plymouth Fury, Deacon tried to make out the other items that lay in there with him. Trying to see in the darkness, what else Jaden had also thrown into this damp space. His cheek was pressed against the leather satchel containing the journal – so he knew that was safe at least. He could make out a round object opposite him. Was it a football? Maybe. This game of his was inconsequential, but at least it kept his mind occupied away from the boredom.

Desperately trying to keep his composure through his impatience, he kept having to tell himself that all of this was determined already. That whatever might happen beyond his control was an unwritten key to the overall plan – yet there was only so much you could convince a decaying mind of. He could feel the heat eating at him again, emanating through the metal bodywork above him. The skin on his forehead was gradually getting tighter. The squirrel he ate did a marvelous job reducing any damage that the sun had done before, but this oven-like heat was now advancing the return of it. This was not as fast a decay, but he swore he could feel it happening quicker. Then again heat was a cruel mistress to the dead, and created a mania which Deacon had trouble controlling, even when he had a body.

Jaden had left a few minutes earlier. After skidding his car to a grinding halt, he got out, but instead of opening the trunk to get Deacon or the journal out, he simply knocked on the top, and shouted aloud "Back soon, Sparky." Then nothing more. He was left wondering not what might happen next, but how long it would take.

He knew what was happening – Jaden was meeting his handler – he just didn't like not being able to make sure it was happening in the right way, and fast enough to stop his baking in the car.

It could only have been be a matter of minutes before he was supposed to be handed over to the Order along with the journal – a needed step for his plan to progress – but instead he just sat in silence, waiting for Jaden to return. Was he the wrong man for the job? His shifting flippancy, and sudden disinterest in the whys, were slightly concerning. But it was too late now.

BANG!

THE CAR DOOR SLAMMED, and the engine started – all in a very hurried fashion. Jaden was back – and in a panicked rush.

"FUCK!!" he shouted from the driver's seat. "SON OF A FUCKING BITCH! FUCK, FUCK, FUCK!!". He smacked his hand onto the steering wheel repeatedly as he slammed the accelerator pedal down as hard as he could. The wheels of the Plymouth Fury spun furiously, before they gripped enough dirt to propel the car forward at incredible speed.

"You gotta be fucking KIDDING me!" Jaden shouted from the front of the car, whilst he sped away down the track.

MEARES AND THE END

Arriving at the Weathered Hearts Inn, Meares slammed his car door behind him. His back was sore and his legs ached, just as they normally did. He arched his back slowly and forcefully, wincing as a dull pain shot up his spine – a good dull pain. One which, when finished, signaled the temporary lessening of his aching back. His spine made its satisfying clicking sound, as a smile crept across his face with the relief.

Having always suffered from sore bones, he had tried all the "remedies" to make his car rides more comfortable. Gel pads, pillows, you name it – he had tried it. But all the quick-fixes and medical breakthroughs only made the inevitable pain much worse. So, he'd decided long ago that he would bin all these "miracle fixes", and just stick with his worn-down driver's seat – just as it was – complete with springs bulging out in the most uncomfortable places. But more comfortable than anything else he had tried.

His expression quickly shifted to a more worried look, as he suddenly checked his pockets. Breast jacket pocket. Trouser right pocket. Trouser left pocket. Trouser rear left pocket. Trouser rear right pocket. Inside jacket pocket. DAMN! WHERE WAS IT?

Turning back, he opened his driver's-side car door, and leaned in.

This was his life. He was dependable. He was hard-working. But he had the organization skills equal to a ball of lint. A very disorganized ball of lint. This was not the first time he had to search his car for something that should be in his pocket.

Inside his rusting car rested a menagerie of discarded junk, filled with old sushi boxes, most of which were empty, but some contained their own ecosystem within their grease-stained white cardboard containers. In between these foul-smelling mold factories lay empty vape bottles which emanated their sickly fruity odor and combined with the smell of decay to make a strange, oppressive stench. It would be natural for one to presume that something had recently died in there amongst all the rubbish – and though not out of the realm of possibility, this was not the case.

Meares could have spent his savings on a new car, instead of hoarding it all for the future which would not happen – but even if he were to live out the day, he would not have traded in his car for anything. He loved that car. It was filthy, sure. It was expensive to run, as you would expect. But it was his. And it had served him very well over the years. Having owed it since he first passed his driving exam, it had borne witness to every major event in his life; from paid sexual encounters, to hospital visits, to funerals, to getting him to every soul crushing job he ever had, to driving him for the last decade to all his work as a handler for the Order. Miraculously, it somehow never broke down, nor had any problem which could not be fixed cheaply. Sure, a spark plug here, a burst tire there, a flat battery every few years. But nothing insurmountable, and a sign to him that he should never replace it. Not until it gave up the ghost and refused to ever run again of its own accord.

Rifling through the debris in the passenger foot-well, he searched for the paper upon which was scrawled the name of his contact, as well as the needed pass phrase – both things he could not continue with this job without. Please don't let it be at home, he thought to himself, dreading that it was still hanging there on his notepad which was attached to his fridge.

"AH-HA!" he exclaimed, as he picked up a folded piece of paper, wedged in between the seat and a paper take-out container – a container which still housed an ancient piece of Japanese Nigiri. This Nigiri – the only evidence of his depression-fueled midnight sojourn to a 24-hour sushi restaurant – was now about seven months old. At the time, he had meant to throw these remains into an actual trash can – as the smell was overpowering the rest of the great indeterminable stench within his 1989 Toyota Corolla – but after a month or two, any strong smell it had once let off was now a thing of the past, as the odor vanished into the background, mixing with the myriad of other rotten smells – so did Meares' memory of having to throw it away in the first place. So this Nigiri took up permanent residence.

THE INSIDE to the reception of the Weathered Hearts Inn was a tribute to 1940s Americana. The owner, Barbara Lennox, was not the person responsible for this. Nor did she have any idea what a typical American 1940s-hotel reception would have looked like to make the comparison. This was just what her Inn looked like. The Inn (she refused to call it a hotel) had opened in the summer of 1941, decorated in only the most

Everyday Monsters

fashionable décor. Its original owner – her father, Stanley Lennox, had painstakingly chosen each and every aspect of the Inn. Personally purchasing every single ashtray in every single room, every vase and every table the vase would sit on, each and every painting that hung on every wall, as well as spending a fortune importing specific wallpaper he thought would appeal to a new crowd of rich guests he was hoping the Inn would attract. Nowadays, unlike other 40s décor, this wallpaper would not be considered retro fashionable. At best, it was seen as a retro-gross design which would be a source of mockery amongst the soy-latte drinking, unicycle riding, hipster assholes from Seattle. Stanley, though, would have disagreed with modern analysis. He always had a love for the newest, bravest and most cutting-edge fashion, the kind of fashion even the most fashionable people could not get on board with, the bold and shocking fashion which only a few could appreciate. So, although the rich guests never arrived in their droves, he would never regret what he had made.

This décor had not changed much since he opened the Inn. Everything in each room was regularly cleaned and polished but never needed to be replaced. Nothing ever happened in this Inn except for the passing through of its ever-changing guests and it was never a place which saw much raucous behavior. There was never any out of control partying, so nothing happened to any excess to even knock over a lamp. The most that ever happened here, the most exciting out-of-the-ordinary thing was the appearance of a pigeon that had flown through an open bedroom window in 1977. It was inside the room, flapping about for about an hour, with the (now very old) Stanley frantically trying to remove it. It became such a talking point for him, that this room – room 32 – became forever known as "The Aviary", and he even went as far as buying its own bird print bedsheets, bird print wallpaper to be put up over the fashionable wallpaper and bird print towels put into the bathroom.

Barbara, though, didn't care for any of her father's history, or the Inn itself. She wasn't that close to him in any case, she had just inherited this business after he passed away. All she wanted to do was to sit watching her Reality TV shows, smoking her Marlboro, eating her burgers and drinking her Coca-Cola (which in truth was mainly filled with Jack Daniels). Now in her 70s, she was extremely obese and did not have any fucks to give about anything anymore. She was too long in the tooth to do anything except do what she wanted. So, she sat grumpily behind her reception counter for 8 hours of each day, the TV on full blast, smoking and drinking until the shift ended. Then afterwards, she would move herself back to her bedroom, with the evening receptionist taking over, there would she continue to watch her TV loudly, whilst carrying on smoking her Marlboro and drinking her Coca-Cola (which was still mainly Jack Daniels).

The whole reception area carried with it a perpetual haze of old cigarettes and whisky. Some of Barbara's employees wanted this to change and had tried to get her to quit, to try and live healthier. They wanted make the reception area a nicer place to walk into, but in her mind, she was living on borrowed time, anyway. It didn't matter what she did anymore. What was the worst that can happen? Death? She'd expected that a long time ago, so would not stand in its way if it wanted to come for her.

IN HER YOUTH, she had been an athlete – though looking at her now, it was hard to fathom her as anything except a glutton. It was after her husband, Gerald, a chiseled muscular example of a man, died in horrific circumstances which signaled her transformation into the unhealthy figure of a lady she was now.

Whilst on a walk through the hills behind where had they lived in California, both Gerald and Barbara – who was then his beautiful wife of 15 years – took the same path on their nice summer's evening stroll. A stroll that they took almost every single day. A stroll that they took in even in the harshest of weather conditions. But on this one hot summer evening, whilst treading on the same narrow path he had stepped on many dozens of times in the past, he lost his footing. Slipping and tumbling down the hillside, he still had hold of Barbara's hand, and much to her shock, pulled her down with him. She was, though, the luckiest out of the two of them. Suffering only a broken ankle, her fall stopped short of the metal barrier between the base of the hill and the busy four-lane freeway which snaked through the hills in front of them.

Gerald, being a lot heavier with muscle than her, was a victim to gravity. His extra weight had propelled him clean over the barrier and directly into the path of a convoy of speeding trucks – all of which took their turns crushing his once impressive physique into a pulpy muck. This all happened as Barbara looked on helplessly, as she screamed at the cars for anyone to stop and help her beloved – but, no one did. Anyone who might have noticed her or what had happened to Gerald just slowed and stared out at the horror.

With her broken ankle in tow, she climbed over the metal barrier and hobbled over to the roadside – waiting for a gap in the traffic. And when one showed itself, she ran over to Gerald, grabbed any part of him she could – a part she thought was an arm, though was in fact his exposed spine – then dragged his remains back to the grass verge. As she got to the grass, her ankle gave way and she fell backwards. Gerald was launched into the air as her arms flung up from the fall –

well, only part of Gerald was. More precisely, his flattened head, attached spine and rear of his ribcage flew (complete with remaining attached organs). She pulled this matter into the air as she tumbled back, and it landed directly onto her as she hit the dirt and grass. His flattened head – complete with protruding burst eyeballs, lolling tongue and brain-smeared hair – fell directly onto her open-mouthed and screaming face.

That was the day the athletic beauty once known as Barbara Lennox died tragically alongside her bodybuilding husband. This was also the day that the fat chain-smoking alcoholic, nihilistic Barbara Lennox was born. But in all honesty, who could blame her for this?

MEARES LOOKED around the reception in impressed awe. He happened to love the décor, especially the clashing colors of the garish wallpaper. Everything here was to him a garish extravagant take on art deco. One he approved of whole heartedly. It was all almost vomit-inducing in its twee-ness. It reminded him of one of his "ex-boyfriends" (what he referred his paid encounters as). Ugly to look at, but owning every aspect of it, to the point of appearing somehow, attractive.

"Can I help ya?" were the words he heard from an out-of-sight gruff female voice. He turned and was met with the visage of Barbara, sitting behind her reception counter, still with rollers in her hair from the day before. Still not giving a fuck about anything. Her TV blared out with the latest rerun of whatever cookie cutter reality TV show she had been recently drowning in.

"Guess ya want a room?" she followed her first question with, her eyes not yet meeting his as she lit a cigarette with her recently finished one.

Everyday Monsters

With a grin, Meares put down the carrier bag which he had held in his hand, then took out a piece of paper from his pocket. This was the piece of paper that could have been lost, if it were not for his foot-well filing system. Looking down at the note, he read aloud from his own scrawled handwriting, "Barbara Lennox. Riddle Dies."

Barbara's eyebrows dipped as she grimaced, then turned to see the man who spoke those words. Riddle fucking dies... Again?!?! she grumbled silently.

"You're Barbara, right? Barbara Lennox?" Meares asked as he took a couple of steps forward to the reception counter.

"So?" she replied with annoyance. "Why it matter to ya? What the hell d'ya want?"

"I'm Meares," he said holding out his hand toward her, expecting a customary shake from this stranger.

Barbara ignored the offer and looked toward her television again. "I don't give a good God damn what you are, say what you want, what that fuckin' Order wants, then get the fuck out of here and leave me in peace."

Meares, still smiling, took back his hand. He was used to people being rude to him in this job. Keep in mind these people have been strong-armed, bribed, and basically given no choice but to assist the Order in whatever they asked. Whether willing or not, they had been contacted previously by an operative who had been tasked to create a database of available locations, items, or even people, these items were to be granted access to, at little to no notice – by someone from the Order – as long as they had a pass phrase. In this case, the available item was her Inn and the phrase had been Riddle Dies. Those words Barbara loathed. Words no doubt concocted by a damaged brain.

Selected locations added to the Order's databases had also been installed with access points directly to the nearest facility

– in this case, to Amorfield. A way for those handlers to pass through items without the risks which came with transporting objects or people the traditional way. It was a portal – usually located within some basement – and one which was heavily controlled and monitored. Meares himself had never even been into a portal. Only items it requested were allowed in. Anything else was summarily destroyed. He didn't even know if it was an actual warehouse at the other side, as he was told it was. He also didn't trust that it was even was a doorway – it could just be a portal to nowhere, to a void or some other existence which existed in negative. What if it was a portal that led to a large machine which exterminated all that was sent through? Like a large cosmic garbage disposal. There was no way of knowing unless you actually went through it. And even if he wanted to travel to any location through these access points, he would never be allowed. He was only a handler, he had to get to whatever assigned location the old-fashioned way.

As for those people conscripted into giving the Order access to what they owned and/or for the installation of an otherworldly portal, they had been paid handsomely in exchange – but it was never a choice for them. It was either take the money or have their life taken for the refusal. In this case, at the Weathered Hearts Inn, the Order could turn up and demand free use of all or any of the rooms on the property. If this happened, the staff would have to remove all current occupants immediately and without question. Meares didn't like any of this business, but he knew he had no say – there was nothing he could do except make the whole process as simple and painless as possible.

"Riddle Dies," he reiterated with a smile.

"I heard that shit the first time ya bleated it," Barbara said as she rolled her eyes. "Now for Christ's sake, when will you leave me the hell alone?"

Meares still smiled at her.

"What you want then?" she asked "A room? All the rooms? How you wanna ruin my business today?" She glanced at him with derision. "Worst fuckin' decision my stupid pop ever made... Even worse than the goddarn wallpaper."

"Just need this reception room for a while, if that is okay? Nothing more. Few hours, tops. Easy peasy."

"Oh, easy peasy? You think that this ain't too much of a cunt-ache, huh?"

"Maybe only an hour," Meares said. He knew this Inn was a regular with the handlers, though he had never used it himself. So, he was in all likelihood the first Changeling handler that ever came here – as he was the only handler who was not 100% human. Because of this, she might have experienced dealing with the Order before, but she had never experienced what she was about to now.

She knew they were all freaks, Satanists, monsters, communists – everything she hated, but she had only seen glimpses at best. She believed that if you didn't have Jesus in your heart, and if you were not a white American, then you should die or stay wherever you were from. She never saw any double standard in this belief. Even one of her tattoos said what her opinion on the subject was; scrawled above her right breast was written in fading ink: "Get with God or Get the Gun". But, and this was a big but – these communists paid – and they paid well. So as long as the money came in, she would leave them be – but not hide her opinion. She was stuck with a deal her father took, and she wanted to cancel it, but as the monthly Order payments kept the place open, she had no real choice but to oblige their needs.

"Also," Meares said as he turned away from her "I need a

tiny bit more from you, I'm afraid." He locked the office door and pulled down the shade over its window.

A look of disgust fell over Barbara's face. "You ain't gonna rut with me ya commie bastard! That ain't the deal. You'd have to pay a crap load more to get in my nether!"

Shocked and raising his palms up to her, his smile fell to a shocked expression. "Whoa, whoa, whoa, hold your horses. I ain't gonna touch you. Sorry, I should have phrased that WAAAAAY differently."

"Then, what the hell ya want?" she asked. Despite her protestations, Barbara was quite offended by his immediate dismissal of her. In fact, if he had persisted, she would have accepted a sexual advance from him. As she would from almost anyone. Young or old. Black or white. Human or whatever the Order were. But for the sake of her pride – or what she had left of it – she just needed to put up a front first, at least temporarily. Despite her politics and her blatant racism, her sexual desires held none of the same ignorance nor prejudice her personality did.

"I just need a few moments of your time, that's all." He put down one of his hands and kept the other extended toward Barbara. He then closed his eyes.

"What you want? I don't wanna—"

That was as much as she could say before she collapsed, unconscious. Her falling weight slumped back into her wheeled chair, and sent them both rolling back across the floor, hitting the wall behind her – it shook the shelves above with a thud.

Keeping his hand up toward her, his eyes opened as his pupils rolled backwards, up into his head, and showed an unnatural amount of the whites of his eyes.

His jaw started to open slowly as his body tensed. Veins appeared over his face as his blood pumped at an increased rate. Each muscle in his body had started to come to life, independently twitching separate from each other. Each following their own rhythm. His skin started to get redder as beads of sweat appeared all over his face.

The pain was starting to make an appearance. Meares wished he had become used to it, like he had with his almost constant back pain. Unfortunately, each time the change was about to happen, the agony was as acute as the last time. It never got better nor worse, just remaining incredibly debilitating in its intensity.

His changing felt like bones breaking, with those broken fragments then shifting on their own power and breaking more, then twisting and reforming again and again. All of this matched with the feeling of muscles shrinking, tearing and growing to different configurations – it felt like this, as this was exactly what was happening inside of him.

Unfortunately, Barbara had a good 200lbs over Meares. Being a changeling, whatever the body Meares was changing into could only ever be a carbon copy if it was of the same size as him. So, with Barbara, he could only become a smaller version, whether in height or width. He could only match lb for lb. The same if the person had been smaller. He could change into a baby, but the baby would be over 5 foot tall.

If only this wasn't an unwavering command from the Order, he wished that he didn't have to change at all, as he had dealt with Jaden for many years, it was not as if he was dealing with a stranger. Yet despite this, Jaden did not know him at all. He only knew his voice and never saw his real face beneath the ever-changing skin suits he wore. They had met many, many times. Had many, many conversations. Even got drunk together on many occasions – but Jaden never saw the real Meares – the Meares he desperately wanted Jaden to see.

As he reined in the agonizing screams through his gritted

teeth, his hair started to grow at speed and start to turn from its murky brown into a bright gray color, matching the hue of Barbara's hair. His face then began to sag, as his beard withdrew into its pores. Looking like a melting waxwork as his face dripped downwards, a sudden snap rang out as his hips broke in two, sending him falling to his knees, screaming. His agony stifled by his determination to try to not attract any unwanted attention. Tears dripped down his sweaty and morphing face – a face that was slowly forming into Barbara's. His palm was still raised and faced toward the unconscious Barbara, who was as before slumped behind the reception desk. It was only when his hip bones broke back into their new configuration that he collapsed onto the linoleum floor in agony, grabbing his hips with both hands.

He hated each and every time he had to do this, but it was the only thing he was ever truly good at. Not that it was a talent. It was his nature. The pain though? Why would nature make this hurt so much? It made as much sense as the male praying mantis dying after mating. Mother Nature was cruel and an often insane force, with no logic or care for what she created.

He would not have to worry though.

He had less than 30 minutes to live.

THE SICARIAN AND THE FURY

Walking through one of the Order's portals, then into the basement of the Weathered Hearts Inn was simple enough. It was an action that did not affect the Sicarian at all. Any side effects were purely for humans to feel. From disorientation, sickness, headaches or in extreme cases, total spontaneous molecular breakdown, there were a myriad of effects that could be felt, but the Sicarian was not of this world, and he was not in his normal body, this body belonged to Vix. So, any side-effects, she alone would feel – and she was not anywhere where her actual feelings were available to her.

In reality, assigning the Sicarian a gender like male or female was incorrect. He was not a he, and she was not a she. It was both, yet neither. It was a singular being who existed without creation, at least that is what the lore said. The Sicarian would assign itself the female gender pronoun when it was in female form, and if in male form would refer to itself with the male pronoun.

She now stood in the basement of the Inn. The bright light from the door-sized access point faded into darkness behind her. The illumination that the gateway had filled this room with was initially blinding, enough that upon arrival she could see everything; Every shelf, every half-empty paint can, every tool. But now the light had retreated back into the portal, so the basement was plunged back into its regular state of subdued darkness.

She walked onto the first rickety wooden step, which led up a single person staircase, a staircase which led straight up to the reception room where Meares now was. The wood beneath her foot creaked loudly, snapping through the quiet of this storage space. As she ascended, her gaze remained fixed toward the closed door above her.

Meares stood in the reception in a state of undress. He had not heard the steps creaking as the Sicarian walked closer. He stood naked, in his new form of a much thinner Barbara Lennox. All the extra pounds of weight the real Barbara carried were now absent in his changeling state. This is what she would have looked like had she not let the tragedy in her past define her future self. She was a fine figure of an older woman underneath all the side-effects of her physical and mental self-abuse.

Reaching down, Meares put his hand into the plastic bag which lay on the floor beside him. From within it, he picked out a plain gray skirt. Grabbing it in both hands he shook the creases out as best he could, before putting it on by stepping into it and pulling it up around his waist. He then went back into the plastic bag and brought out a floral-patterned pale shirt as well as some flat soled black shoes.

When he was fully dressed in this garb, he was far from perfectly turned out. There was no makeup. No tights. No underwear. No finesse. No care for his overall appearance, this was a rough-and-ready disguise. Enough to hide his identity and to fool any people who knew the person whom he had copied. Despite the weight loss, no one would doubt that he was indeed Barbara Lennox. This was partly due to time constraints, but also because he hated women's underwear. Bras hurt. Knickers hurt. They all hurt. How women grinned and bared through that discomfort, despite being impressive – was stupid. The same went for makeup. All uncomfortable aspects of female life he could not bring himself to entertain.

For each job, he had to know only the sex and age of the person he was needed to change into. He needed this so he had a ready stock of clothing for each type of person he was mimicking. The clothing size would always be the same, as he could not change his mass, and he chose not to be smaller in height, so all that was needed was appropriate clothing for their age range and sex. The only thing he did not know beforehand was their chosen style, which was why the clothes he chose were plain and devoid of any real stylization. He didn't want to wear anything inappropriate or clashing to their usual look, so went for simple plain patterns, and muted pastel colors.

He walked around the staff side of the reception desk and grabbed the real Barbara from underneath her shoulders as she slumped on her chair. He wheeled her unconscious body backwards across the linoleum and into an adjacent storeroom. Though he was happy that the chair she fell on had wheels, it was still not an easy job. Moving someone of that weight was a huge task for a man of his size. Yet she had to be moved and he was the only one there to do it.

Within the slightly cramped storeroom, he looked down at Barbara slumped in her chair. She was deep in her forced unconsciousness next to the bucket and mop. Her arms hung heavily from her huge frame as she snored lightly to herself.

She would of course be fine and would wake up the moment he transformed back to himself, severing the connection between them. She would feel exactly as she did before, with no aftereffects. The link that had been established between them was only temporary and could not hurt the other person physically. It only ever hurt him. It only always hurt him.

Closing the storeroom door behind him, Meares adjusted the floral shirt he was wearing. He then took in a deep breath; A moment's pause for what was to come. He checked his watch. Done in time as always, he thought to himself, priding himself on his timekeeping skills.

He then walked behind the reception, grabbed a nearby stool and sat in it. Taking on Barbara's previous position. For a few minutes, he planned to zone out; To daydream as he did before each job. Sat in silence within another life, in the calm before the storm.

His thoughts dashed around his head in a dreamlike haze. Would Jaden want to have sex with this female form? he pondered to himself as he imagined multiple scenarios. What would be the harm in asking? After all I could always pretend to be someone else, he thought, an actual woman for all he would know.

Back in the early days of changing, he was very curious about having sex whilst as a woman and went to a bar and offered it up to the first drunken lout he met. That back-alley experience was dirty, unhygienic, sloppy, stinky, but the best sex he had had in a while. So, when he had time and the inclination, he did it again. And again. And again. It became a fun pastime. Yet despite the sordid pleasure it brought, he'd decided to stop over the past few years and instead chose to remain alone. Despite abstinence making him feel alone and unloved, he simply didn't have the time to indulge any more.

He didn't know why he was so attracted to Jaden. That

man was a corpse after all, but there was something about him that Meares could not quantify. An X factor that piqued his interest. A mystery wrapped in an enigma.

Turning around, lost in his daydream, Meares was snapped back to reality when his gaze met with the Sicarian's as she stood at the top of the stairs that led to the basement. She stood, motionless, staring blankly at him.

In this bright daylight, her injuries from the fall in the quarry could be seen clearly. Her face was a fresh mass of scarring, which, unseen by Meares, almost covered her entire body. The Sicarian had done her best to repair the damage from the quarry, the internal organs were placed back inside where they belonged, the skull had been repaired, the jaw reattached, the skin pulled back together – but she could only do so much. She could rebuild but not refine. So, the scars were thick and rough. In their seams, fusing these wounds together, within the very skin itself, lay many parts of flies: wings, legs and torsos of these insects were all buried along the lines of each scar, now part of this newly reanimated body. Their presence a needed component of the Sicarian's healing ability. Even her eyeballs, which were previously burst, were now reformed with parts of flies embedded along their wounds.

In this state, when the wounds could be clearly seen, she looked monstrous. Not that she cared, this was just a temporary body after all which held no importance except to tether her to this reality. A mere vessel of no other importance, she had no care that it was in such a horrible condition. It walked. It could talk. That was all that was needed. Anything else was out of her realm of thought.

"Can... I help you?" Meares asked nervously.

"Do you know me?" came the sternly toned voice from the Sicarian.

"Did Mikko send you?" Meares' voice wavered as he spoke.

The Sicarian let a small smile creep across her scarred face. "Where is the book?"

Up until now, Meares had totally neglected to see the flies that buzzed around this scarred woman. He just now noticed the wounds, and though having his own body rip itself apart to change, he felt sick at the sight of blood or wounds. And the state he saw this woman in now, filled him with dread and nausea.

Then he noticed the flies. She stared back, still blankly as he began to take in the full picture of who was standing here in front of him,

No.

Wait.

It can't be.

The Sicarian then walked slowly toward him from the entrance to the basement, to behind the reception counter.

"I asked… Where is it?"

"I…" he began, before his words trailed off, his attention on her grotesque appearance.

"The book written by the corpse. Where?"

"He… He will bring it. He is due at any moment," Meares said. He had trouble keeping his thoughts together as he realized that he was in the presence of an Elder. "I'm just waiting for him."

"Who brings it?"

The reception door then opened. The Sicarian and Meares turned at once to see Jaden enter the building with a smile on his face.

"Him," Meares said lightly.

The Sicarian's expression t turned sour, as if she was looking at her intended prey. He was in danger and had no idea what was going on, but he knew from her stare towards

Everyday Monsters

him, that this strange scarred woman meant him no good will. Why? He did not know, but could feel that it was because of Deacon. Because of this job – maybe because he knew too much? Maybe this was the last mistake he would ever make? Maybe she was just in a bad mood? His smile dropped as he tried to quickly assess the situation, as he tried to quell the rising sickly feeling in the pit of his stomach.

"Jaden!" Meares spoke in a panic, his mind now racing. He felt powerless as he had no power compared to this being standing beside him.

Jaden glanced back at this fake Barbara Lennox.

"it's me..." Meares uttered weakly, hoping for some recognition.

Jaden may not have known the face, but he realized who it was from the voice. "Meares?" he asked. "That you?"

Meares nodded within his female body. His eyes darted around to the Sicarian then back to Jaden. His wide expression tried to warn Jaden as much as possible. He hoped that Jaden was perceptive enough to sense the danger. Anyone else, Meares would have just stood by with a poker face. But this was Jaden.

Jaden's attention though was on the Sicarian. He stared as a few of the flies which swarmed around her, then landed onto her face. One then walked over her cheek and squeezed its way into her tear duct – pulling itself through the small hole, causing her eye to bulge outward for a brief moment.

It dawned on him who this was. For anyone who knew of the Elders, knew of the Lord of the Flies, knew of how they possessed bodies to carry their beings in this reality.

Deacon was right.

Deacon had warned him

Meares gathered all of his might. He knew he should be quiet. He knew he should just let this Elder do what they needed. But he could not contain his fear. "RUN!" he shouted to Jaden, pleading for him to escape.

With this command, Jaden's eyes widened.

He didn't need to be told twice.

Furiously turning to Meares, the Sicarian let out a bellowing angry growl. "BETRAYER!" she screamed at him. Her right hand shot up and grabbed him by his throat, her left arm quickly raised toward Jaden. From her left palm, the skin split open and unleashed a torrent of flies which broke forth into a large thick spew, spreading across the room with shocking speed and swarmed into Jaden's chest like a cannonball. The force knocked him backward onto the floor, sending him crashing into the coffee table, smashing the vase which had rested on it; the first vase to break in that Inn since its doors had opened.

Turning to Meares, her mouth started to open further and further, until it was as wide as it could go – her expression reflected her murderous fury.

Coming from deep inside of her and past her lips, another huge waterfall of flies shot out, all covered in a thick black liquid. So many were now forcing themselves out of her that her mouth started to split at either side, ripping slowly up her cheeks into a ghoulish smile. Her expression showed no pain at all and only expressed her hate and madness.

The flies moved as a swarm with such aggressive speed into Meares' face, it forced his mouth open. This extreme volume of attackers hit him with a supreme power and a thunderous buzzing, straight into his throat, barreling down his windpipe and into his chest. As they streamed into him, they started to fill up his lungs and then in turn, his stomach. Those that could not get in via the mouth, made their way through his eyes, bursting his eyeballs within seconds, breaking their way into his very skull.

Everyday Monsters

This torrent showed no sign of abating, as more and more winged assassins shot out from inside of the Sicarian at an impossible rate. The constant barrage continued into Meares and broke their way throughout his body with incredible speed and a grotesque force.

Meares' stomach, as well as his assumed female chest, started to swell with the insect's numbers increasing exponentially. His skin started to rip across his belly as the flies broke out to their freedom. As they started to ascend up to destroy his brain, his changing ability began to short circuit. His body started to change back into his male self. His bones broke and bent backward, as his skin loosened and stretched – all whilst this attack was occurring and the flies worked at speed to break him apart.

ALL OF THIS destruction happed so quickly that Jaden hadn't even made it off the floor at this point.

Meares' attempts to scream were now futile, as within seconds of the attack commencing, the flies had torn through his vocal chords, forcing him into unconsciousness soon after – a slumber he would never wake up from. Though such a horrifying way to die, it was thankfully very short. Despite the Sicarian realizing that this betrayer had passed, she continued her attack despite that, enjoying the destruction as much as she could.

Meares' last thoughts as his being was ripped into nothingness, were of Jaden. He only managed to hope that his friend was able escape this fate. There were no flashbacks of his life, no visions of his happier days. Just that one, quick, futile thought.

As his body emptied of its insides, the Sicarian broke her hold on Meares and dropped his now broken, twisted corpse to the floor. His remains now permanently stuck in mid-change, forever left as half of both sexes. He was a mass of broken skin, liquefied organs and crushed, pulped bones. As he lay on the floor with his body in its mixed sex state, his insides pooled out of the burst remains. The flies escaping their victim swarmed back into the air around the Sicarian – back to their master.

Vix watched all of this from within her mental prison that the Sicarian had trapped her in. She screamed from her darkness in terror and heartbreak. No one heard this except the Sicarian – who found her primal fear very arousing.

JADEN AND THE ESCAPE

Walking up at the door to the reception of the Weathered Hearts Inn, Jaden's mind was in a daydream, as Meares' had been earlier. But unlike Meares, his thoughts were of the future away from the Order and this job. He was done thinking about that stupid journal and the status of Deacon's severed head. He was instead dreaming of the vacation he would take. He hadn't had a break in many years, so pondered what he would do. Maybe he would buy a big meal to regenerate totally (which would take a substantial amount of flesh to complete), then he would travel somewhere looking like a real human. Maybe Iceland? He'd always wanted to go there, see the fjords. See the northern lights. Wonder how much of a bonus I'll get from this? he thought to himself.

Opening the door to the reception, he walked in with a smile.

"BETRAYER" was what he heard moments before he was hit in the chest with an almighty force. Thrown backwards he slammed into the wall behind him. His leg caught the table to his left, sending a floral vase that rested on it crashing to the floor – smashing it on impact into many porcelain shards. That vase itself was so hideous, that if Jaden had seen it on any other day, he might have smashed it anyway to put it out of its awful misery.

The roar of the flies that swarmed at him were deafening. After slamming him in the chest, they came at him en masse, trying to keep him pinned to the floor. Pushing him downwards with all their collected might. Their buzzing roared like a chainsaw next to his ears. It was painful to witness and even more grotesque to look at. Each fly seemed to be coated with what Jaden could only guess was motor oil. He knew better than to presume anything about this Elder. He had heard the scary fables about it. Every child growing up around the Order knew of the Sicarian. It was the enforcer for the Elders. Each of the five were ancient beings, and unlike most other children's stories of Gods and monsters, these stories were all true. Every child knew that when the Sicarian came into this world, it was for no other reason than to destroy something. As the attack was on him now, he knew he was in the way of what the Sicarian wanted, and he was in a danger that could bring with it death for the undead. Though happy to hand Deacon and his journal over, he could tell by the situation that there was going to be no negotiation. No payment for services rendered. This Elder would take what it wanted and leave no witnesses. It had not given him a chance to protest or comply. The fact that he was being attacked before having any allowance to speak and explain, spoke enough of what it intended. He was obvious collateral damage and was to be disposed of. This all proved one fact, the journal must be important – but he still could not fathom how. Though it pained Jaden to think about it – he knew Deacon had told the truth. Sure, he was vague and annoying in his answers, but he had warned him. Dammit. He could have listened. Really listened and made preparations, instead of just walking into this building blindly.

Ripping his arm from the grasp of the attacking swarm, Jaden let out a grunt. They dispersed into a thick cloud for a second, before regrouping and renewing their advance onto him again.

He managed to sit up and scramble backwards with both his hands, as he kicked away large swathes of these things off of him. Despite this, they kept on with their attack – as a unified violent force.

Rolling out of the way of another attack, the flies smashed into the bookshelf behind him, splintering the shelves into pieces, causing the dust-coated books which rested on them to cascade into the air, before falling haphazardly onto the floor.

With speed, he scrambled to the door – but not before catching a glimpse of Meares. In that brief moment as he looked back, he saw his handler being ripped apart by the swarm protruding from the Sicarian.

THE RECEPTION DOOR to the Weather Hearts Inn swung open as Jaden sprinted out in a panic. The immense fly swarm closely followed behind, but as the heavy door closed it cut off their link to the Sicarian, and as it did, hundreds of thousands of oil-slicked flies that flew with murderous intent toward Jaden all dropped to the floor in a heartbeat. All motionless as their connection had been severed.

Jaden noticed this as he glanced back, and in that moment smirked through his anger and fear. He raced to the car, opened the door and got in as fast as he could.

. . .

"FUCK!!" he shouted in exasperation as he slammed the car door behind him.

Turning the engine on, he glanced in his rear-view mirror – which pointed toward the hotel – and he saw the Sicarian step out from the reception. The moment it, or as it looked, she, placed one foot onto the ground outside, the hundreds of thousands of dead flies, all at once burst back to life, raised off the dirt and joined the huge swarming plague that now encircled her.

"SON OF A FUCKING BITCH! FUCK, FUCK, FUCK!!". He smashed his hand onto the steering wheel repeatedly as he shouted – but his mind screamed at him that he had to leave. NOW!

He stomped his foot hard onto the accelerator pedal after turning on the ignition. The wheels of his Plymouth Fury span in the dust for a moment, before gaining their traction and propelling the car forward at speed. As he skidded away, the wheels left a large plume of dust behind them.

Continually staring back into his rear-view mirror, Jaden saw the Sicarian was advancing fast upon him. The swarm had now become a large dark cloud, as her pace sped up into a run. As she was at full speed sprinting after him, her whole body suddenly exploded into a mass of flies and became part of the cloud of the attacking plague, chasing him as he drove away.

"You have GOT to be fucking KIDDING me!" he exclaimed whilst speeding away as fast as he could.

The swarm was almost upon the speeding Plymouth Fury as it made its way down the dirt road, away from the Weathered Hearts Inn.

It was in this moment that Jaden realized that he would not win this race. That was the last thing he thought before the swarm descended upon the car, then flipped it over, sending it careening into a tree – crushing the engine block in an instant.

Before he lost consciousness, Jaden saw – though would not remember – the Sicarian reform from within her swarm. The flies rebuilding her body from its destruction, just as it did at the quarry. Her wounds now exponentially increased in number, which made her appearance even more horrifying. As she walked over to the smashed-in windscreen of the car, she crouched down to meet his semi-conscious gaze. She smiled her sickeningly vile smile at him. "Nice try," she mumbled to herself as the buzzing of the flies increased in volume, and he got pulled further into the dark.

THE CAPTURE OF THE DEAD

Johnstone had his orders. His long laundry list of things to do. All things that were to be completed after Deacon was handed over to the bounty hunter. And he had done as many of them as he could.

The next order that Deacon left for him to fulfill was to arrive at an address at a certain time. He didn't know why, he didn't know who he was meeting, if anyone. He knew little, as Deacon was never that detailed with his orders, though they were always to the point and concise. This information was never that burdened with other associated information which some people might find key. He was a vague man in life, in death and undeath. Some people might have found it rude and unhelpful not being given every scrap of information, but Johnstone appreciated it. He preferred simple short instructions. He had no need to know details. As the details were never really that important. Nor could he process the information that well. His brain was not as developed as a normal adult's one, but instead a mish-mash of other brain parts. It was not a finely tuned machine, but it served him as best it could.

. . .

STANDING in front of the cracked oak tree, Johnstone looked down at the destroyed Plymouth Fury.

The front of this once-beautiful car had been crushed to almost nothing, the roof was caved in, the trunk had been ripped off. Johnstone walked around this lump of twisted metal, looking at all the gnarled and wrecked parts. Trying to figure out what he was there for.

As he walked to the car's open trunk, he crouched down and looked inside, but saw nothing in there except a single cracked bowling ball. Deacon's head and the leather satchel containing the journal were gone. Not that he knew that they were ever there.

HE STOOD up again and glanced around. A building stood in the distance, a sign nearby pointed to it. "Weathered Hearts Inn". The tagline on the sign stated a home away from home. Johnstone found that very amusing and let out a booming laugh. It was funny to him because the Inn was currently on fire. Billowing up large plumes of smoke into the blue sky. The flames lapped up over the roof consuming the entire building. And before he left, he had – as ordered – set fire to Deacon's apartment, so the Inn truly was a home away from home.

"YOU GONNA HELP me out of here?" Johnstone heard. His laugh was cut off, and he turned and looked into the passenger side cracked window on the crushed car. There, trapped under the steering wheel, and looking out at him, was Jaden.

"You?" Jaden looked up surprised, as he now recognized Johnstone. "The fuck you doing here?"

"Coming to find you, I guess."

BARBARA'S BAD DAY

Barbara woke from her unconsciousness with a jolt. Twitching as if lightning had just struck her.

From outside of the room she was in, she could hear the fly swarm – not that she could know what was happening. Its collective buzz getting fainter as it flew outside, following the Sicarian away to chase the Plymouth Fury.

"What in hell's bells is going on?" she slurred groggily as she stared at her watch. Was she imagining that noise? "Erin? Erin? That you?" she called out, hoping to hear the reply of the evening shift receptionist.

She moved her considerable bulk to get out of the chair. Slowly and uncomfortably, she used her small arms to lift up her weight to get to her feet.

Eventually standing upright, she steadied herself on a nearby shelf. Catching her breath, she had no idea of evil that just exited her business, or the violence which lay on her reception floor.

. . .

Looking at a dead body in any condition is a horrific experience.

Seeing a body mutilated – like Barbara saw happen to her husband, was exponentially worse, and in almost all cases; mentally scarring for those unprepared.

Now Barbara was about to see her second mutilated body. Which would be two too many for most anyone's lifetime.

This one in particular, though, was much worse than anything she could have ever foreseen.

The mass of skin, guts and shattered bone was almost indistinguishable as being either human or animal remains. It was the fact Barbara could make out a small parakeet tattoo on one part of remains (which normally would have been on her neck), that she could clearly recognize part of her own face amongst the gore – complete with her large mole.

One of these remains' burst eyes stared back up at her, emptily.

Her mind could not process any of it.

She didn't have the imagination or knowledge to guess what this was. So, Barbara Lennox's body did the only thing it could think of doing; at that moment, her heart suffered a colossal myocardial infarction, and exploded within her chest.

A heart attack that no one could ever have recovered from.

She fell to the floor, dead before she landed.

Face first into the gore of Meares' remains.

Barbara Lennox – RIP.

PART III

A VIOLENT PATH

A HEAD FOR INTERROGATION

The interrogation room was perfectly circular and imposing. Not until seeing it would anyone realize how the lack of corners on the walls could affected a prisoner's psyche. It lent an air of impossibility to where they would suffer.

The walls were made from pentagonal cut stone. Each was so large that no man could lift one on their own. Each precisely measured two meters in diameter, with the walls themselves stretching up precisely fifty feet in height, upon where this circular wall ended to a plain white stone ceiling.

There were no lights affixed to these walls and none hung from above. All of the illumination within this room shone upwards from a floor level light source. A seemingly modified dentist's chair lay in the exact center of its stone-paved floor; The chair where the victims of all of Amorfield's interrogations were made to lay. Beaming out from a gap around the circumference of its metal base came a bright white light. A light which reached across the room in all directions and refracted off from the white circular walls, dissipating up their curved height. The design of this light, like the room itself, was entirely specific, intentional and created for the singular purpose as to enhance the interrogations which would take place here. (Or, if they were given their more apt name, torturous executions.) The light beamed out from the metal base, casting shadows of anyone who stood in their way. Shadows which stretched high upon the walls – creating what appeared to be a large dark monster behind those asking questions. The victim would be shrouded in darkness as the light beneath them escaped out, yet the chair they sat in blocked all of their illuminations. It was a genius, yet simply made design.

Around this chair, after the gap where the light poured out from, lay a ring of slatted metal grates which circled around the base. Over the years, these grates had swallowed hundreds upon hundreds of gallons of blood from the victims above. This blood, after venturing past the metal grates, traveled downwards, past the confines of the interrogation room and into a structure below. Though believed to be, the interrogation room was in fact, not the lowest point of Amorfield – there was another below and it was not a place where anyone would wish to venture. The blood from the victims would pour down through the grates from above and be finely separated into four streams. These streams would be split, each to seep down one of the four walls of the room below. The pouring coating the walls like a grotesque water feature, as these streams trickled evenly downward. Down and further down. This room was not meant for living things and was one that made the tall ceilings of the room above miniature in comparison. This was, in essence, a stone-lined pit. It reached down hundreds and hundreds of feet, with no doors or windows on any of its four walls. This pit was a vessel for the remains to be thrown into from above. Many, many thousands of victims had been processed in the interrogation room. After they were questioned, if deemed necessary (which it almost invariably would be) the chair would give way, sending the decimated corpse downwards, as it tumbled over itself into the pit below. Joining the myriad of other discarded bodies.

At the top of this room of death, circling the top part of a wall, was a ring of brilliant white lights, which fed up past the dripping blood, into the interrogation room above, to give it its illumination.

This room was already half-full. Over the years, the remains within had turned from being solid upon entry, to now being liquefied into a meaty slurry. A thick gelatinous lake of decayed flesh and malleable bones, which hungered for more sacrifices to be cast into it.

Some higher-up employees within Amorfield – those few who knew about the existence of this room – had at times, pondered what would happen if this pit should fill beyond capacity - When no more could join the rancid soup within. Though it would take many centuries more to do, with many more thousands of bodies needed, it would eventually have to reach its limit. The running joke was that Amorfield would either have to move, or give up interrogating. It was the former that was the likeliest of these two scenarios.

With the frequency that this room needed to be used, along with the number of victims that were cast into the lakes of death below, the smell produced from this pit seeped throughout the entirety of the complex. The stench coupled with the high heat permeated throughout every room of Amorfield. Everyone could smell it, though no one without knowledge of the pit would ever know where it came from. If anyone was transported to this facility, into any room, having never been before – they would immediately sense the creeping death from deep within every fiber of their being.

Each part of their subconscious would scream at them to run. The smell alone would alert their unconscious primitive mind to the fact they should leave, that nothing here was any good. For those that had been here before, the dread was what was used to keep workers in line. Here no one felt they could ever step out of line, despite having the faith to not want to, the sense of foreboding in the complex insured it would never be the case, due on no small part to this pit.

WHILST STARING at Deacon's severed head, which had been placed on the middle of the interrogation chair, the Sicarian paced slowly. Walking around the circumference, around this body-less prisoner, her lips slowly cracked a cruel smile, as she took one slow step after another. Never breaking her eye contact from him.

As with everywhere the Sicarian went, dozens of flies followed. They flew, buzzing loudly, over Deacon. Each taking turns to land on him and eat their fill – a miniscule bite of flesh here, a morsel of blood there.

Deacon grasped tightly onto any last moments of his life that he could. The skin on his face now missed large chunks of itself, exposing the dried bone that existed below. One of his eyes had been punctured. From within this socket, from inside his brain, flies escaped after entering, feeding, then scuttling back out onto his cheek. The black viscous liquid covering them left tiny marks as they scurried over his dead and pallid skin.

His other eye was half-closed from exhaustion. He had been tortured significantly more over the past few hours. Though the pit below remained empty of any offering, as barely any blood remained within him to fall down. The walls below would remain barren of any sanguine offerings from

Everyday Monsters

him. The best they might hope for would be a dried husk of a skull.

Deacon knew this was undoubtedly it for him. He knew he would die today and held no illusions that any other eventuality would arrive at his metaphorical feet. Yet, he did not regret a thing. This was what he intended. This is what he needed to do. He needed the balance to be readdressed. He needed his plan to be realized in order for the next step to begin.

He felt smug.

Despite the barrage of violence being meted out on him, he was still laughing inside. Amused that his captor had no idea what she was doing or really looking for. With all the facts of the situation, she would have left him alone – knowing that any actions against him were not only futile but predictable. If she kept him alive, he would fail – but that was an impossibility in his mind.

He was glad that his inner thought was secure from her; she had no power over him like she did others. He was dead and no-one could see the inner thoughts of a deceased brain. He did not hold all the cards, though. He knew as much as he could, but only up to a certain point. He knew what he had to do, but not what others would do beyond his plan. He knew the path up to his death. He already discovered years ago that this was the point where his light would fade out, but he did not know exactly how. After his death, he could only hope that the plan he put into motion would be completed, but as with all magic – you can plan and plan, but nature has a way of subverting even things that normally should not comply to its steadfast rules.

For Deacon, watching the plan was like watching a stick traveling along a river. Keeping track of it was not a problem – keeping track of the surrounding water at the same time, however, was the impossible portion of the task. He knew where the stick would end up, but did not know the purpose of each and every droplet of water that existed within that river. At the end of the day, no matter what, the stick would always end up at its destination. It might be delayed for a while, but as long as the river flowed, it would reach the end. Yet in a world of infinite possibilities, Deacon dreaded that he could only really plan each part of each moment up to this point – after was what he dreaded. But what did it really matter? He would be too dead to witness it... He hoped to all the Gods in creation that he was right and would be able to breathe again someday.

He knew the Sicarian. He had met her in the past. He had read her entire history. Had learned all of her hidden truths. He didn't know the face she wore, but he could sense her signature malevolence which eked out from her pores.

The Sicarian had said nothing to him at all. Not one word during his torture. He was just cut and beaten for her thrill, to appease her sadistic appetites. Now, with his torture finished, she just slowly walked around his chair. Her flies decimated him in slow motion. She recognized this man. She had hunted him in the past to no avail. He was elusive and knew how to hide from all kinds of tracking. Now, though, he was here – finally in front of her – finally her victim. She did not hold any malice towards him for evading her over the years. She respected his skill at running. But her respect did not negate any owed fury that was to be met out upon him – and with this fury, she held nothing back.

He was nothing more than her victim. Deacon, as he chose to call himself now, would soon be nothing more than a memory – and as she believed, no longer be a potential danger to her and her kind.

She didn't really need to bring him here to Amorfield. She

didn't really need anything. The journal itself was what she needed – and it was safe after its journey having been intercepted. Though she wanted to read it. Though she wished to know what this corpse had inked onto that parchment. To read the future he had written. She wanted more to kill him. She wanted to feel the rush of his demise first. She had seen the effects of his previous work and knew that the journal was his primary mission, but her bloodlust was first and foremost her reason for her being which could not be ignored or relegated.

After she discovered his head in the remains of the Plymouth Fury, she was quite shocked. An emotion that she rarely felt. As soon as she met his gaze, she stared at this impossibly living head. A condition she had believed to be an exaggeration or a misheard descriptor of Deacon's current condition. As soon as she saw him – all she could really feel was an unbridled lust to finally end his life. Something that she felt was not only a long time coming but deserved. It was a shame though, as he was a marvel of science and magic combined.

Here he was, a prisoner in the chair of pain and death. She had glanced at the journal and had sensed a danger in its inked symbols. She presumed they were to be written in Catigeux symbols – her language – but they were not. They were not in any language she could read. She knew the danger of presumption – so had to find out what language this was in. What cypher was used to make these symbols unreadable. Deacon told Jaden they were in Catigeux, but he had lied. Knowing this man, she thought, this could be made from the darkest and most powerful magic – possibly even something older than her. Nothing could be left to chance or ignorance of the unknown.

Symbology in the respect of magic was complex. On their

own, standalone symbols were nothing special and held no power. They had meaning of course, but it was only when they were in a sequence that the real power was exposed. That was the principle of magical writings. The runes or symbols or commands used were solely part of a whole, so could not be understood until all of the symbols were read. It was also the meanings of the symbols not written that were of great importance. Magic was as much about omission of language as well as language included in order to create the deeper meaning. The Sicarian knew that as long as she could not read this book, the more danger there could be, she did not want the author to be alive though, as she could not trust any truths to be forthcoming from his treacherous mouth. Instead she would get any answers from his death.

"Aren't you going to ask me anything, you fetid bag of putrid shit?" wheezed Deacon with his weakened voice. His remaining eye fluttered as he tried to fight off the inevitable darkness from enveloping him just yet.

The Sicarian smiled to herself. "I do not need you alive to find the answers I want..."

Deacon's next few moments were felt slowly filling with dread. He had lived the past decade knowing this path, but saw the Sicarian's glee. He panicked as to what it was that he did not see; whether this was a bluff of genuine confidence from her.

"I guess... this is goodbye?" she uttered, her words almost dripping out from her lips with an air of evil. "I supposed you may have met the leech before, correct?"

This was a prime example of the dangerous unknown. A missing piece of a puzzle not yet completed. The leech. The goddamn leech. How did he not know that this thing was still in existence?

The fact that the Sicarian was not working alone was in

itself part of the unknown equation, as she existed primarily in solitude. She would normally destroy any being who even tried to assist her. She was perpetual isolation and decay in a physical form – and now she was working with the leech – who somehow still walked the earth? Well, that was something that he could not have foreseen.

This Leech was not the same creature as the small blood sucking animals which shared its name, but was something worse. Something that was supposed to be dead a millennium ago, yet somehow it was here with the Sicarian.

This could undo everything, Deacon thought to himself. How had he not seen the path splitting so soon? He should have known this was a possible eventuality. He knew where he would end, but with the leech, the new path could be far removed from what he had planned for the future.

The Sicarian sensed Deacon's dread about the leech. Because of that, she felt the warm glow of cruelty crawling throughout her stolen body. She knew he was scared of chaos, so her mentioning the Leech brought that chaos in, and allowed it to reign over his death.

OUTSIDE OF THE INTERROGATION ROOM, three floors up in the Administrator's office, lay the Moogle. Sleeping atop the three sets of remains from his recent execution, he snored loudly. The executed prisoner's limbs and innards created a grotesque mattress for his monstrously blubbery body.

It would be foolish to think that dreams were absent from such a creature's slumber. Of course, this creature was not a mammal or any kind of known genus – but here he lay, curled up amongst his grotesquery, twitching slightly at a nocturnal fantasy. He was reliving the moments he had just experienced, over and over again. It was his reason to be. It was his joy. His chosen purpose and most adored pastime was to end the lives of the guilty – it was all he knew and all he wanted to know. Nothing else existed for him of note. It was Mikko that gave him the additional guidance he needed – the guidance which showed him the joy of relishing the calm before the storm. To eat the fear before the flesh. To extend his pleasure for far longer than only enjoying the brief moment stealing life and gifting death. Yes, he deemed all those he ate guilty. But his measure of guilt was simply not being able to run away.

Mikko was sat at his desk at the other side of the room, deep in thought. The Sicarian's presence was not part of the calm he craved for in his life. Yet he had to obey and bring this Elder forth into a chosen host's body. The presence of this strange Journal (which the Sicarian had since kept referring to as an "offering") was something Mikko ruminated on considerably.

Ever since he became the Administrator of Amorfield, he'd been told to keep an eye on those who would seek to undo. To look for the written word on human skin. To look for particular symbols in texts. So, he did that as best as he could. For years asking the same questions over and over if anything written was involved in any work the Order did. But every answer was a "no". Soon the cause lost its meaning and became a standard question which was always denied by others. It was something that was considered a joke amongst the hunter community – a joke they didn't really understand the root of.

But when the call came from the handler about what his collector had found, Mikko asked about skin pages and symbols as he normally would – and he got the reply he didn't anticipate. It was then that the dread crept in. He had been issued one command if anything like this was found – to enable the Sicarian to cross over. So that is exactly what he

Everyday Monsters

did, not before going into the room of light first, to double check that was what they wanted. Hoping that they would deem it now unnecessary.

He had foolishly thought that what they were looking for was just an old superstition. He had never had the dubious honor of calling forth the Lord of the Flies before and calling this unmaker was a portent to him; a sign that all that was will soon not be, and all that will be will have no order – so no place for him. A bit of paranoia on his part, but still something he genuinely felt.

People would be mistaken for thinking that Mikko's faith in the Elders was out of love or devotion. For him, this was not like a religion where you would blindly deify a constructed image. He was not in the habit of giving love to something imaginary and unproven. This was his voluntary servitude to beings that were creators and destroyers of the universe. One did not revere or love them, one simply lived in awe and fear of them, whilst playing their own part to ensure that they were not left dead in their wake. From this awe and fear, he followed the Order's demands to the letter. He gladly ended countless of lives of those who showed any inclination for the slightest disobedience to them. He would do anything that was asked. No matter if he agreed or not, so he held others up to the same standard.

As someone who could hear thoughts unspoken, he had heard mild dissension in every employee's thoughts from time to time and would always forgive that – he just would never forgive such thoughts in writing or speech or being. That what he presumed the journal was – a written manifesto to overthrow the Elders. Elaborately made of skin. So, understood what would happen if the threat was not quelled with extreme prejudice. He knew why the Sicarian was sent. He just felt it was a rocket launcher used to kill a fly.

Of course, Mikko wanted to read the journal – who wouldn't? His deities seemed to be in fear of it – any sane being would be curious enough to ask why they felt such an emotion? Just because it was on skin? Because it was symbols not writing? But he kept all thoughts to one side. He saw the journal for a moment when the Sicarian walked through the access point with his predecessor – more correctly, holding his severed yet somehow alive, head. "Pleasure to meet you again, Arius," Mikko heard himself say to the head as it passed him by, gripped by the hair in the Sicarian's hand. He had no inclination to call this head by anything other than the name he had known him by, when he was the Administrator before Mikko.

Mikko then asked the Sicarian if the journal was what they thought it was – but was met with a threat of evisceration if he asked one more word from her.

So he retreated to his office instead.

THE STITCHING OF DEACON SORBIC

"Deacon Sorbic is not his actual name, you know?" Johnstone said matter-of-factly. Then again nothing he ever said could be spoken in any other way. As a Golem, he was unbridled by any ability to speak lies, or speak with imagination and flourish. Golems were simple, in the fact that they could only ever tell the truth, not through any choice or higher morality – but they did not possess any ability to deceive. Being a manufactured entity, they were made up of – and not always in entirety – human body parts. They may have had human brains, human limbs, but the spark was not there that allowed them the ability to be one of the flawed creations, such as humans were. It would be like telling a computer to do one thing, and it choosing to do something else instead. It was just not possible, unless the computer was programmed to oppose any issued direct command. It was the unknown spark of humanity that gave humans that ability to connive, and Johnstone was not a human.

"What's his name then?" Jaden enquired, now sitting opposite the Golem.

Johnstone shrugged. He knew some morsels of the story – the parts Deacon found relevant, but not all. "It was never important to know."

"Not important?" Jaden replied.

"He's not that man anymore, anyway," he said. "The man he is now, soon will not be. And then the next part will begin."

They were sat within an old and decrepit stone tomb; a mausoleum which rested in the center of a large abandoned cemetery. They sat on a couple of grave markers which were positioned around the circumference of a large stone coffin which rested in the middle of the tomb.

Johnstone picked up a large cloth sack from beside him and emptied what was inside onto the top of a coffin. The chopped up remains of Deacon Sorbic tumbled out and on to the cold old stone.

"You don't know his real name, you killed him, and now you're helping him?"

"He's my master. I do what I'm asked by him," came the blank reply.

"Why all this though? If he's your master? Why not just do it? Just walk into Amorfield and get him—"

"No one can just walk in. You know that, right? You worked for them," Johnstone replied, cutting Jaden off.

"Only person from the Order I know is... WAS... my old handler – and he... just..." It hit Jaden that the person who had just died was the only person he spoke to regularly; dare he say it – was the only friend he had.

"I'm sorry for your loss, by the way..." Johnstone spoke the words, but he was just saying what he had been taught should be said in situations like this. He felt no actual sadness for anyone about death occurring. He was made of death, after

Everyday Monsters

all. It was just a part of the evolution of life for him. But as Deacon had taught him, humans saw death as the villain. They saw all lives passing over to nothingness as tragedy. "But no, we're not going to Amorfield to save him. That's just the distraction. The convolution of events so we can do this. Did you think that we were going there now?"

Jaden had no reply. He glanced around and then shrugged at the Golem. "I have no fucking idea what you're doing."

"What d'you think we're doing then?" Johnstone asked.

"It's a fucking cemetery... How do I know? Not like you're telling me anything." Jaden was feeling like it might be time to leave. "What the hell am I here for, anyway? I just nearly got killed by that Sicarian asshole. He, she. Whatever... they included ME in this. You told me I could help stop it, and that this could go back to being normal – If I followed you. So, you tell me what I should say?"

"Deacon couldn't walk into Amorfield, he's one of the banished – so he could only get in there if escorted. Thus, he created a myth that posed danger to those in charge, so they would have no question but to take him there. Anything less than that threat would be ignored. So, them doing that, meant they would not see the real myth waiting to be made real." He motioned to the body parts on the coffin in front of him. Jaden was no closer to understanding than he was before the Golem spoke.

"And now we have to commence."

"Commence what?

"You may not understand the whys, but you're important to all of this. I don't know how, but you were where I was supposed to find you. And you were supposed to come here. Deacon made it so. He saw your life before. The role you played in the universe. The strength you had, and still have."

"Life before?" Jaden asked.

"You don't understand it. You can't. No one can see it yet. He's creating a diversion – done so they have no idea that we're doing this. There're paths we gotta take – whether we want to or not – like this one. But the moment he dies, we have to prepare, then we'll have to act fast and quick, before the path ends. Before they know—"

Jaden had spent the past 32 hours with Johnstone. After the car crash and the Inn burning down, Johnstone had rescued him from the confines of the crushed driver's seat. He had asked him to join him on the mission to beat the Sicarian. Out of anger for his close brush with death, he agreed. He wanted out of this mess and for life to revert to how it was. But he also wanted out of the car. He could have just said fuck you and walked away after being helped out of the wreckage – but no matter what he did though, he could not bring himself to leave. Even though he really, really wanted to.

The pull of needing to stay here was the thing he wanted answers to the most.

Johnstone took off his suit jacket and reached into a large full rucksack which lay on the floor behind him. From within it, he removed a large hunting dagger and a sewing kit. "It's about completing the paths we live to make new ones." He placed these items beside him on a grave marker, as he then proceeded to remove his shirt, his eyes never losing focus on Deacon's limbs laying on the coffin.

Though the Golem had told him what was about to happen, it was still something he didn't understand or approve of. Yet he was here nonetheless, about to help a Golem rip himself to pieces.

"Get ready to take over, when I can't reach any more," the patchwork monster said. His large hand reached up to his shoulder, his finger pushed itself into the seam between his attached limbs. He then slowly ripped out the thread which attached that limb to his torso. Jaden winced in empathy as he watched. The sound of snapping thread and ripping flesh was grotesque – yet did not affect Johnstone at all. He felt none of it. Even if he could, he would still carry on with as much determination. His master commanded it, after all, and his Master's word was gospel.

Deacon had given the Golem the gift of not feeling pain, which was not something that all masters did for their creations. But as he knew what lay ahead for Johnstone, he had to do this one kindness.

After the thread around the circumference of his shoulder had been torn out, Johnstone lifted his arm up towards Jaden – who looked back at him curiously, "Guess you need me to pull now?" Jaden asked.

Johnstone nodded, his expression blank and almost sad.

Sighing, Jaden stood up from the small stone marker he sat on, leaned over and grabbed the offered hand by its wrist. He then started to pull hard, but to no avail. Realizing that this was not an easy job, he placed his foot on the coffin in front of him for purchase and pulled harder. Using all the strength he could muster, he gritted his teeth. Slowly the fused flesh tore away from the adjoining torso and after a couple more yanks, Johnstone's arm was removed from the socket with a loud cracking and disturbing "pop" as the bone disconnected from its socket.

Johnstone glanced at the open wound on his shoulder, then back up at Jaden. He nodded to him in thanks. Jaden smiled as he lifted the detached arm up and, with the palm towards his other hand, he gave himself a small round of applause.

Johnstone did not react, and Jaden immediately regretted his poor attempt at levity. Quickly dropping his smile, he put the Golem's arm down. He then grabbed the matching arm of

Deacon's from off the coffin and handed it to the Golem, who took it from him gingerly.

With the connecting bone exposed at the end of the Deacon's arm, Johnstone replaced this where his old arm had been – popping Deacon's arm bone into his exposed shoulder joint.

It clicked into his socket as if it was meant to fit. He then let the arm flop down as he reached to the coffin top and grabbed a prepared needle and thick, almost twine-like, thread.

Starting with the part nearest him, Johnstone stabbed the needle into his own flesh, then jammed it through to the meat on Deacon's now attached arm. Fumbling with the difficulty of doing it himself, Johnstone realized that this was a much more difficult operation than he had originally anticipated.

Jaden watched for a few moments at the clumsy attempts at stitching with his left hand, then stood up. "Here, let me," he said, whilst walking around the coffin to where Johnstone sat. Without even a word of thanks (or complaint) Johnstone dropped the needle, letting it hang over his chest to rest onto his arm.

Jaden suddenly regretted offering to help. Sure, he would still do it, but he knew he would have to attach both upper thighs, meaning he would be working right next to the Golem's penis, balls and asshole.

He considered just dropping the thread and leaving right there and then. He pictured himself shouting "Fuck this bullshit!" and striding off into the sunset. But it wasn't to be. Penis, balls and asshole it was. He was too polite to not do it.

"And then what? What's after this?" Jaden asked. Trying to create some more discourse to distract from the horrific work he was undertaking.

"We wait."

"For?"

"Not what, who."

Jaden still didn't appreciate the vagueness, but was more concerned with his dread at attaching the thigh. Imagine how sweaty and gross it is down there, he quickly thought, like a fucking vinegar swamp. In a situation where the fate of the world was allegedly at stake (though he only had the Golem's word for it), in a reality where a severed head could talk, where a monster just tried to kill him (a monster which he previously thought was just a boogeyman story told to kids to keep them compliant) – the fact his mind was stuck on this part of his journey, the part of having to work next to a giant's groin was something he was quite glad about – at least he wasn't dwelling on the danger itself. Just on his eventual proximity to a Golem's undercarriage. They were going up against a being that humanity had made into their version of the devil. What humans saw as the most ultimate evil – but no; Jaden was only dreading being next to a fat man's sweaty butthole. It was a preferable dread for sure.

ALBERT WALKED the halls of Amorfield with wavering confidence.

He had to keep his thoughts unthought.

He couldn't let Mikko hear any of them.

Now more than ever he had to be strong.

This was his chance.

His one shot.

His only shot.

His time had finally come.

He had just been informed by some operatives in the field about the location of Johnstone and Jaden. About them traveling eastward from the Weathered Hearts Inn together.

They had to be part of it, yet Mikko could not know this. This was not Mikko's problem to solve. This was his own. And he had to be their hero of the day. He had to earn the rewards from the Elders.

S<small>ILENCE WAS</small> what he would have wanted to have in his mind, but instead, he couldn't help thinking of what he was about to do. No matter what he tried he couldn't silence the thoughts. So, did what he always did. Grabbing the nearest song in his head, the song he always used to camouflage his mind, he started to hum lightly. He sang in his head with all his might.

Death's wanting, Light's dying. Dark is rising, I gave you all the chance. He stared forward wide-eyed as he sang silently and walked down a hallway with renewed purpose.

Concentrate, Albert, concentrate.

Turning a corner, he knew that he only had two more hallways to walk down, then he was at the access point, the place where he could do something which would signal the end of the unworthy Administrator, Mikko.

I know that, Fires that follow, Ground be swallowed today... his mind blared, pushing all other thoughts into silence.

Blood drying, Silent crying, World be swept away – turning a corner he almost burst into singing the song aloud, as he concentrated on it so strongly.

In this house of pallid walls. The door was ahead of him.

Found you bled. He reached for the handle as he took out his key card with his other hand. Here you are, Albert. Thank you, fate!

He swiped his key card across the metal card reader on the wall.

Hour to hour. The door light that was red switched to green.

Everyday Monsters

He breathed a sigh of relief for a moment.

In your eyes... Opening the door, he was met with the imposing stature of the Moogle blocking his entrance to the access point. This beast stared down at him. Breathing heavily, drooling huge long ropes of saliva from his gaping grinning mouth, his black hidden eyes terrifying Albert to his core.

"Words I said will Echo On?" a voice uttered to the same tune, breaking the silent tension.

The Moogle stepped back a few large grotesque paces, to reveal Mikko standing and with a self-satisfied grin upon his face.

Albert's mental wall fell down from the shock. For the first time, he had no protection from his current thoughts being heard.

"Now why would you be thinking about locking the access point?"

Albert stood frozen, staring at his accusers.

"There are two others? Very interesting Albert... Now tell me, why are you hiding this finding from me?" Mikko asked, then smiled at the answer he found in Albert's mind.

"Oh really? Now I normally would not do this. Judge a man on the evidence of his mind, but these are some extenuating circumstances, wouldn't you agree?" He looked to the Moogle, then nodded,

Albert was able to speak one single word before the Moogle – with his skin tags audibly vibrating – lunged toward him. "Sorry—" he began.

The Moogle's stomach then opened wide toward him, as it lunged and bit through his body – slicing him clean in two before another word could escape. Albert fell dead in less than a second. The blood and innards from his body slopped to the floor as they sprayed their liquid up the walls.

Specks of blood had managed to fly far backwards across

the room and hit Mikko on his patent leather shoes. In disgust, he glanced down, then immediately took out a napkin from his pocket, leaned down and cleaned the spot of blood off. His footwear was immaculate at all times and despite the given situation, he had to ensure it was always the case.

In the last milliseconds of his life, Albert had seen something he never thought was possible. As the Moogle's chest enveloped his soon to be decimated body – in the very moment before this thing had crunched through his ribcage, eviscerating all of his internal organs and sending him into the eternal darkness – he saw something in there with the Moogle. Something deep at the bottom of its cavernous chest-mouth. A light. A strange, dull light. Before he could form a thought as to what it could be, it had all ended for him. Not with a scream. Not with a whimper. With nothing but the sound of his body being crushed.

The Moogle's stomach ate its victim loudly, opening and closing as it chewed up Albert's body. Each time his stomach-mouth opened and closed, it made a loud wet smacking sound, like a child eating toffee through a megaphone.

Mikko presumed Albert's last words must have been an apology for his blasphemous actions. Sorry, Mikko. They made me. or Sorry Mikko, I did wrong, please forgive me. But in actuality, Albert intended to say Sorry, but fuck you both.

Little did Albert know his actions would indeed be the undoing of Mikko that he had wished for. He just had to pay the price in his own blood for it to happen.

It was an end which Albert would not have wanted as he did not wish to die, but if he knew how things were to progress with Mikko – the effect that his death would have on Mikko's future, he would have died with a smile plastered over his round, sweaty face.

DESTROY, DISCOVER, REBUILD

Mikko held up the receiver to an old rotary phone within the access point room, its white cable curling its way back to the hub which was affixed to the wall behind him.

He stood silently, listening to the tone ringing. Waiting. Waiting for someone. Waiting for anyone to pick up at the other end.

He glanced at the remaining bloodstains on the floor in front of him, the last remnants of Albert. The final evidence of his body that was now being licked clean by the Moogle; on his haunches, lapping up the blood from the floor with his long and calloused tongue. Mikko considered this to be an unfortunately grotesque and violent end for someone who had – up until then – been a stalwart worker. Dedicated. Unwavering. Mikko presumed he had heard every thought Albert had from their many years of working together. From hearing about what he wanted to eat that day, to whom he wanted to have sex with. To that damn song. Over and over again. Echo on, or something? He had only ever heard that blathering nonsense in Albert's head. Did he write it? Steal it?

Mikko disliked music in general so would have no way to find out. But he knew that song more than most others, solely due to Albert.

Nothing he read in this man's mind had ever been out of the ordinary, or even against any status quo. This worried him. When and how was Albert corrupted? It must have been corruption! Mikko could not fathom any other option. The thought that Albert hated him? Impossible. Why would he hate his Administrator? Albert had worked there 7 days a week and never left the complex. When could anyone have gotten to him? Was it Arius? And, more importantly, why wasn't anyone answering the damn phone?

He needed the Sicarian to know of what happened – of the corruption that spread out to further than they had presumed. That it was more than just one man – Arius must be part of a larger cabal. A cabal which included the Golem and a zombie which Albert hid in his mind. This Order might have been huge, might have had an immeasurable number of followers – but it only took a tiny thorn to incapacitate a lion, after all.

He hung up the phone, exasperated, as no one picked up.

He then dialed another number.

He had to tell the other Administrators.

They had to know of the danger.

As Mikko talked frantically on the phone, the Moogle finished licking the remnants of his meal. Like all executions, for him – one was never enough. The hunger was unbearable and only satiated for the fleeting moments when he swallowed the flesh or lapped up the blood. After his meal, came the vacuous pain from within his core. A hunger which invariably amplified his rage. He was a creature of fury driven

Everyday Monsters

by a need to feast. He needed another meal soon. He always needed another meal soon.

He heard Mikko talking, telling other Administrators what was happening, as well as who they needed to look for. For such a secretive man, he was telling a lot of people everything he could – Mikko's anxiety rose to an unmanageable level and this was all he could think of to do.

He hung up the phone after the fourth call, looking relieved. He had shared his panic amongst his peers; all of whom would keep watch for the two men in question.

Hearing unspoken words from the Moogle, he then sighed. "Yes, I know, my friend... It might not be the most intelligent idea I've ever had. But what else could I do? All eyes are better than 2, after all."

His friend, meanwhile, was sat in the corner of the room, running one vile, fat-filled finger over his quivering belly lips. Smearing some blood off those lips, and onto his finger. He then brought his finger up to his mouth and sucked it like a child at their mother's teat.

"Well, what can we do? We cannot do this alone. Especially as she is not available."

The Moogle looked up at Mikko, still sucking the blood from his fingers.

"Send you? Why? We were ordered not to get involved. Besides Albert's plan failed. And sending you to get them welcomes them here!"

Mikko looks half-annoyed and half-concerned at what the Moogle had silently replied to him. "Yes, you could kill them... But what if you don't find them? She would be furious."

The Moogle replied without words.

"Yes. Yes, I do trust you. Of course, I do!" Mikko rubbed his eyes with his thumb and forefinger. This conversation was taking a familiar turn; started with Mikko stating facts, which the Moogle (intentionally) chose to not understand. Then would ask more questions until, finally, Mikko would relent and let him do what he wanted to anyway.

"Fine! Okay? Go if you must! Just be quick about it."

With surprising speed, the huge bulk of the Moogle stood up. His face showed his large, bloodied, yet victorious, smile. He knew how to work Mikko and he did it well. A primitive mind like his was sometimes the best weapon against an intelligent mind. You cannot win an argument with someone so simple. They believe what they want, and other factors like logic and planning make no sense to them. If they believe one thing, then you could show them the facts disproving it all – but they will just label you a villain, then believe all you say is all a lie – FAKE NEWS!. There is no winning in those situations. The Moogle knew that this was the case and relished it. Across monsters and humans, "fake news" was always the rallying cry of the imbecile. He wasn't as dumb as everyone thought he was, though. His brain might have been limited in its capacity, but he knew how to win over this vastly intelligent man.

Mikko walked over to his gargantuan friend, looked up at his monstrous face, then noticed how pleased he was with his win. "My friend. Please consider staying here. They'll be caught, no matter what."

The Moogle walked heavily over to the access point; a large shadowed doorway against the wall at the far end of the room. As he did Mikko heard some of the Moogle's thoughts.

"You can't say that!" Mikko called out to him, "That's blasphemy!" he exclaimed as he heard an insult about the Sicarian. The Moogle then turned and looked at Mikko for a moment.

"Oh," Mikko said, hearing the Moogle's reply. "You now think you're too stupid to be blasphemous?"

Everyday Monsters

The Moogle grinned a sickly grin, then turned back to the access point.

IN A PREVIOUS LIFE, Mikko could have been a much more powerful man than he was here. Some believed he had total power now, but in his mind, he was just a puppet. He was a voice box for the will of the Order, spending his life passing down the rules and regulations to the masses beneath him, all whilst governing over his nominated sector and the conduit to the Elders. Sure, the masses of those followers saw him as a man of immense influence and power, but he did not see what they believed. It was like saying that a newspaper was powerful, instead of the actual words that were printed within it. The paper itself could only viewed as powerful because of the words – not despite them. Like that paper, he was viewed as powerful because of the Order's words. He was nothing without his position and it was the same here – he saw himself as having no power to really stop the Moogle, especially as he was secretly glad that someone was doing something.

The Moogle stood in the shadowed access point as Mikko walked up and stood beside him. Putting one hand on his friend's sweaty, pockmarked, skin tag laden shoulder, he spoke the words: "May the light lead you, my dear friend."

The Moogle raised a hand and placed it over Mikko's.

"I know. You don't have to keep telling me. You'll be fine. You always will be."

Stepping out of the access point, with his other hand, Mikko pressed a button on the wall beside them. In an instant, this doorway became a blinding pool of liquid light, illuminating the room with its glow. Mikko squinted at the brightness as he looked to the Moogle. This light was one of the few things that broke through the shadows of the Moogle's eye sockets, allowing his eyeballs to be seen within their consuming darkness. These eyes, strangely, looked very kind and were a light hue of green. The antithesis of what anyone would guess his eyes would look like.

"Destroy. Destroy. Destroy," Mikko said with a smile as the Moogle walked into the light and disappeared.

Saying Destroy. Discover. Rebuild. was something that the Order had indoctrinated into them. Humanity believed in Question. Analyze. Discover. as their preferred method of fact finding, but throughout the years the Order took a different route, and believed that only real truth could be discovered within the remains of what once was:

- Destroy anything that stands against you. No questions. No mercy. Decimate with extreme prejudice.
- Discover reasons behind the root cause with clear 20/20 vision. No emotions such as anger or fear should block your way.
- Rebuild what was destroyed with something better in its place, or nothing in its place at all.

THE ORDER WAS VERY MUCH in favor of burning bridges and employing a scorched earth policy. If any person was brutally honest with themselves, they would agree that this was the most expedient way – the best way to demand compliance amongst those it dealt with. To know that one small infraction would result in immediate and unemotional execution? That was a powerful deterrent. To know that if anything stood in their way it would be destroyed no matter what? That notion was terrifying to go against.

As to why Mikko said Destroy. Destroy. Destroy. to the Moogle was a joke between them – Of course, the Moogle would destroy everything in its path even without this belief, but instead of then looking for answers and rebuilding, he was more than likely to either start sleeping on top of, or rut with the remains. So, Destroy. Destroy. Destroy. was what the saying had become between them. Mikko accepting of the reality of his friend's needs and abilities.

Mikko walked briskly through the hallways of Amorfield. After seeing his friend off, he was now tasked with the unenviable mission of finding the Sicarian and telling her about Albert, as well as the others in league with Arius. He knew he had to tread carefully whenever he talked to one of the Elders, and it caused him to break out in a cold sweat. You never knew which way a deity's temperament would go when given news. They could be pleased or they could be furious – either was possible in equal measure.

The wind blew a chill across the smoldering remains of the Weathered Hearts Inn. The flames had long since been quelled by the fire services. The building was now been cordoned off by the investigating police officers, with long strips of yellow "caution" tape lining the now blackened ruins.

Of the 29 rooms housed within that Inn, only three guest rooms had been unoccupied. All of the others were booked with guests. These bookings were mostly traveling businessmen or long-distance truckers. But there always had been a regular turnover of young men and women who chose to stop here for a night on their way to the "big city", a place where they would fulfill their dreams of becoming a star. Unlike the hundreds of identical dreamers who passed through here – kids on the exact same mission as they were, with exactly the same plan and dreams as they had – these kids would tell you that they were different to the others that passed through. These kids would make it – there was no question of maybe in their minds, as well as no failure to consider. They were not like the other wannabes. They were the ones! The special ones. Invariably, these kids were the popular people of their town. They were the youths that won all the local accolades in their unknown Podunk hamlets. So, if the mayor of whoeverthefuckcaresville thought these particular people were stars in the making, then think of what they could achieve in the big city? Look out world – here I come! they all thought.

If any of the particular dreamers who were in the Inn when the fire hit had survived, they would have gone on to their chosen "big city" the next day. They'd have gone to every audition they could find. Auditions where they would have seen that all the other kids had exactly the same dream as them, as well as having way more talent than them. The feedback from the auditions would have referred to their attempt as "prosaic" – and because of their poor education and naivety, they would presume that this was a compliment. Ultimately though, they would get rejected. The next step in their journey, these kids would try to find any job they could to afford them food and a place to live. Whether waiting tables or becoming a cashier – that soon would not be enough for them. The pay would be too little to get by as their savings disappeared. They had to try harder to get a better job, to get an apartment which was sanitary to stay in, unlike the hovel they found themselves stuck in. They could not let this stand

Everyday Monsters

in the way of them making it! This delusion and poverty would go on for months in a cruel cycle, until the depression would take hold hard and fast. Drugs and booze would help them temporarily forget their woes for a few fleeting moments – but the pittance they earned would run out too soon each and every week. Their hunger would rise, as they would spend their food and rent money on more drugs and more booze. Anything to quell the depression deep inside of them – to make them feel anything except the despair which consumed their lives. That in turn, made the meager wages disappear even quicker. The more alcohol they drank and the more narcotics they took, the more unreliable they would inescapably become, inevitably losing their terribly low paid work. Then faced with the choice to either find a new job, in an attempt to fight off homelessness, or to buy more drugs and booze to silence the demons – they would choose the latter. To get the next fix fast, they would sell their bodies for the price of a hit – but by now, they were already junkies – and no one paid much money to have sex with someone in that condition. Only the dregs of society, the desperate and the twisted would venture to the neglected nether regions of these broken and beaten youths. This spiral continued further and further down and showed no sign of ever changing. Whether one or ten years later, they would eventually die from an overdose, a sexually transmitted disease or be murdered in a drug- or sex-fueled related situation. Their estranged parents would eventually be found back in whoeverthefuckcaresville and would come to the "big city" in order to pick up their child's broken body. These parents would, of course, be distraught at the loss of their little baby. This "baby" who had followed the same damned path as scores of others had before them. Now this "baby" was just another statistic. If they had just called home, things would have been okay, the parents convinced themselves. We would have sent them money – helped them out. Brought them home. These parents of course totally neglected to remember that their child did, in fact, call them. They did ask for help and money – but their parents thought that any money given would be spent on drugs – which it, invariably, would have been. So, in reality, they had rejected their child in their hour of need and instead of blaming themselves for the corpse they had to pick up, they ret-conned what had happened and created a fantasy of tragedy to help them both sleep at night. If there was a heaven, if these kids could look down at their broken lives, they would have thought to themselves "Maybe I should have died in that fire at the Weathered Hearts Inn, instead." This was what the investigating police detective thought to himself as he looked at the spot where two such kids had met their fate. He saw these types come and go, but had never heard of any of their dreams coming true.

Detective Scott was an officer who had seen too much of this kind of tragedy before. It made him very weary; the kind of weary that pushed him to end each night by passing out from drinking more whiskey than anyone should.

The top of a four-poster bed – where two such kid's bodies were found – had originally been made of the same wood as the rest of the bed's frame, but had been replaced by a thick plastic sheet (after the original wood had got infected by termites.) The aging handyman who had been hired for the job of fixing the top of the bed had no idea that his quick fix would eventually turn deadly. He took this shortcut without foreseeing that the plastic would one day be melted by the heat of a raging fire. The liquid from it would then pour down onto the bodies of two sleeping dreamers, encasing them in plastic as they burned to their deaths. These kids had gone to sleep happy, fresh from celebrating them leaving their hometowns. But fate took a harsh turn; In the hours after toasting their soon-to-be famous careers, instead of giving them their bright glittery future – fate gave them death by suffocating and burning them in boiling plastic, a plastic which turned into a shell over them as the high temperatures faded.

"Fucking tragedy," Scott muttered as he moved on from this burned bed, which had been encircled by yellow police tape.

The rain had started to fall, spitting down from the clouds above, through where the Inn's roof used to be. The fire had swept through and eaten the majority of the building, leaving the rooms exposed and bare to the elements, each strewn with charcoaled debris. The building was now a charred maze of half-standing walls, destroyed furniture and ember-eaten beams. Its second floor – where the guest rooms had been located – was now just a graveyard of what the fire had consumed and shat out. Naturally, the corpses themselves had been removed and the scenes thoroughly examined as the police came and went.

Detective Scott did not have to be here. The police's work was completed, but he felt that one more final attempt to look at this place, a last glance to make sure nothing was missed, was needed. Though he returned of his own volition, he shouldn't have taken a step onto the first floor. The building was not stable anymore and the whole floor been condemned – but he was never a man to care much about Health and Safety Regulations. The truth had to be discovered. These people's families deserved that much at least. The fire he watched burn seemed too strange to be part of a normal accident, so much so that he knew that something was amiss. Something didn't add up. He had to figure it out.

The ground floor had been home to the reception area

(where Meares and Barbara met their end), the dining room, the kitchen and storage – but all of these rooms were now only frames of scorched wood and plaster, which housed the remnants of what used to be inside of them. The fire had spread unnaturally fast through the Inn, consuming everything within its sight within moments. Somehow even the metal objects had caught fire and subsequently melted – betraying the laws of physics themselves. These flames had also spread out onto the gravel stones of the driveway, all of which set had been alight. The fire crawled out over the stone path and over any cars that happed to be parked up in its way. The flames then burning and melting the metal into the ground. The firemen and policemen who answered the call would never be able to explain how this was possible. The investigation itself would eventually be swept aside and never talked of again. It scared them too much – which it would naturally do. What happened was nothing that had an explanation that any common sense could make head nor tail of. Detective Scott would never fathom how this fire raged at such speed and heat, let alone melt things it had no right to do. He saw this fire move as if it were a living monster, consuming everything in its wave as it moved from room to room like a rampaging bull.

The families of the victims would eventually be told that it was all caused by bad wiring, that all of this was just an accident, which was a fault of no-one except the owner, whom they found the remains of.

Detective Scott looked around the second-floor honeymoon suite as the rain poured onto him through the open roof. He would soon become part of the very cover-up that he would have railed against, if he had survived to hear the judgement of it being deemed an electrical fault. His family would soon be told that he died as a result of the injuries that he'd received 12 hours earlier, when he was standing alongside the firemen, fighting the blaze with them. He suffocated from smoke inhalation. He was a hero and his memory lauded as he tried to save the victims. Though he shouldn't have got involved in fighting the fire, he did anyway. He was a great man. Taken before his time... No other explanation of his passing was possible. Humans were too ill-informed a species to fathom what the truth could have been, so had to make a fantasy to convince themselves of.

For years to come, the ruins of the Inn would remain a vacant skeleton. That was, at least until the fear of that fire was no longer a residing memory. When no one in emergency services, nor in the nearby townships remembered the reality of the fire, the ruins would be demolished, sold and rebuilt on. But that was over a decade away.

Shining his torch on what used to be a television in one of the bedrooms, Scott looked pale as he took a breath. He had seen this scene earlier in the day, but needed to see it once more. The TV itself had melted, and looked as if it had transformed into something else; remolded by some other force, it now resembled an attacking alien – with many plastic and glass tendrils reaching out across the room from its wooden stand. These "tendrils" pierced into many parts of the bed opposite it. The tape outline from the bed had left a charcoal silhouette of a person that had the unfortunate luck of being in these tendrils' way; an unsuspecting male guest who was skewered to death before the fire even reached his room, taking his life before any monstrous flames could.

It was this way all the way throughout this Inn. The bodies of the guests were of course, horribly burned – but it was obvious to all the investigators that most had had died by other means. Other... impossible means.

. . .

A crash downstairs alerted Scott, waking him up from his deep thoughts of what might have really happened here.

He turned on the spot, his flashlight illuminated what the moonlight could not. Through the destroyed open roof, the rain was falling even heavier upon him. His police issue hat and coat provided only temporary protection from this oncoming deluge.

He heard another crash. Whatever it was, it was nearer.

A thundering, repeating booming rang out. The sound of the footsteps of a giant. A giant who was getting closer by the second.

"Police! Who's there?!" he shouted, withdrawing his pistol and pointing it ahead to the partially standing doorframe. The hallway the other side of it still had a part of its roof intact, which kept the hallway dry and in darkness, managing to avoid the moonlight. His flashlight did nothing to penetrate the hallway's shadows. Whatever might be there was out of sight. But definitely there. He could sense it.

The rain started to beat down with torrential might, heavier than it had fallen for many years. As if the heavens now opened and screamed at Scott to run. To run NOW – or at least to save himself from the horror that was about to be forced upon him, by turning his own pistol on himself – hopefully ending his own life before he met what was coming straight at him.

If only Mother Nature could scream those words.

Oblivious to his fate, Detective Scott stood his ground in this storm. Gun and flashlight pointed shakily towards the dark hallway in front of him. The falling water illuminated itself in the beam of his torch as rain poured over the brim of his hat, splashing droplets onto his face. The visibility between him and the doorway had become murkier as the

Everyday Monsters

rain fell faster, creating a thick rainy veil between him and his death.

Maybe I imagined that crashing noise? Maybe there were no footsteps? Maybe part of the building was collapsing? he thought. Yeah. That must be it. He smiled nervously to himself. Of course, that was what it had to be.

THEN, from inside the darkness of the hallway burst forth a vision of pure terror. The Moogle appeared in the moonlight and without a second's pause, ran at Detective Scott from his shroud of shadows, his stomach-mouth open wide towards his intended victim. Each footstep he took echoed with a booming crunching sound, as the floorboards buckled under his weight. A sound that seemed be louder than the sound of the storm.

A war cry was loosed by this monster as he continued his attack. Sounding like nails down a blackboard, this screech made most people reach for their ears in pain, but before Scott could register any discomfort – let alone pull the trigger of his aimed gun – this attacker was upon him. Slamming his stomach-mouth around the detective's arms as he enveloped them, snapping them clean off by the bicep. Scott screamed for help as this monster's stomach chewed on his arms, opened wide again and bit clean into his face and chest – ripping them with ease off from head and body.

DAYS LATER – when the other police officers would find Scott's remains, they would find the back half of his body in one single piece – complete with 3-foot bite mark showing that the front was clearly eaten in one bite by some creature. Further down the street, near the crashed Plymouth Fury, they would also find a large pile of animal feces. Feces which would visibly contain parts of Detective Scott within them – with his police badge resting on top. Polished. Placed intentionally.

It was because of this hideous fate that this officer would be remembered dying in a more heroic way; what else could they have said? Eaten and shat out by an unknown monster?

A TIMELY DEMISE AND A LEAP OF FAITH

He could no longer feel anything at all. Not even the flies that crawled over his face.

His nerves were severed and deceased.

The end was so close, he assured himself.

It was happening a lot later in the day than he presumed it would. He knew he had his plan, but the timetable of that plan was intrinsically malleable; all had been dependent on circumstance. He thought with the Sicarian's trademark rage, he would have been cast into nothingness many hours before.

He looked up at his gleeful torturer. She was now on her haunches on the chair itself, staring very closely into his one remaining eye. She had an open-mouthed smile from cheek to cheek, as she slightly tilted her head, looking at him from an ever-changing angle. Taking everything about his condition in with joy.

The breath in his mouth was stilted and shallow as he spoke. "You think you have won?" he croaked weakly – trying his best to smile.

"Won? Me? No. Not at all… I'm just waiting to watch you

die." She moved closer to him, and whispered into his ear, "I want to enjoy it all, you see?"

Deacon slowly blinked over his unburst eye, his strength dissipating. "I would like to say I won't give you that satisfaction… But have at it…" he managed to say.

Moving in even closer to his ear, the Sicarian continued, "Whatever you think you had planned… It will all be over for you soon. Do you feel it nipping at your heels, yet?"

"I… embrace the end." His voice was almost a whisper.

"I often wondered why anyone would care if they lived or died. They can't stop its determination. Whether after a year, a dozen years, a hundred years, or millennia. It comes for us all… We shouldn't even think about it. It's part of all of us."

Deacon tried to speak, but could not. His mouth could only slightly open and close.

The Sicarian moved herself backwards off the chair and stood up straight. "So, this… your death… this is a gift to me from you," she said as she clasped her hands together in fake reverence. "A gift that I deserve more than anyone else on this spinning rock.".

Deacon's eye fluttered as he exhaled weakly. He had now taken his last breath. His eye and mouth remained half-open as he faded away into the ether, a bit later than he thought he would.

The Sicarian took a pause as she solemnly looked down at the now deceased remains of Deacon Sorbic.

"Underwhelming," she muttered aloud. "Very. Fucking. Underwhelming."

"Excuse me?" came a voice from the back of the interrogation room.

The Sicarian glanced over her shoulder and saw Mikko,

Everyday Monsters

standing by the door looking as if he was about to be chastised for interrupting her. He was carrying Deacon's journal in his hands.

"I don't mean to disturb, but I have some news," he proffered apologetically.

"Nothing to disturb," she replied as she motioned to Deacon's head. "He's now passed over."

"Did he answer all you wanted?"

"I never asked him anything," she replied, almost mad at the question.

Mikko closed the door behind him, walked over to the center of the room where the interrogation chair lay and glanced at the now lifeless head of Deacon Sorbic. He was quite surprised by this turn of events, at the lack of questioning.

This man was of such importance to the Elders, that the Sicarian came to collect him personally. When they found out that he – the banished – had written something that potentially carried a great power. He presumed the Sicarian would a) extend his life for extensive interrogations or b) ensure that he would not expire, so that he might be taken to the other realm. Mikko could only presume that she lost this prisoner from a lack of her control at the beginning of the interrogation A fit of rage – which was something she was known to be prone to succumb to.

He knew the ease at which any interrogator could lose control and resort to primal urges. He had overseen thousands of them. He knew the ways of torture all too well. Unlike his monstrous friend, his method was more of a mental torture – as with physical torture, it was all too easy to take things too far. Though normally, after he had coerced the information from his prisoner, they were never to be released anyway. This process – on his watch anyway – was a one-way journey. The only way they could escape was if they were innocent, which none ever was. In the end, it did not really matter if this process went too far, as it always ended at the same destination; The prisoner's death, followed by their corpse feeding the pit below.

He preferred the less physical methods, as he didn't like getting his hands dirty. He was an obsessively clean man. He needed to be clean. A drop of blood or other bodily fluids that might land on him, would make him retch. So, because of this aversion, he never killed them by his hand – he simply gave them a choice.

He would open the floor beneath the chair and make them an offer – to take a leap of faith. Jump into the pit below. Prove their worthiness to the Order. And if they did, their sins would be forgiven and they would be saved. They had to trust in the Order, after all. He would tell them that this was the first time he had made this offer. That no one had ever been potentially worthy before. He told them to be the first... This was of course a lie. They eventually jumped into the pit of bodies below all too willingly, casting themselves to drown amongst the liquefied flesh and bone; becoming part of the horrible depths, that lay in wait for its next offering. By doing things this way, there was no killing by his hand. It was a clean and expedient death, with no clean up needed.

"You think you could do better than I did?" the Sicarian asked Mikko. "You think I failed?"

Taken aback, he looked at her wide-eyed for a second. "I... No... Of course not."

The Sicarian held out her hand to him, and he passed her the journal. Her eyes fixed on him sternly. "Lost control? Is that how you think of us? Prone to emotion? You don't think that I have other, better, ways to find information out than asking someone living?"

She heard my thoughts? Mikko wondered in an instant.

"You think your abilities are solely your own to master?"

She can hear...

"Who was this Albert you are thinking of?"

Caught off-guard, he quickly searched for words.

"He was corrupted?" She turned, then motioned to the severed head upon the chair, "and this meat had followers?"

"Yes... Two..."

Suddenly the Sicarian advanced a few paces on Mikko, an instant wave of rage filling her. Though her voice remained low and controlled, her eyes spoke a different tone, "And you ended his life instead of bringing him before me?" she seethed through gritted teeth.

"No. It wasn't—"

"Then you told others?" she accused, "before your GOD?"

"No. Please... Let me explain."

"You killed a man who could tell us more about a potential conspiracy... You allowed his life to be eaten away? And now what? You want others—"

Mikko interrupted. "We're handling it for you. We didn't want to disturb you here. I presumed—"

"NEVER PRESUME!" she bellowed at a frightening volume.

Her demeanor suddenly subsided again. These back-and-forth emotions unsettled Mikko. The Sicarian knew this all too well, as a small smile crept over her face. "Though honestly. You're not to blame. Nor is your pet. You did all of this with the best of intentions, correct?"

Speaking to the Sicarian was both terrifying and confusing, her actions and emotions contradictory and unpredictable. Mikko tried to remain calm as she paced around to the other side of the chair in deep thought. She gripped her journal, which she held tightly in her hands.

Nervously he thought to himself, that he was a dedicated follower. He had proven his worth time and time again. She must see that.

"Please. Give me a chance. I can make this right. We will find the conspirators and bring them to you. I'll do anything you need..." Mikko uttered. He felt regret that he'd allowed Albert to be punished. He wished he had just paused for a moment and considered his actions. Weighed up the eventualities from his actions a bit more. Just held him prisoner – not made him a meal. But he also felt slightly annoyed that he had no authority in this situation, when Albert was his employee. His to deal with.

Turning to him, she smiled, and without a moment's pause pushed a button on the floor next to the chair. It made a high-pitched metal clanking noise as a lock disengaged itself.

"I need you..." she started to say, as she grabbed hold of the side of the interrogation chair and pulled it towards her. It pivoted from its attached head, and exposed a two-foot diameter hole which led downwards, into the great pit below. A thing Mikko had done previously, many times. The stench immediately grew more potent as it filled the air uninterrupted from its depths.

"I need you... to show me how contrite you are... to prove your worth."

Mikko felt the cold chill of ironic inevitability approaching.

Wolfgang "Rodeo" Imhoff Jr. had been an actor in the 1940s. His rise to fame was meteoric yet very short-lived. Known as a stuntman during his early career, he quickly ascended to lead actor status for a major Hollywood studio, becoming a staple in their western and gangster films. His rugged good looks and impressive physique stood him above his contemporaries. In the short space of 6 months he had gone from being an unknown stuntman to being toasted as the talk of tinsel town. The trades had then almost constantly been filled with coverage of his private life, as well as notifications about his exciting upcoming features. During his 2-year career, he had starred in over 22 films – unprecedented for an actor of his fame to be so prolific. But Imhoff Jr. was in it to win it. He knew he could not stop for one moment or he might lose what he'd set his sights on. He had to claw his way to the top and fight to stay there. Fight with everything he had.

His catchphrase, which appeared in many of his features, was a saying he had heard as a child. Words from his father, which he now made his own: "This ain't my first rodeo". Whenever his character needed to exclaim that he knew what he was doing, the studio writers would work this catchphrase in. The audiences ate it up every time. People would shout it to him as he drove past them in his Bentley. When he was flanked by beautiful women in the fanciest restaurant on Sunset Boulevard, he would say it to the adoring crowds, who all waited to catch a glimpse of him. To hopefully get his autograph.

It all came to a head on his 22nd film "Rodeo for Betsy".

During the first scene they had to shoot, he was to ride a bucking bronco – and being a stuntman he always insisted on preparing his own harnesses and safety equipment. He couldn't trust anyone else to do this. He knew better – well, he thought he did. This time though, he didn't secure his belt to the safety rope. A rope which was intended to pull him upwards, out of harm's way at the slightest sign of trouble, far from the danger of the rodeo bull.

The bull, as bad luck would have it, bucked when it shouldn't and threw him forward with such force that he lost his grip on his handles. The safety crew pulled the rope to swing him out, as had been planned in an emergency – but the harness was not attached tight enough.

He flew over the horns and landed on the ground in front of the furious animal. Before the safety crew could reach him and before he could scream, the bull then proceeded to attack. Rearing up in fury, it then stomped down onto Imhoff Jr's cowering body – smashing his bones apart, then goring him using its horns. Attacking him until his body lay in pieces. Chunks of bloodied and twitching meat and splintered bones.

That was in fact – and most ironically – Wolfgang "Rodeo" Imhoff Jr.'s first Rodeo.

Since then, his legend had been forgotten, not helped when a studio fire in the 50s lost all the masters of his films, coupled with the industry burying the further news articles of his death, so they could cover over their failings. Besides, it was only a matter of weeks before they found their next lascivious story to feast on. Another shocking story to force down their reader's throats. Even his iconic catchphrase had been taken from his mouth. 40 years later it become attributed to another film, stealing his only remaining legacy away.

This was exactly what Mikko was most worried about; Being forgotten. In addition to this and making it all the more ironic, he was the only person alive today who still remembered who Wolfgang "Rodeo" Imhoff Jr. even was.

But soon, no one would remember either of them. Their memories forever lost to time and space.

"I will save you, you know? I just need you to prove yourself," she spoke as she looked to him with a kind smile.

Could she mean this? She would really save me? he thought in the depths of his mind.

Everyday Monsters

She nodded slightly in response to hearing his silent pondering. "The light leads you. Let it save you. Let it wash your sins away. Rebirth is the only option for any failure."

He had used these words so many times before. He had said the same to hundreds of the dead which now floated beneath him.

I will be saved, he believed as he followed the damned and fell towards the brown and red lake of rot beneath him. He willingly took his hundred-foot fall to show this God he was worthy. I will be saved. She will see my devotion. His was not a big sin, after all – just a small misstep – a misunderstanding at best.

His legs smashed on impact of the landing, his thigh bones broke and exposed themselves through his hips. This lake of the dead was not like water. It was akin to hitting concrete.

His screams, though piercing and alarming, were futile – as far above him, the chair had now swung back into place, the bright lights which shone high above him – the ones which filled the room above them with their illumination – were now all that could be seen.

I will be saved, he kept thinking to himself – over and over. He kept repeating it as the human remains he lay broken upon gave way like quicksand and swallowed this new addition deeper, pulling his dying body downwards.

Mikko's cries and shrieks, his pleading screams to the Sicarian – all went unnoticed. He had pictured the Sicarian standing up there, just about to swoop down and save him. Ready to repair his wounds and save him from this agony.

The Sicarian, though, had already left the room far above, taking the head of Deacon and the journal with her.

Mikko died in the pit where he sent so many people before him. The executer had become the executed. Though he believed himself to be a perfect follower, though he did everything that he was asked, he was punished. On this one occasion, where he took extra initiative. Where he took authority. He had paid the toll. He knew that the Sicarian's cruelty had no limits, but thought he was above her judgement. He knew that she relished the deaths which she doled out – but thought he was one of her chosen.

In the end though, it didn't matter who or why she killed – it was all done on a whim. He was not the first follower that she would kill for a lesser infraction. She hoped he would not be her last, either.

This was, after all, not her first Rodeo.

Somewhere in the middle of the country, the Moogle stopped in his tracks. The rain beat down hard on him as the moonlight struggled to illuminate the surrounding vistas.

Something was wrong.

Something had just happened.

Mikko... No.

He somehow knew that his friend was no longer alive.

His breathing quickly became stilted and out of control. He started to growl as his breath got faster and faster. Louder and louder with each quicker breath. It ended in a crescendo, as his stomach and his mouth opened up in a sudden audible rage, as he let out a terrifying roar. A scream of hate, straight towards the heavens.

PART IV

THE FACE OF GOD

THE LEECH

Long thought extinct by the few who were even aware of the creature's existence, the leech was a singularly evolved organism. A being which could survive indefinitely as long as it could feed. Its main source of sustenance came from humans, though it was not averse to feasting on the odd animal if fate dictated it or if there was no other option. This being was one of a kind. There had never been any other like it, nor ever would be again. It was an anomaly which should never have come into existence, but by happenstance and a miscarriage of magic, it did.

Unlike its namesake, the water-dwelling bloodsucking worm, this leech did not actually drink blood. Nor was it a slug-looking creature. It did not consume anything which could be measured or extracted by normal scientific means. This leech feasted on the unquantifiable and unmeasurable essence of a life. All the experiences, intelligence and personality was sucked out from the intended victim. The leftovers from any of its feasts, though, did not die. Not straight away anyway. What would be left behind would be a worse existence than if the leech had just killed them. They would be abandoned in a state of living torment. The leech took all the important parts of their lives, so what remained was a living ghost of what their victim once was. Leaving them as a barely coherent mess, with no reliable memories or thoughts left to tether their personality to. People often mistook these victims as drug addled or demented, senile or just outright insane. And in the case of animals, what was left was normally seen as anything from rabid or merely violently feral. Its victims almost always displayed similar side-effects from the feeding. Their body would slowly begin to rot, starting from their extremities first (usually their fingers or toes). Their skin would begin to blacken and swell, cracking and bleeding when moved. These wounds would invariably get infected – so would result in the victims developing a texture of yellowing fleshy tree bark as the pus softened the cracked and swollen skin. Their bones would then twist and gnarl, resulting in the victim hobbling, until their movement had been completely taken away from them, when they would become bed-ridden. It was not just their body that would rot either; next would be their minds, making the victim initially seem to suffer from memory loss, but the dementia-like symptoms would soon increase as the mind turned on itself, as the brain cells cannibalized themselves and as the mind started to die, the victim would become consumed by psychosis and rage without any obvious cause.

It would also amplify the victim's dominant personality trait. If they were a sad person by nature, the sadness would grow to insurmountable proportions after the feeding, usually resulting in suicide attempts. The leech did not like this though. If the victims had a narcissistic personality – which were the kinds he preferred – then that aspect would be amplified. Their steadily rotting brain bolstered their self-belief to such a degree that they became screaming lunatics who never saw the truth of their situation. Their narcissism exploded to a blinding degree – stopping them seeing the truth of what they were now. Making it safer for the leech to continue.

The leech loved to watch his victims' lives, after he fed upon them. He loved to see their future play out without what he fed on; the glue that held them together. Which is why he loved to feed on chronic narcissists so much. Watching their lives unravel as they were left ruined, screamed about their worth, when they were in fact worthless. Screaming about their brilliance, when they were imbeciles. Screaming about how beautiful they were, when they were now just rotting, inside and out, was a marvel to behold

This rotting process could take years to complete and if the victims were lucky enough to live to the end of that process – which few were, as usually they either killed themselves, were killed by others, or were victims of unfortunate accidents – their bodies would eventually collapse in on themselves. Physically as well as mentally. Their nose would collapse first, then their forehead, then their chest. They would live out the remaining years incapacitated and a grotesque shadow of their former selves. Any autopsy that could be performed on any of these deceased victims, would show that the inside of their brain had almost entirely rotted away. Yet as they would find no cause for this, it would be considered to be a natural, though puzzling death.

The leech was aroused at the steady decline of its victims' lives. It pleasured itself when it saw the mental and physical rot which spread through them, all because of the feeding. The fact that their resulting insanity protected his identity was secondary to his desire to watch their decline. It was not though, an evil being at all. It prided itself on only feasting on those who were terrible people to start with. Ones whose deaths would make the world a slightly better one to live in. It had its code and morals – but that didn't stop its arousal at seeing the devastating effects it left on them.

With the sustenance it had extracted, it also acquired all the victim's knowledge, which it would always use to its advantage. Because of this, it believed that there was no point in feeding off a pauper or a stupid person. All a pauper would give it was emotional distress with no real substance to devour. All a stupid person would give it was their stupid delusions and ignorance. Its victims of choice, its favorite subjects to feast on, were successful artists – those who were makers of things – the more successful the better. Deluded self-believers that had been lucky enough to be rewarded with success was what it hunted for. I had no artistic ability itself, so its power to take another's ability, and an ability which had been proved to be successful, was delicious. What did it do with all the acquired artistry it drained from the victims? Nothing. It just left it in its mind. Locked away. An unused prize it could masturbate over.

With the knowledge it acquired, it could also acquire their victim's wealth, leaving them with nothing but the rotting skin they had been cursed with – unknowing as to why or how their fortune had disappeared.

It once fed on a movie starlet back when Hollywood was still called Hollywoodland. A starlet who was had been a cruel and awful woman – a fact made worse due to the fact that she was stunningly beautiful. She regularly left a trail of broken hearts in her wake. Ones she left destroyed as she ascended to grasp her fame and power. After the leech had left her, its feasting had made her a contorted and grotesque mess. Over the subsequent months, she became afflicted head to foot in severely rotting flesh. Her body twisted itself over as if she had a sideways hunchback. She had been such a cruel narcissist in life, that when the rot took hold, her delusions of her worth multiplied exponentially. She was found broke, homeless, hobbling naked down the city streets – screaming at any man she could see, that she was beautiful. Demanding to know why they did not want to fuck her. Within her failing brain, she saw all their revulsion as proof that they were misogynists and bad people, because she was irresistible. She was, and would always would be, a STAR!

STANDING AT 6 FOOT 2, the leech looked like a typical 30-something year old male executive. One whom worked within some part of the entertainment industry. Someone who constantly took meetings. A charming man. A man who set up multimillion dollar deals for breakfast. This was the kind of persona it adopted to get to its victims. The position it convinced others it was a success at. It had given itself the name "Mark", and this was mainly a joke just for it – as the people who fed on were its marks. As for its surname, it chose it at random every time. It did not matter that no one had heard of it, or that it had no credits they knew – it could charm its way into any room, into any meeting. It could get anyone to give it access to what it wanted. The shell it wore on the outside appealed to his victim's lower intelligence. A shell which it could change whenever it wanted, but for the last 9 decades, it had not needed to change a thing. This was its winning formula. Its winning face. Though male in look, it did not identify as a male. It was a hermaphroditic creature with both sets of genitals. It could alter its skin to any gender, so aligned itself as an "it". It was an "it". It was a proud "it".

If anyone looked very, very closely at its face, they would be able to see two very thin lines – one horizontal, and one vertical – running the width and height of its features. From chin to forehead and from ear to ear, the line crossed over themselves at the tip of its nose. It occasionally covered these lines up with makeup, if it was to walk out in the daylight, but most of the time it never had to. People in the entertainment industry were too self-involved to ever truly look at the person talking to them in any great detail.

When it fed, this cross-section of lines would open up like a flower, each of the four flaps of skin opening outward from their meeting point at the tip of its nose. This would reveal a large circular mouth inside – almost as big as the opening of skin itself. This opening would be surrounded by small fleshy tendrils, along with a multitude of sharp serrated teeth. To feed, it would need to place its victim's cranium up to its now exposed circular mouth. Its four sections of open skin would close down on the victim – holding them in place with their teeth, as well as tendrils. It then would feed on them, sucking everything away from their mind. When finished, the victim's face would only be affected by looking noticeably older. The rot and insanity would take weeks, if not months, to begin displaying.

A STRONG, repetitive slurping sound echoed throughout the cold room, as a string of saliva pooled onto the cold metal floor within the leech's chamber.

A naked, diminutive pale male body, aged in its 60s, lay upon a metal table in the center of this room. His face was unseen as it was covered by the leech, who was bent over the man, feeding upon him. Its four flaps of face skin were open and attached. Its head and throat undulated with each sucking motion as it drank. A muffled scream wailed in futility from within. No one would ever hear this, not in the place they were. This room was soundproof and secure.

Everyday Monsters

Saliva mixed with a tiny amount of blood and dripped from around the leech's "lips" and joined the spit pool onto the metal floor below.

This room was steel lined in every direction. All 4 walls, ceiling and floor looked exactly the same – 6 highly polished square steel slabs, each 5 meters in diameter. The only difference between them was the outline of a large metal door on one side. Each surface was highly reflective and caused any reflections to appear to stretch an eternity in each direction anyone would look. Resembling a room from the depths of a cruel funhouse, the walls each reflected a reflection of a reflection of a reflection, continuing on forever. It was ironic that the leech only wanted to feed on narcissists, as it was one itself; The worst of them, in fact – this room was a testament to that. At the same time that it fed on its victim, the eyes on its skin flaps would stare at its many reflections all around it. As it imbibed their essence, it would be watching itself; the all-powerful Leech. Feeding on the weakness that was humanity.

This old man on this metal table had been a novelist, an artist, a filmmaker. A real renaissance man from within the entertainment industry. A man with great wealth. The leech had found him by happenstance, as it usually would – nothing would ever be highly planned, as the leech believed firmly in fate – and it was never let down by this method. It managed to get into this man's inner circle with promises of movie deals, art gallery shows – you name it, "Mark" could do it for this man. This man, though believed to be a great imaginer by his fans, was in fact a despicable example of humanity. A cruel abuser. Something those close to him knew but were too afraid to do anything about. A worthy victim for the leech. Someone who would be better off being damned.

. . .

After months of promises of a golden future, it had tricked this man to this metal room and was now feeding on everything that he was. This man had millions in the bank, houses in the Hollywood Hills, but the leech had no primary interest in these. It wanted to taste the knowledge of creation. After it was done, this man would have little ability left to create anymore. His once brilliant prose would now be reduced to childish phrases, his detailed artwork would now be stick figures. He would be nothing of what he once was – but being a narcissist before, meant he was much worse now, so he would not see the missing brilliance in his work, and his "yes" men would not let him know either.

Despite the want to imbibe artistry being its primary focus, the leech was not stupid. With the knowledge acquired, it would have opportunities to take money, property and almost everything else from his victim without anyone knowing what happened – and of course, it could not let that opportunity always pass. Yet, it would not take all. It knew the money would be passed eventually to the victims' families, so only took 1/3rd of whatever wealth he could find. This would amass over time, and net the leech a comfortable existence.

This latest victim was to be dropped back, under the cover of darkness, at his mansion in an unconscious state. When he would wake, the same thing would happen to him as had happened to others countless times before; he would remember nothing of the leech's feeding and believe he just had a bad night's sleep. After a few months of carrying on but neglecting to see the lack of ability left in him, the man would not see his "empire" crumbling, as everyone else would. His brain would sense something was wrong, but be unable to pinpoint a cause. He would be left powerless, untalented, screaming. A man who now foolishly believed he was still who he once was, and that he still had the ability which the leech had stolen with glee.

Those people around the old man would see this rapid decline. They would have no idea of the leech or what happened, so would put the man's deluded behavior down to an increasing madness caused by an illness, or possibly drug addiction. This was why the leech's gifted fate was a lot worse than a quick death. A quick death that the leech felt his victims didn't deserve. His victims earned their fate.

THE LEECH BROKE contact with the old man's face, with its circular mouth now exposed as it pulsated, swallowing its last mouthful of knowledge.

A mobile phone started to ring in its pocket. As it did, the leech's four flaps of skin closed back in and reformed its male face – restoring its chiseled good looks firmly into their place. Answering the phone, it smiled a sideways grin, the whole conversation spent looking at its reflection on one of the metal walls. Loving the view.

"Hello?" it said assuredly in its adopted west coast drawl.

The smile soon dropped from its face, as it heard what the voice on the line had to say. "I'll... be right there, I guess?"

It had to go to Amorfield. It had never been summoned before. What did it do? Did it feed on a forbidden person? Fuck. It knew it broke the rules occasionally... but why now? Why was it being called? Why didn't it ask them on the phone? Dammit Leech! Stupid Leech!

It started to break out in a cold sweat as it still looked at itself in a reflection. It hated anything which wasn't something it controlled – but it knew that as the Elders protected it, it would need to do all the Order asked.

Looking down, it saw the old unconscious man on the

metal table. With no time to return him to his own home – and instead of allowing him the damnation of the downward spiral into madness, poverty and rot – it decided to do this man a kindness, out of expedience. Putting its hand over the man's neck and with a terrifying ease and speed, it dug in its fingers deep into the skin and ripped out the man's throat – tearing it out all the way down to his spinal cord. There was no chance of the man waking during this execution; the feeding left this old man so close to death's door that even the pain of choking to death on his own blood would not allow him to stir from unconsciousness.

The leech let the handful of meat and windpipe fall to the cold floor. As it licked its fingers clean, it turned, then opened the large metal door.

A NEW REGIME

The Order was simple in structure, yet complex in method. There were the Elders at the top of the company ladder, with a few administrators below them. Like any good religion or cult, those at the top chose those on the level below to pass down their holy words. They would never sink so low as to address anyone themselves. These followers, though, were many. The monsters in the shadows of existence, across all realms, were innumerable – and over 2/3rds of them were followers of this faith.

Amorfield might have been the only complex that the Elders chose to travel to in this realm, but there were many equally powerful complexes worldwide spearheading the faith, each with scores of believers following the orders of their Gods. Though like all churches, the further away from the reality of their Lords they get, the more they create fictions about them, and ignore the violent realities of their creation, real or fiction. So the further away from Amorfield you go, the more fervent and dedicated the followers are.

The administrators at the head of each of these complexes had remained the same for decades, the personnel at the top rarely changing. Yet now – at the complex called Amorfield – the whole regime was in upheaval. There were now many empty shoes to fill.

It was a follower called Essa who had been given the highest opportunity by the Elders; the opportunity to take over from where Mikko had left off. The moment he had sank down amongst the rotting bodies in the interrogation room, Essa had been immediately called upon.

After walking out of the room of light – after receiving her promotion – Essa stood almost hyperventilating. She had just been given the veritable keys to the kingdom – but had no idea what she was to do. She had no idea what was expected of her.

In the white room, Mikko could hear their commands easily within his mind, his power translating their intentions perfectly. Essa on the other hand, had to hear their voices aloud, and try to understand their meaning, through the words spoken only, which was not an easy task. Mikko's power could decipher intention through any words, Essa had no such power.

The gills on her neck opened and closed with every breath she drew. Her large black eyes glistened from her panicked emotion. Her wide mouth hung open as her breath traveled past, stilted and heavy.

She could only think of one thing – the Moogle. That beast would not be happy with her taking over his friend's position... at all.

Turning, she walked slowly down the hallway, each step wobbling from her nervousness, her mind awash with confusion. Why me? she thought over and over, in the fugue of her imposter syndrome. She had worked in the lower levels of the complex for years. She had always worked on her own, keeping herself to herself, collecting information about the world outside – then sending it up to the Administrator to review. Her employment had been to discover any information on anything that would expose or threaten those that the Order protected – all online. A safe and repetitive job of trawling websites and forums, which she enjoyed.

She pressed the button to call down the elevator, as she wiped her brow with her other hand. She had to go up to Mikko's office. No, she corrected herself. Her office. It was her office. She had to remember that. She was now the Administrator. She was now the Goddamn Administrator.

THE LEECH WALKED into the main reception area of Amorfield.

This circular, stone-lined and grandiose room was adorned with seven statues around its circumference. Seven statues which each represented the Elders by their elements; fire, water, wind, earth, birth, death and renewal.

This room was empty bar one figure – a receptionist – who sat behind a single stone table. This skinny, pale, sexless being wore no clothes nor accessories. Its smooth and hairless head had no eyes, no nose nor ears – only a mouth. A wide and lipless mouth.

The leech walked up to this stone table; its stomach had been turning over itself from the transport through the access point, a feeling it was trying it best to not focus on. Its demeanor remained assured, yet still had a tinge of apprehension about it. It still had no idea why it was summoned.

It was supposed to be in hiding, but despite that order it still lived its life as it wanted; feeding on the higher echelons of society. They must have found out. They MUST have, it thought to itself. There was no escaping the Order. Running would be of no use. No one had ever escaped them as far as it knew. So, it would face its accusers and do anything it could to ensure that it could walk out of here. Anything. But then again, what difference did its actions make? It didn't affect or concern them at all.

The Sicarian, of course, had known what the leech was doing, and still kept a strict watch on it. Keeping a close eye in case it ever risked getting discovered by humanity. She needed it after all. She could not afford to punish it, yet, or risk its compliance in any sense. So, she just watched from the shadows, via the administrators, ordering the clean-up for any potential issues that arose. She had no intention of punishing it today. But with the Sicarian, intention took a secondary place to impulse.

"I'm here to see Mikko?"

Upon hearing this from the leech, the receptionist turned its attention forward, with its eyeless head staring at it.

"The administrator is deceased," it said in its weak, emotionless and genderless voice.

"Excuse me? What?"

"Yes," the receptionist confirmed. Looking down for a second, it then brought its head up again, and stared at the Leech despite having no features.

"Who... Are... You?" it asked slowly.

"What about Albert? Where's he? Can you get him for me, instead?" The leech asked, ignoring the question.

"Dead. Dead. Dead. All dead."

"The Moogle?"

The Receptionist cocked its head to the side at this – surprised that anyone would want to see that monster. "That... That thing is gone from here. For now."

The leech was processing the information it had just heard. No one in the management of Amorfield were here. Dead or gone. The Receptionist stared back without eyes. Silent. Waiting. Offering no more information.

Everyday Monsters

"So, who's in charge then?" The leech asked, wanting answers.

"Who... Are... You?" it asked again. Its voice turned into a rasp.

Without a word, the leech remained silent, as its face slowly peeled out and opened up its four sections – displaying its circular mouth.

"Ah! You are expected," it said, as it then looked up towards him again "I had presumed you... extinct... before I was told you were to be called in..."

It then pressed a button on the desk, unlocking the set of double metal doors sat at the far end of the room.

It pointed backwards. "Go... In..." The smile on its face extended, and reached to either side of its head, showing its entire set of jagged broken teeth.

"Who wants to see me?" the leech asked as it started to walk towards the now open doors.

It looked back as it got to them. The receptionist pressed the button again, which started the mechanism to close them. The leech moved further inwards to avoid getting caught between the doors. Its expression fell flat as it heard the receptionist's parting words. "The Sicarian..."

It stood in the hallway, facing the recently closed doors and swallowed hard as the access to its exit was now closed. There was no turning back now.

Turning around, he was faced with a small fishlike creature who silently stood, staring up at him. This was Essa and she was fulfilling her very first duty as Administrator. "I'm Essa," she said, extending her scaly hand to him.

It disregarded the offer with a slight smile. "You'd do better than to touch someone like me," it said. Even though it fed on people through its mouth, a single touch to anywhere on its body would drain the energy of the unlucky person it came into contact with – or in this case, the unlucky fish-person.

Essa did not know how to handle this and quickly withdrew her hand. She felt instant shame rise within her. Then, uttering a weak "Oh," she turned down the hall without looking at her guest. "She is expecting you. This way," she said softly.

As she walked, she heard the leech's footsteps closely following behind hers. She felt like she had done something wrong. He was probably offended by her offer of a handshake. He maybe hated her kind and did not want to get near her scaly skin. Her thoughts covered these questions and more, as she beat herself up mentally and continued to doubt her ability in this newly awarded position. She should never be around people, she concluded self-deprecatingly.

Arriving at the end of the hallway, she opened the door to a large chamber. Turning around, she didn't meet the gaze of the leech. She was convinced of the handshake having offended it. "Wait in here, please."

"Do you know why I'm here?" it asked hesitantly.

"No. I'm sorry. No," she replied.

"Damn. Okay," it muttered as it walked further into the room. Glancing over its shoulder, it offered a smile towards its chaperone "Thank you", it said – but the small fish creature had now gone. The door began closing on its own.

Looking around, it was slightly in awe at the opulence of the golden room it now stood in. A large room with no windows, complete with a granite 12-person table positioned directly in the middle of it. On that table, resting silently, was Deacon Sorbic's severed rotting head. Lying next to it – his Journal.

The leech walked over to the table cautiously. What is this? it thought.

Everyday Monsters

"Beautiful, isn't it?" A female voice spoke from the other side of the room. Looking up in that direction, the leech saw her. The Sicarian, in the flesh. It noticed how her body was in quite bad disrepair, her host body not looking like it could be healed much more.

After hearing its thoughts, she replied "This old thing?" whilst motioning to her body. "This will last me just fine... and if not? I'm sure I can get another. Why, are you offering?"

The leech met this question with a polite but nervous smile.

She walked over to the opposite side of the table, put her hands onto the top of one of its high-backed chairs, and offered the leech a smile in return. "You're not in trouble, don't worry."

The Leech hadn't asked but was relieved. It knew that the Sicarian could read thoughts, that did not bother it, what did was her sadism. A sadism without a code. That was something which dwarfed even its own appetites. It knew that anyone's survival after a meeting with an Elder was only a 50/50 proposition at the best of times, as they could – and often would on a whim – willingly end the life of anyone for any reason they cared to invent.

"You are safe. I assure you. You are here because I need your help. My ability doesn't stretch to the dead. Whereas yours can."

The leech kept its poker face, but inside was relieved.

Leaning in, she picked up Deacon's head by its hair and threw it over to the leech. It caught it with both of its hands. "I just need you to work your magic with this. I need some answers he wouldn't give in life. Ones he never thought for me to see."

Looking down at the partially decayed head, it felt

nothing. There was no life to drain. No energy. No thoughts to imbibe.

"You want me to feed on this?"

"It is of the utmost urgency, I assure you."

The leech tried to remain calm. "But... he's dead."

"And?" she said in mock confusion. She enjoyed speaking to the leech. Always so nervous. Hiding his fear through stoicism. A welcome change to those who couldn't stop crying or pleading.

"If I feed on the dead, I have to give some of myself to awaken their mind."

"And?" she continued. She knew exactly what the leech needed to do.

"And..." It looked down at this dead head in his grasp. It had no choice. It had to do as she asked. Hopefully it was freshly deceased enough that would only need a slight part of its own essence to navigate his mind. But this head looked very old. Very dead.

"May I ask if this is optional? Do I have a choice in the matter?" it asked, as it looked up toward the Sicarian.

"Of course, you do. You always do," she said, walking towards it around the table, not once breaking eye contact. "Do the work asked... suffer any consequences, then go back to your life of feeding on the rich and famous. Or..." She stopped as she reached where it was standing. Her smile slowly fell from her face as she continued, "Decline and face what I am capable of. Your choice all the way."

"What... What would that be? What are you capable of?" it asked. Why did I ask that? it thought in a sudden panic. It was not a brave being. It had no desire to anger the Sicarian, but feeding off the dead could be a death sentence in itself. If it fed too much, or navigated into a part of the mind that may have been too damaged, it could suffer worse than meeting the end of its life. It could get trapped within in its own mind, unable to ever escape. It had only fed on a dead person once before. And it was something it never, ever wanted to repeat.

"What I would do to you? I will leave that up to your imagination, suffice to say that it would last a long time... Nothing short of an eternity."

It heard her words, and knew it had no choice in this matter, at all.

ESSA STOOD in what was Mikko and the Moogle's office, a dank stone room. At one end sat the Moogle's execution chamber, complete with various rotting remains adorning the floor, remnants of his recent wrath. And at the other end was Mikko's table, complete with the Order ledger sitting on top of it; the book which wrote back to its reader. A direct written conduit to the Elders – a book where the administrator received their commands and gave updates. The room of light, on the other hand, was reserved for more urgent commands. The administrator would write into the relevant column – then a reply would appear in the column next to it. Opening the ledger, she saw all of the runic symbols that Mikko wrote. The Catigeux language was something that Essa had not had to use for many years. Most families in the Order taught it to their young, but it was not often in anyone's adult life that knowing that language would have any benefit – but now she had to. She was glad her memory was flawless, as if not, she would have been in trouble and had to have re-learned the language from scratch.

She wished she could leave all of it. She was not a follower of the Elders despite being raised into it. In her mind, she just worked there, as was the case with many of the workers in Amorfield, where some did not care about the Order itself.

Though they obviously believed in the Elders' existence, they just didn't care for the religion that had been created around them, or the blind dedication they demanded. Essa and others like her were here for the wage and out of habit. Most had worked here for decades and knew no other life. Not like a fish creature could get a job at a Target, after all.

Now away from her previous, much simpler job, she just wanted to leave. Live her life away from the death that this new position would no doubt bring with it.

In the years before she joined the employ of the company – when her family allowed her to travel the underworlds in an effort to "find herself", she had met many others that were different like her. Different in a way few "monsters" were – ones that were untouched by cruelty. Ones who had never been subject to the barbarism which humanity often wrought upon those who were not normal. Those untouched by this lived genuinely happy, peaceful existences in isolated realms away from the reality of man. Surviving off the land which they chose to farm. Self-sustaining everything for them and their families. This was a reality she wanted for herself; a life without violence, without fear.

Also, no one had quit the Order before – not that she knew of, anyway – there was nothing in place within the rules of employment which seemed allow such a betrayal to the faithful. People had been banished before, but she would rather leave amicably. She did not want to change the Order's opinion of her. She didn't want to be made a pariah to the beings whom she worked for, either.

Maybe she could do this job for a few years. Keep working hard, whilst squirreling away some money, so that she might be able to afford her eventual departure? She couldn't have refused this new appointment to be the Administrator, that in itself would have been punishable. So, she would plan and prepare her exit before the role itself would consume her. After all, there was now no mind reader like Mikko, no-one to hear her thoughts of rebellious escape. No one except the Sicarian, whom she had to make sure did not hear inside of her mind.

She glanced to the end of the room, where the recent executions had taken place, and pondered the fate that might be met upon the executioner; the Moogle. Of what waited for him upon his return. She did not know whether he was ever coming back, or if he was now gone for good. The Sicarian told her that he would face "only consequences owed." Which, though noncommittal and quite vague, sounded like he would only be censured, and not condemned for whatever his crime was deemed to be. Maybe he was only guilty by association to Mikko? Maybe now they would force a bond between her and the Moogle? She hoped to all the Gods not. He terrified her – as well he did anyone with a sane mind.

LIFTING THE VEIL OF DEATH

The Leech's real face was fully exposed, its four facial sections gaping open wide as it lifted, face first, Deacon's rotten severed head up towards its circular mouth.

It had been told what it needed to do by the Sicarian – find out the cypher to this journal's symbols. Search his mind. Find where Deacon hid the secret, as well as ensure that these were the only pages he produced. The leech did not know why any of this was important or needed. But there was no choice and this was not the place to question.

Upon being asked how long this would take, the leech had no definitive answers. A dead mind was unlike a living one, mainly in terms of navigation. When entering a resurrected mind, the memories that would be present would inevitably be in a "survival mode". The brain would somehow know it had died, so would fight to remain alive the best it could. The leech being there would not be ignored, like it would be within a living mind, as a living mind is so active, its presence would not even be noticed – but a mind with nothing to focus on except its own mortality would notice a foreign presence

Everyday Monsters

within it, and react with hostility and desperation. The subconscious would presume this interloper was some kind of bringer of death; a death it would sense was very near, so would fight with all of its might.

It did though, neglect to tell the Sicarian one thing. As this man to be leeched upon was an obvious Zombie, it might not have been possible to feed on him at all. Some beings are not edible for the leech. The Sicarian for one – as her brain was not her own, only a host. So, in that case, it would only be able to feed from the host's mind. Moogles are another – as they do not actually have a brain like humans do. As for Zombies, it just did not know. It had never met one before, let alone wished to feast on their rotten deceased flesh.

The leech's plan was that if there were no answers within this dead man's mind, it would just make the answer up and hope that the Sicarian would not hear his hidden truths. Failure would also be an inability to complete the given task. So, even if it was not possible to find the answer at all, it would still be punished.

Its folds of skin enveloped the sides of Deacon's head, as its tendrils dug their way into the skin, through the skull and into the decaying brain. Its circular mouth covered the head's nose, mouth and eyes, as its skin started to ripple with the undulated sucking of this feeding. It did not know what it might find, but only hoped that it could survive it. It needed to survive this. This couldn't be its ending.

As it connected to the dead head, it gave up some of its energy to it, to kickstart it. It felt its strength depleting but forced itself to carry on.

It moved its hand, palm downwards, and held it above the journal, which laid on the table in front of it. From the skin on the palm broke forth hundreds of tendrils, all flailing wildly downwards as they grew in length. As it placed its hand on the top of the journal, the tendrils wrapped around and burrowed within the book itself. The holes they created were imperceptibly small, like fine needle punctures. Visible under scrutiny, but not damaging to the naked eye. The tendrils burrowed harmlessly through the skin-made pages, as they attempted to use the journal's familiarity with Deacon to gain entry and focus into his mind. A key to the correct door, beyond which laid the answers the Sicarian looked for.

DARKNESS. Nothing but darkness drifted past it, as it descended deeper.

Beneath it, coming into view in the far distance, was a pinprick of light. Far, far away but coming closer at a gathering speed.

From within this pinprick of light, things were staring to emerge: as the light grew in size as it fell closer downwards. Tall buildings came into view. A whole city landscape was being brought into the light beneath it. This mind was being woken up and starting to re-create its mental vista; the landscape where the leech hoped the answers lay. The answers he was too scared not to find.

The city beneath it got closer and closer. The wind rushed past its falling body. The faster it fell, the more the buildings beneath came into a clearer view. It soon fell by the tops of the skyscrapers within this imagined city, continuing its free-fall downwards. Faster and faster. The asphalt of the street beneath came toward it with a terrifying speed.

Landing with a thud onto this street, the descent came to a sudden and uneventful halt. Nothing in its body broke. No bones shattered or even dislocated. No cuts or bruises appeared over it. Nothing even changed in its being. Its body, in reality, would have just burst and smashed open upon impact on this street, hurling it into an instant and violently horrific death. As it would, if it had hit any solid object at hundreds of miles an hour. But here, it just landed fast and instantly, without any mark of damage on or within it.

Standing up, it glanced in all directions. The streets which lay around it stretched out 50 or so feet in each direction. Beyond them lay nothingness. With each passing moment, this dark nothingness retreated, revealing more and more of the city; foot by foot – this city built by Deacon's resurrected subconscious mind.

The leech's eyes darted hurriedly as it covered each corner of this ever-growing place. They would be here soon, it thought. They would be wanting to fight for their life, which they did not want taken away from them so soon.

Taking a few steps backward, it stopped in the partial shadows cast down by an awning over a small entrance to a closed dive bar. It glanced up and noticed the sign above the doorway which said "Sorbic's". The walls either side of this entrance were adorned with posters of future gigs taking place here. These live bands: The Zombies, Grateful Dead, Deacon Blue – all bands listed with names that related to Deacon in some way. All the photos of band members on these posters were also, each and every one, Deacon. Each member, whether short or tall, fat or thin, black or white, male or female – each had Deacon's face. This was a natural kind of occurrence within a person's mental landscape. Their subconscious created everything which could be seen, felt or tasted. Some minds created their landscape to be a city – like this one. Some had space stations. Some farmland. The leech's preferred mental locations were mazes. It liked them as the secrets were always hidden in the center, unlike places like this city. Not that it wanted the easy way, far from it. It loved a challenge, and a maze – even a mental one, was a puzzle with lateral and logical aspects to it – the cities, space stations, farms or whatever other locale were not solvable things in their very nature, had their answers always hidden in more abstract and meaningful places to the victim, that the mind alone knew. So, it took more time to find what it might be looking for. At least it had the journal. This would shine a light on to where it needed to go, the part of the mind that still would recall what it was and the workings of it.

As a general rule, male minds favored space stations. Female minds favored seashores or cities. The places within people's minds mainly were dictated by what they could imagine. The more natural the environment, the more assured and developed the mind, and the more grounded in reality the person was. Having feasted on artists and creatives for the past few decades, the leech was used to the more unnatural places, as the victims were full of neurosis and delusion. The most memorable it had experienced was when it walked within a living painted world. The whole landscape was an ever-changing place made of paintbrush strokes – each item within it having been made of oils and pastels. The closer you got to anything, the more "finished" they became, with the opposite happening the further away you walked.

Here, though, it just looked like a city – similar to New York or London. The personalization of posters and bar name aside, there was no real difference between this and reality. This person was very well grounded, logical and with no delusions. Quite a shame, really, as it expected more from a zombie. Though for a dead mind awaking, it really couldn't expect more than what was here, best have fewer surprises after all, especially considering the potential dangers here and in the reality it came from.

. . .

IN THE ROOM with the Sicarian, the leech's hands moved over the journal. The tendrils removed themselves from inside the book and found different paths to burrow within it. They traveled through every part, the handmade spine, the pages inside. Its pointed and fleshy ends gently pierced through each area they could cover. Slowly and assuredly.

The Sicarian watched silently. She marveled at the leech sucking on Deacon's head, as a small smile sat over her face. She had always been impressed by this creature as it was something that existed outside of reality. It was an aberration. A bone fide one-of-a-kind.

WITHIN THE MIND, the darkness crawled back even more, exposing more new streets and more buildings. The leech looked up towards the receding night. It saw that each building the relentless brightness uncovered was taller than the last. Each of these successive buildings appeared to lean progressively more inwards to where it was standing. Glancing around at the complete skyline, encircling the entire area, they all appeared to bend in towards his position like a giant claw – as if even the landscape was telling the mind where he was. Pointing to his exact location.

IN THE REAL WORLD, sweat broke out over the leech's body.

A NOISE. Something a few streets away. A crowd? It sounded like a crowd. As if a riot was starting to build up, this increasing clatter of murmurs got louder and louder, and the murmurs soon became shouts.

Closing its eyes for a second, it knew the source of the

noise was where it had to go – and judging by this sound, the people there might be expecting it. They sounded angry and numerous. Opening its eyes again, it moved on, keeping to the sides of the buildings, hiding in their shadows as much as it could.

It could hear the clicking sound of a window opening above; it looked up and saw in the open window on the second floor of that building, a woman with Deacon's face leaning out. Falling into a panic at seeing this invader – she quickly reached out and closed the window shutters, then the windows behind it.

The sound of a single pair of rushed footsteps behind it caused the leech to turn. It saw a small child (also with Deacon's face) running across the street, and into the doorway of an opposite building.

Dammit, it thought. They were not only becoming aware of him, but were starting to react. Fear was the primary emotion these avatar type creatures would feel. They would run and hide first, just like any creature encountering something they had not seen before.

But the fear would not last long. Not here. It would soon give way to anger. Then would come the rampaging violence to destroy what was not meant to be here; just as cells would attack a virus.

Turning a corner and into a narrow alleyway, the leech was relieved to see that there was nothing else here with it. No mob of the subconscious, waiting to enact their fury. After seeing those few afraid figures, the leech worried. It had hoped that – having just woken up – this corpse's mind would not have had time to populate itself with any physical representations, and instead would be empty and without emotion, but that wish was just too good to be true.

Moving hurriedly down the alleyway ahead, it ran past a

collection of partially torn posters which stated "Sorbic for Mayor", complete with photos of Deacon dressed in a suit, grinning happily at the camera. These posters had a blue screen-tone effect to them, which lent them a retro 80s air. If the leech had stopped, had it read these posters closely, it might have decided to end this trip immediately. Each poster was adorned with the tag-line "You are not welcome here, Leech." Had he stopped, had he read, he would have decided to face the Sicarian and simply lie about what he'd found. Any mind, even one that was dead, should only know – at most – of a foreign presence there. It should never have known what that presence was. Not who it was – but instead of seeing this, it just moved on, towards the opening of the alley, where a few large trash cans sat.

It ducked behind one of these cans and took a moment to breathe and think. Whatever the cause of this riot-like noise was, it was located on the other side to where he now hid. He tilted sideways and peered through the gap between two of the trash cans – hoping to catch a glimpse of what was happening.

Behind him, the posters of the would-be Mayor Deacon started to move. Each Deacon in the poster slowly turned their heads towards where the leech hid. Their smarmy Mayoral smiles dropped quickly, as they turned into a hateful stare, focused only on the insurgent. Anger overtook the previous emotion which had been printed on their faces. One by one they reached forward and pulled themselves out of their paper confines, reaching out into this "real world" of the city alleyway. The blue screen-tone effect on these images stayed with them – even after escaping the home of their poster; they were still what they were before – two-dimensional printed paper.

The leech peered through the trash cans, to what

appeared to be a couple of hundred people all clamoring in a large pile for something in the middle. Climbing over each other with no care for who was beneath. They each scrambled into this pile, like rabid creatures chasing their prey.

IN THE ROOM, back in Amorfield, the leech's tendril-exposed hands now forcefully clasped either side of the journal. Its face pulsated as it sucked – faster and faster – on this head gripped in its mouth. It was sucking in desperation for the answers.

THE PAPER MAYORS advanced upon the unsuspecting Leech. Their blue screen-tone effect lent their look a terrifyingly unnatural air. One of these paper men reached out its paper-thin hand and grabbed the leech by the collar. Turning, terrified, it staggered back, yanking itself away from this attacker.

As it pulled away, the hand of the paper mayor tore in half. Being paper, they were prone to the same weaknesses that all paper was. Seeing the ease of this damage, the leech stood up and ran at this man with both hands on the attack. As it grabbed this attacker, it ripped him clean in half. Both thin sheets of paper fell slowly to the ground. The mayor screamed loudly as he was bested, though not loud enough for the huge pile of people outside of the alley to be able to overhear.

The leech stamped on this mayor's face, its boot-print remaining as a red stain on the blue paper.

The other mayors advanced en masse. The leech was grabbed from behind by one of them, who yanked its head back by its hair. One of the other mayors punched the leech in the face with his fist. His paper arm rammed into its open

Everyday Monsters

mouth, up to the mayor's shoulder. The leech fell, choking on this paper gag. Struggling to breathe, it bit down as hard as it could, ripping through its attacker's arm.

Pushing itself away from them, it stumbled as it proceeded to cough up the rest of the paper rammed down its gullet.

Wiping its mouth, it stood upright to turn to the mayors. It then ran at them with a destructive intention.

THE SICARIAN STOOD next to the leech, who was still feeding, whilst gripping the journal. She moved her head closer to it – right next to where the severed head was being fed on. She stared at the process from less than an inch away. Getting closer, she sniffed it. Like a dog sniffing another of its kind – she was learning more about this creature – staring in obsessive examination.

Deep behind her eyes, from the darkest recesses of her mind, Vix watched this play out in torment. No end was in sight to the anguish she had been trapped in.

LEAVING the beaten and torn paper mayors behind, the leech decided that it had to do something quickly and without any hesitation. A braver decision than it normally would make – but these were extenuating circumstances. It had to get this done and get the fuck out of this dreamscape in one piece.

Now standing, staring at the human pile which reached up almost 100-feet-in height, the leech watched as men, women and children – all with Deacon's face – clamored on top and between one another to create this human monolith. All seemed to be trying to make their way in to see something within the pile's center; something that shone a bright light within the pile itself. The light which broke through and outwards from the frantic mass. This must be the answer, it thought to itself.

None of these piling Deacon avatars paid its presence even the slightest shred of attention. Not like the paper mayors did. Instead they remained totally focused on climbing on the pile.

Looking around, it noticed that – apart from those in this pile – there were other people in the area. Others who were now starting to notice its presence. Ones who were slowly starting to advance towards it. From inside buildings around the large city space, as well as from other posters and even from reflections in windows, the city knew full well that it was here now. By the paper mayor attack and these people's demeanor, it was obvious that it was not welcome.

IN AMORFIELD, the leech clutched the journal tight to its chest. It was its focus in the dreamscape, to show it what it needed. It was the only way it could make sense of the place it traveled within. Going in blind without a focus was suicide, as the journey could be placed anywhere, instead of where it was now. In the figurative belly of the beast.

IN THE DREAMSCAPE, the light within the pile now shone significantly brighter, at the same time that it clutched the journal tighter in the real world. What he wanted to find was right there – and just announced itself with its brighter light.

Running toward the pile of people, each scrambling their way to the light, the leech climbed on, hoping that they would not pay it any notice, as they seemed solely focused on this light. The avatars from the streets behind him, though, were now advancing as a crowd. Each wanting to destroy this invader – but at present were not near enough to stop him climbing up this human hill of Deacons.

Trying to claw its way through these the avatars was easier than it presumed. Akin to crawling into quicksand; as soon as it moved its body between two avatars at the top, the motion of the ones surrounding him – trying to pull themselves forwards – pulled him deeper first. As it sank into this mire of flesh, the light from the center got brighter and brighter the nearer it got.

The chasing avatars had now reached the pile and followed him furiously.

The Sicarian was still watching closely, as it started to twitch and emit a moaning sound which rose above the sound of the feeding. It twitched as someone in the dreamscape pushed him in the pile. Suddenly, its shoulder was pulled back for a second, its head flung to the side. All movements it replicated on its body pile descent. Its physical body reacting to the motions made in Deacon's mind.

Pulling its way over a shoulder of the avatar in front of it, the leech fell through a gap, falling at least fifty feet downwards. It hit the ground painlessly as it looked around. This huge mass of people was hollow in its core. They had created a fluctuating, living dome. It glanced at the huge array of avatars reaching inwards, grasping toward the light in the center, all seemingly unable to fall through like it did. They all moaned in unison, stuck in their places – none seemed to notice it as it landed within them.

Without more hesitation, it turned and scrambled towards the illumination in the middle of this space. Toward the object emitting this light. The closer it got, the dimmer the light became. As dimmer the light became, the clearer the object within became.

All around it, the arms from the Deacons in the dome lunged and grabbed at the light feebly, being too far away to touch anything.

In the center of the dome, within the light, the leech began to see something that it wished it hadn't. It didn't want to be the one to tell the Sicarian this news – being so well-versed in dreamscapes, it knew the symbolism that each dream spoke in. It knew exactly what objects here meant in the real world and only had to take a quick look at this, to know what its meaning was; the journal was not real. It was a distraction. A trick made for the Sicarian.

Within the light, a white rabbit sat on its own, its fur crawling with flies. Its body crudely held together with thick stitches which broke apart in places. Looking up at the crowd of lunging avatars, the rabbit twitched its small nose. This was the representation of Deacon's journal within his dream. And the leech had been guided to its location. This was, most tellingly, a white rabbit – meant for people to follow to a fake land; a very blunt and obvious metaphor.

"INTERLOPER!" was the scream heard. A scream that made the leech turn upward to those who shouted it. One of the chasing avatars had made it through the last row of other Deacons, and now pointed towards him. It repeated its scream "INTERLOPER! INTERLOPER! INTERLOPER!"

"INTERLOPER!" came the same voice from another body within the dome ceiling. The leech turned back and saw a female avatar with Deacon's face, screaming at him the same way.

"INTERLOPER!", "INTERLOPER!", "INTERLOPER!" more and more of these chasing Deacons made it through the last row of avatars, screaming the same words in the same voice.

Slowly, the avatars which lunged for the light – the ones that formed the dome itself – became infected by these cries. They, too, started to turn their attention toward the Leech.

One of the avatars then fell from the ceiling in the dome, landed on its haunches with a grunt – then sprang to its feet with incredible speed and without pause, ran toward the leech unleashing a battle cry. Quickly a second followed suit. Then a third.

The first one smashed into the leech, sending it crashing to the floor. All the while the screams of "INTERLOPER!" made a deafening chorus.

WITH THE SICARIAN, the leech was pushed backward by an invisible force. Smashing into the wall behind, it crumpled and collapsed onto the floor. The head of Deacon was still fixed in its maw – the leech still feeding as it fell into a heap. The journal spilled out of its hand as it fell, its tendrils flailing wildly from its palms, with nothing to attach to.

A PILE of avatars crawled over the leech. Despite being able to scream "interloper" they were simultaneously in a brain-dead state; Hungry. Feral. Bloodthirsty. One of these attackers opened their mouth, lunged hungrily and bit into the leech's shoulder with terrifying force and ferocity. The leech screamed a terrified scream as this avatar ripped the chunk of flesh away.

All the while, the rabbit stared silently at them, twitching its nose.

. . .

In Amorfield, the Leech's shoulder burst open, the skin ripping apart, and jettisoned a spray of thick blood. An invisible force had bitten off the same section of flesh as the avatar did within the dreamscape.

An avatar crawled over to the leech and took a large bite from his thigh, ripping the muscle with a wolf-like ferocity.

Another burst of blood in the real world – its body reflected the dreamscape attack in perfect synchronicity. What happened there, manifested here in real time.
    Without hesitation, the Sicarian reached forward, grabbed Deacon's head by its hair, and yanked it forcefully from the leech's mouth.

The pile of avatars swarmed over the leech like maggots on a corpse. In an instant, they were all pulled away – caused by the Sicarian's actions in the real world – and all ripped backwards in the same direction, far away to the other side of the paved area they were in. Now exposed, the leech's body displayed the extent of the frenzied attack. Blood spewed from his mouth in a torrent, as a wound in his chest displayed his ripped-out lung to the elements, his heart lay next to it, beating fast and erratically.

The Sicarian threw Deacon's head across the floor as the leech's chest burst open. It was now alive again – raised awake from its death by the feeding, biting at the air with a look of rage toward the Lord of the Flies.

She turned her attention away from this living head and back to the leech. She bent down with determination to its massacred body, and with a stern expression she moved the flaps of its face over its open circular mouth – reconstructing its human appearance.

"Tell me!" she shouted at it.

The flaps of its face held together weakly, though sagged and slightly slipped apart. Its eyes were barely able to focus as it drifted away from the dream city and back to Amorfield. It tried to look at her as best it could. Even with these wounds, it was scared of what the Sicarian would do.

"I saw..." it uttered weakly through the spluttering blood from its mouth, as its exposed and ripped open lung forced the last parts of the air from it.

"Tell me!" the Sicarian barked with urgency

"I...," it coughed. "Help... me... Please..."

"After you tell me!"

"Please," it barely managed to gurgle in reply. It tried its best to grab some air through the blood it drowned in, and through its only working lung.

"I promise. Tell me, and I will resurrect you!" she said, almost panicking. The nearest to a human reaction she may have ever had, outside of rage.

"The book..." it strained.

"WHAT?! How do I read it?"

"Distraction..."

The Sicarian heard this word and quickly fell silent, in thought.

"It's a... trick."

The Sicarian turned quickly to see Deacon's head – who now lay there, smiling a wide triumphant smile toward her.

Screaming with rage, she scrambled over to him, picked him up, and started to smash his head on the metal floor. Over and over and over again.

The fact that the head would only be alive for a moment more, until the leech's power wore off him, was not even a consideration for her. Her fury needed to be expelled. She didn't know why he did this, but promised with each slam of his head, with each bone that cracked beneath her hands, with each piece of brain matter that smeared onto the floor – that she would destroy all that had been involved. She cared less about the effect Deacon wanted to elicit in her, and more about the lustful hate and anger she aroused herself with.

THE LEECH BLED out and died within the next few moments. Died waiting for the Sicarian to do what she promised for it. – but she had no inclination to save it at the moment. If she had her calmer head on, she would have not thought twice, and saved it in an instant. Yet her rage blinded her mind. It was a one of a kind – someone she could have used time and time again in the future – someone the other Elders wanted alive, but all she knew was that Deacon must be destroyed and those that followed would feel the same pain.

The last few smashes of the pulp that used to be Deacon's head squelched onto the polished floor. No part of him could be clearly detailed anymore. There was nothing of his face left to identify. Each part of him was now smashed into nothing but gore.

She screamed to the heavens in a violent frenzied anger, as her body suddenly burst into a gigantic swarm of flies with rage.

. . .

Everyday Monsters

LATER, when she would reform from this explosive scream – in an even more damaged state – she would see the Leech now laying in the room, dead. She would regret not saving him – but do so only for a fleeting second.

ESSA, sitting in the dark of her new office, listened to the silence. It was deafening and all consuming. She had been sat here for a while, not knowing what she was to do next. Everyone she had spoken to in Amorfield alluded to Mikko, the Moogle and Albert's absence not having any impact on their positions, or day to day workings. So she was lost. They seemed to not need anyone telling them what to do. So, what did they do? she pondered. Was the Administrator merely a caretaker? Was it everyone else who ran Amorfield?

She had a call with the other Administrators – but none of whom, predictably, were forthcoming with any advice on what she should do, or detailed what they did. So, she waited, for many hours, staring at the phone on the desk. Looking at the ledger pages.

IT WAS in the early hours of the next morning, that within the ledger – which sat open in front of her – symbols had started to appear in ink in the far-right column – one by one – written from somewhere else. Still awake, Essa looked down at them as they appeared, reading them. If she had eyelids, instead of large black fish eyes, she would have widened them at what she was reading.

"Oh no..." she uttered weakly as she realized what she was being asked to do.

AND THEY ALL FELL DOWN

The coffin in front of Johnstone and Jaden was now open and exposed the fresh corpse within. Beneath this dead male, naked body, lay many, many others beneath it. All of which lay in varying stages of progressively worse decomposition the further down they went. Despite the appearance of being a normal coffin in a normal mausoleum, this was, in fact, an entrance to a deep pit. A pit that reached down further than anyone could see. It was a mass grave dating back centuries, which from the look of the fresh corpse on top, was still one that was in use to this very day.

Johnstone, with his newly stitched on arms and legs, wore his suit jacket again. This jacket and trousers hid the significant size differences between his currently attached limbs – his old ones now lay on the dirt floor beside the coffin. His bulky black torso was no longer held up and adorned with matching appendages; instead by thin, white, old legs and arms. He did not seem to mind, though. It was part of the plan he was created to follow, after all.

He took his knife and reached down to pick up one of his

old limbs; his right arm. He placed the blade at the inside of the wrist and cut the skin all the way down the arm carefully.

Motioning to Jaden, he held up the arm to him – shoulder outwards.

"What d'you want me to do?"

"Hold it by the bone as I pull," Johnstone replied.

Jaden, confused, reached up and grabbed the bone joint sticking out of the end of the arm. Johnstone, at the same end, put his fingers into the flesh and grabbed the two flaps of skin either side of the incision he had recently made. In one movement he pulled this skin off the arm, de-gloving it with ease.

Jaden – wide-eyed – held the skinless arm in his hands. He could see the inside of the Golem's old skin now. It was adorned with hundreds of tiny written symbols.

"You can throw that away." Johnstone motioned to the arm Jaden was still holding. He then leaned down and picked up another limb from beside the coffin.

"That writing... On... on the skin." Jaden motioned as he dropped the skinless arm.

"This is the real offering, the book was a lie," Johnstone replied in a monotone, his attention fully on the task at hand.

After all the limbs had been skinned, Johnstone placed the pile of his old skin into the rucksack beside him. Each of these skins were covered on their insides with the same kinds of symbols.

The skinned appendages, meanwhile, were left in a pile behind Jaden, as he wiped the blood from his hands, onto his shirt. "So, who wrote that book if it's a lie? You? Deacon?"

Johnstone smiled. A strange thing to see on a Golem. "Looked good, didn't it? I was proud at how good I made it."

"Okay, so what needs to happen next?" Jaden asked whilst staring blankly down into the pit of dead bodies. "I would ask what the fuck everything I just did was for, but you wouldn't answer that, would you?"

"I don't know. I wrote the book because I was told to. I knew it was a lie, but can't say why, really. I know we have to get here. I know I had to do this. That's it."

Johnstone knew he had to get to this very moment. The moment of him standing in front of this very coffin, with the bounty hunter by his side. Deacon was very, very clear on the actions that needed to be done – where Johnstone needed to go and what he was to do. Yet, despite being told that he would have somebody with him – Johnstone still felt alone in all of this. He had tried to explain everything to this man, but his words seemed to make matters more confusing. Maybe he didn't understand the words totally himself. There was so much here that he did not comprehend, and he liked Jaden, but was sure Jaden didn't like him. But it was all going to plan, a plan he never questioned. Whilst sitting in front of Deacon as he gave the orders, all Johnstone could think was, if this was so important, if Deacon could usurp the Elders in some way, if this was really as big as he said it was – then why had the Order's army not been dispatched? Why did the undead solders, that lay in wait for a purpose like this, not be raised to ensure the plan died in its infancy? And why would he trust this plan to a Golem? He never asked these questions out of obedience to his master. It was not his place to question – so he never got any reply to his thoughts. Not that Deacon would have given him any answers which he could have understood.

"We wait? For what?"

Johnstone looked at Jaden. "I just know we had to get here... And then... We wait for him."

"Well, can't we close the fucking lid so we don't have to

smell this shit?" Jaden asked whilst motioning to the deep pit of putrid rot that sat before them. "And who's gonna come, eh? A severed fucking head?"

Johnstone wondered why Jaden was asking so many questions. Hadn't Deacon proved that he was above any doubt? "I'm not sure what we are waiting for. He didn't say."

"And you didn't think to ask?"

"Not at all," Johnstone replied.

Jaden, meanwhile, was somehow still intrigued. He had just helped a large reanimated, stitched together corpse replace his limbs with the limbs of his former boss. A boss that he himself had killed. Then he skinned his old limbs which were somehow written on before they were removed. Now... Now they were waiting... Waiting for what? His whole mind still screamed at him to leave, but something was still making him stay. Stay despite knowing that being here put him in harm's way.

"Do you at least know what this is?" Jaden said, pointing to the coffin.

"I don't know for sure, but I think it may be a—"

In an instant, a bright light emanated from Johnstone's eyes and mouth. He screamed aloud, cutting off any more words of his potential answer. The light beamed out blindingly, blocking any ability to see the Golem's actual eyes or inside his mouth. There was now only this light – pure and white, shining out like a floodlight, illuminating the entirety of the mausoleum into a bright white blindness.

Shocked, Jaden backed away. "Jesus fuck!" he exclaimed under his breath. "What in living fuck?" he continued to mumble as the light came screaming out of the Golem. Frantically looking around, he tried to find something – anything – to defend himself, but the room was so bright he could barely focus on any single object.

With his hand searching the floor blindly, he managed to grab one of the old skinned arms on the floor. With the bone tightly in his grasp, he stood up again and held it upwards, defensively, in the direction of the brightest part of the light pouring out of this Golem.

Though screaming as the light broke through him, Johnstone was not in pain. He was, in fact, not even present at that particular moment. He had been forced into unconsciousness within a millisecond – the scream coming from his throat, was not even him screaming.

The light cut out as Johnstone fell off the grave marker he was sat on, and slumped to the floor next to the stone coffin.

Jaden still gripped the severed arm like a baseball bat, his eyes darted around in a panic, as he readied himself to attack any danger.

But instead of an immediate attack, there was now silence. Nothing was here, except the unconscious Golem and him. No more light. No more screams.

The Sicarian stared down at Essa, who was now stood looking meekly up at this deity. The body of the leech lay dead on the floor nearby; drained of everything living within it. Its body was now merely a dry husk.

On the other side of the room lay the smashed pulp that used to be Deacon Sorbic's severed head.

Essa spoke softly. "I can put out an alert if you'd like? All the hunters and shamans could find them, I'm sure – it would just take some time."

The Sicarian did not answer, instead just felt comforted by her spent rage. Essa had informed her that the two other beings which the Moogle was in chase of were Deacon's old Golem, and an ex-employee of the order – a hunter she had met before. When they were last spotted, they were many miles away from any access point, but had been tracked.

"Are we sure they are even part of this?" Essa asked.

"One was his slave. The other ran," the Sicarian said quietly. "The fact they are together, says a lot. They are mobilizing."

She picked up the journal from the table and handed it to Essa. "This was nothing, but you don't create nothing unless it masks something. And they know what that something is. So, we need to find them."

Essa opened the book and flicked through the many pages of symbols and writing. "What shall I do with this?"

"Burn it. File it... Just keep it away from me if you want to continue to live."

Essa without another word backed away and left the room. If there was one thing she was good at, it was disappearing from people's sight. She was terrified of the Sicarian, but she did not feel nervous in her presence – as if she elicited a calming influence over others in order for them to be less guarded. As soon as Essa left, the terror within her returned. She had to make sure these two traitors were found. She had to bring them back – as well as the Moogle. There was no room for failure – not on her first day. Of course, these two might be innocent and there might not be a conspiracy, but this was all the Sicarian's call – whether it was a wrong or right one.

The Moogle, on the other hand, she had no idea what to do about him. He could not be contacted. He was rogue without Mikko to keep him in check and there was no way to stop him doing what he was obviously going to do – whether he was ordered to stand down or not.

. . .

The Moogle ran across a field in the dead of night. There was no electric lighting in this area. No houses. No towns or villages. Not even any farms. Just wild fields and the moonlight.

Though the downpour had abated for a while, it would soon return. The storms had left the fields he ran across slicked with rain.

He ran on all fours through the overgrowth, like a silverback – knuckles down, with his legs doing most of the work. His breath was heavy and he grunted from each exhalation. His blubber flailed behind him as if it carried little weight.

He was not slowing in his pursuit.

He could smell them on the horizon.

Despite the heavy rainfall washing so much away, that particular scent of those two enemies he'd first smelled at the Inn were unmistakable to him. They were not far from here – and when he eventually found them, he would take them back to Amorfield. Their bodies, though, would not be breathing, or in one piece.

In his mind, he was doing no wrong. He followed Mikko, not the Order – but, as Mikko followed the Order – he, by default, did too. These two he hunted were needed to be found. Even though Mikko was against him leaving, he knew he could find them, as he had done a hundred men before. Mikko's hesitance had been continually unfounded and the Moogle's approach always succeeded. So, he would get them. Bring them back in pieces. All would be good again. All except the passing of the man he was now doing this in memory of. As he had felt Mikko fade, he'd felt his mission become more necessary, and their fates were sealed. He would have tried to keep them alive before, but now. Now there was only death in their futures.

Everyday Monsters

. . .

JADEN SAT on his haunches above where Johnstone lay on the dirt of the mausoleum – he was now coming to. Jaden put one of his hands on the Golem's shoulder. "You ok?" he asked.

The light now gone from his eyes and mouth, Johnstone looked up to Jaden and smiled widely.

"Hello there, friend," he said calmly, his voice carrying a different sound than before.

Jaden's brow furrowed in confusion at the response.

"I'm glad you made it, laddie," Johnstone said whilst getting to his feet, with Jaden's assistance. As he stood, he stumbled. Due to the size and bulk of his torso, his thinner legs were difficult to balance on.

He glanced at the pile of skinned arms and legs, then reached down and felt the stitches between the legs and hips. "Not a bad job at all," he said under his breath.

He then looked at Jaden and noticed his look of confusion. "Ah... Pardon me."

"Huh?"

"Let's get this pleasantry bullshit out of the way, shall we?" He held out his hand. "Deacon Sorbic, pleased to meet you again."

THERE HAD BEEN a report of the Moogle, seen 121 kilometers due east of the remains of the Weathered Hearts Inn. Essa looked over a large map on her office wall, as she marked this location with a pin.

She had previously attached other pins to this map; where there were sightings of the Moogle, as well as where the two fugitives had been seen. There was also a large red dot on the map, which showed the location of Amorfield.

She traced the general direction ahead of the path from the latest sighting – looking for a town, a marker. Anything. But there was nothing in the path they seemed to be travelling to. Nothing until her finger went over an area marked "Potter's Field".

She smirked to herself. Were they there?

A Potter's Field was traditionally a place for the burial of those unknown, unclaimed or indigent people. In this case, it was an abandoned cemetery, once home to the deceased of Parsonsvale – A– a growing town dating back to the early 1800s. A town which, on one bright spring morning, fell victim to a cataclysmic earthquake. This was the first and last earthquake to ever hit that area, one which the people who lived in nearby townships saw as a sign from God. That He must have destroyed Parsonsvale due to its base morality – akin to the biblical city of Sodom. It was the only explanation that their narrow minds could muster to explain such a tragedy. Why would God take the town if there were any innocents there?

All that was left behind, the only thing not swallowed into the earth, was this nearby cemetery.

Over the following years, towns came and went, but all stayed far from the site of the old cemetery of Parsonsvale. Yet they all still used that same cemetery to house their own deceased.

By the mid 1920s – after the last town had gone, the cemetery was repurposed fully by the Order.

Jaden looked at Johnstone – or Deacon– or whatever he was. The patchwork man had just said the impossible; that his other body died, but the Golem's brain inside was partly made of his old brain, so enabled him to continue the plan in this body. Frankly it all sounded ludicrous.

"So, where is he?" Jaden asked the man claiming to be Deacon.

"He's here too. We're one now. Melded together like yin and yang. A big mental orgy." Deacon laughed aloud.

Jaden just stared. This was too much.

"Come on now. We gotta head down there." He pointed down into the coffin.

"Down there?"

Deacon looked into the pit of the dead.

"What are you talking about?" Jaden asked, still stuck on the details he was missing.

"You'll know everything soon... I'll tell you what I know when we get there... We just gotta scarper before they find us here. It's not safe."

"They know we're here?"

"I've no fucking idea. They had the leech. The fucking leech! Dammit. I have no idea what's happening now. I've been living in my own preordination for decades. But now it's over. I'm not used to this bullshit unknown."

"A leech? The slugs?"

"THE not A. You never heard of the leech? Don't you read?"

Jaden shrugged. "So, what do I call you?" he asked.

"Excuse me?"

"Deacon? Johnstone? Which one. Which name?"

"Call me either. I'll answer to both. And I am both and neither, or call me by my real name, Arius."

"Arius?"

"That's the one."

Jaden turned his attention to the pit, then to Deacon who

saw his look of concern. Being one with Johnstone, Deacon could remember how Johnstone had tried to explain, but came off as vague. So, he needed to rectify this if he wanted Jaden to join him.

"First off, please don't be scared by the fact you're here. I know you want to run, but can't bring yourself to, right?"

Jaden didn't reply to this. He just stared at Deacon.

"I am sorry you've not had the satisfactory answers you want." He motioned to the inside of the pit. "You see here? This is the pit of the condemned bastards. Those who have been deemed... undesirable?"

Jaden glanced down at the rancid bodies.

"Rapists, murderers, tormentors... A place to bury those who deserve to rot for eternity, in the company of their peers... And as you can see, it is still in use." He looked up at Jaden. "This is also our doorway. You see, the dead hold...," he paused as he looked for the right words. "...untapped power... The condemned dead hold the most power. Unimaginable power. They are evil at their core, so their core is potent."

Deacon moved around the coffin to where Jaden stood, with one hand on each shoulder tried his best to reassure this confused zombie. "Johnstone tried to tell you what he could, but I'm afraid he didn't see all the path... And that's on me. I didn't explain it all right to him. And I should have. You have to know that he meant well."

"You're right by the way. I do want to leave."

"But you can't, right?"

"Yeah."

"It's 'cos it was written that way. Some may call it prophecy, some may call it destiny, but there are certain routes in this life that have to run as have been written. Some parts of this life are non-negotiable... Let me put it this way. You know when you do something but it is something that you would never normally do?"

Jaden didn't reply.

"Those things are determined. Of course, not all can be like this, only a rough guiding path. With me so far?"

"Not really. But why the fuck am I part of this?"

"That answer is... difficult... I know you have a large gap where your past was... But we have met before."

"I know that."

"No... We have met MANY times before. You, me and Gobolt, the Wolf."

"I have no idea who that is, you get that, right? You keep bandying it about like I'm supposed to know."

"I know. Nor should you. We didn't know you as you are now. We just set you on the path. I have never met Jaden. Just the person you once were."

"Once were? Who am I then? Who is Gobolt as well?"

"That will need to be left unanswered for the moment. Time is catching up with us... But I can say that here, we're at the crossroads. And you will want to go again. But I think until your purpose is done you will have to stay. And won't be able to go no matter how much you want to." He picked up the rucksack. "I don't know what lays in store for us down here. I hadn't got that far in the story. But I know this... this is more important than all of us. And I wish I could give you the opportunity to leave if you wish it. To go and forget all of this. Sit back and watch the world burn. But fate's a cruel bitch, and your reward is a long time coming."

"What... What has this to do with the Sicarian? With me? With anything?"

Deacon smiled. "We really haven't got time to find out."

"Please."

Deacon paused for a moment. He owed Jaden as much

explanation as he could give, but now was really the worst time. "All of us were created by someone's plans, someone's paths. And they don't want me to interfere again as I did before. That's what they want to stop. They need to control the path and destroy those who seek to change the path. Especially the Sicarian. And I created the journal as a way to mislead them. Well I didn't make it. Johnstone did. But that's beside the point."

"What? What the fuck are you talking about?"

Deacon smiled again. "Please. Just come with me. And you'll meet the real creator." Grabbing a knife from the inside of his jacket, he leaned over into the pit. "The path though... is going to be tough... and quite gross... But we've got no other choice."

He then stabbed the knife into the corpse at the top of the pile and started carving it open, down the body, opening it up from the gullet to groin.

THE MOOGLE RAN across the fields. His destination got closer. The Potters Field cemetery lay on the horizon. His grunting grew louder and louder as he got more and more angry with each step.

"I'M afraid to say that in order to ascend to the light, we gotta descend through the dark..." Deacon said as he climbed up onto the coffin.

A loud roar broke through the silence of the surroundings – noticeably getting closer to the mausoleum where they stood. Both alerted, their attentions jolted towards to the large closed door which led to the outside; the outside where the roar now approached.

"Fuck. They found us way quicker than I thought they would." Deacon exclaimed, shocked. Turning he ripped open the chest of the corpse – wide-open. "All that fucking preparation and it only gave us a tiny fucking head start. Fucking typical."

The Moogle sniffed the air as he ran, his fat undulating around him with each heavy step. Through the rows of stone he moved, smashing through grave markers as he headed towards the mausoleums at the center of the cemetery. Their odor was so strong, he could taste them.

His mind was singular.

His mission clear.

Destroy. Destroy. Destroy.

Jaden stared at the Golem which housed Deacon's mind. He watched as he climbed into the open chest of the corpse – pulling the large rucksack behind him.

Before he put his head in, Deacon looked up to Jaden and said the words, "through the flesh comes the new world…"

Jaden was lost with what to think. But felt the undeniable urge to follow.

From outside of the mausoleum, the roars and crashes were getting so closer. Much closer.

"Let's go change the fucking world, eh?" Deacon said, as he climbed down fully into the corpse. His feet disappeared inside as he pulled himself downwards.

One arm at a time, he crawled through dead flesh ahead of him. Through layers upon layers of solid rotten walls of meat and filth.

He crawled downwards and downwards.

He could only hope that Jaden was following him.

Destroy. Destroy. Destroy.
The Moogle smashed into the door of the mausoleum – ripping out part of the wall with ease.
Destroy. Destroy. Destroy.

The Sicarian looked at the map on the wall of the Administrator's office. Her finger traced the path from where Amorfield was, past the pins tracking the Moogle's movement, along to the Potter's Field cemetery.

"You are quite right," she said with a growing smile.

"Should I send anyone there?" Essa asked, wanting to please the deity which she was in the presence of. "We can have them within the hour."

"No," came the reply.

Essa's heart sank. Had she done wrong?

The Sicarian turned and walked toward the exit. She did not look at Essa for even one moment before she left. She just spoke as she exited the door. "They will not be there long enough. They are going somewhere much worse than this plain of existence."

PART V

RED SANDS

THE BANISHMENT

Life throughout all the realities in existence was simply about balance; That which is born, must also die. That which can be done, can just as easily be undone. That which is light must exist opposite the dark. That balance must always exist. That is the essence and meaning of life. Simple and without question.

This is why immortality cannot exist, as it provides no balance. Nothing always was. Things have always been created, or come into being another way. There simply cannot be a life without death. Even the Elders were created at some point in the past. With what came before the Big Bang – the void of existence – nothing had ever existed. So, all had to have been born. Thus, all must be able to die. The start must have an end. There was no being in any realm which could not be killed in some way – it is only that some are a lot harder to kill than others. People often mistake life without decay as immortality. The Elders, for instance, would exist for an eternity if untouched, but they could still die in the correct circumstances. They just do not have vessels which slowly wither and expire like standard life on earth does.

. . .

Before Mikko there had been only one other Administrator at Amorfield. A man named Arius. In his 50s, he was the person who would later take on the name Deacon Sorbic – but unlike then, as the Administrator he was human, well as close to human as one could get. His only power was that of living. By the time he was made a zombie, he was already over two hundred years old.

He was a big proponent for enforcing the balance. His work as administrator believed that light and dark, good and evil must play into each and every decision. He saw the truth as something which was sacred, yet not for everyone. The beings that he was the Administrator for were, by and large, reviled and vilified by society. So, it meant he had to create balances where he could. Humanity did not look favorably on the different and those different were looked on as evil and ungodly.

As the Administrator, he was well versed in towing the company line and propagating any misinformation to keep the Order out of humanity's gaze and away from their pitchforks. A misinformation propagator – this misinformation, he made more than a duty, he made it an art form of deception. These lies that he spread were in no way nefarious and evil, not everything the Order did could be considered that black and white. Despite Arius carrying out the Order's zero tolerance and extremist demands, he also, primarily, protected its followers more than anyone else had or ever would. Of course, his reach was somewhat limited as he was only one man. He could not stop every human from hating difference. He could not save all of those who were monstrous – he could not stop every lynching of the demons, aliens or witches, that humans believed they were punishing.

Everyday Monsters

A primary example of one of these artistic deceptions, concerned the beings known to the masses as vampires – In reality they were only small harmless creatures. Skeletal, pale, fanged and nocturnal. In the lies he created, they were made suave, evil, strong, merciless, sexy, charming, and more importantly deadly. Able to bite a victim and turn them into a "child of the night". A romantic notion – and one that has served them well, all in order to protect them.

The weaknesses these creatures were born with were also fabricated or exaggerated. Sunlight? They were nocturnal creatures, so simply could not see that well in the daylight – that was all. They would not burst into flames at the sight of the sun. Garlic? Like dogs and grapes. They just could not digest that food. It wouldn't kill them, though. Stake through the heart? That would kill them – as it would most living creatures.

It was this convoluted concoction of falsehoods that was the stroke of genius from Arius. Giving people the information about the small amount of ways vampires could die ensured their continued existence. They were made impervious to everything else. Most of their enemies throughout history had shot or hung them on sight. But now, this new legend made people believe it would be futile to even try those methods. Best run! Run from the vampires! They are stronger than us, were their new and implanted thoughts.

Few would try to fight what they thought might be a vampire, yet in reality, these creatures had a lot in common with a flock of pigeons – you could simply "shoo" them away with ease if you wanted to. All they wanted to do was to exist in peace. They craved silence, in which to live out the rest of their lives. Without any "intervention" from humanity, each of these creatures could exist until the end of time itself, or pretty damn close to it.

Like pigs, vampires lived in a naked state, dwelling in the mud and filth within forest areas –- yet despite that, they were very clean creatures. They didn't soil where they slept or fed. They didn't sweat, or molt. They took their baths in wet mud or water, whichever was most accessible – all in silence. Blissful silence. Safe silence. A silence Arius did his best to ensure.

Originating from the south of Ireland, vampires tended to hide far from sight, making their warrens under the roots of trees. Their history being a trail of persecution, they had no choice but to always be on the run, settling in any land they could find – up until the point that they were chased off again.

It stayed the same until a struggling author was contacted by Arius in 1890. He was informed of the existence of these creatures and paid handsomely to write about them. He was a human given the rare chance to see reality behind the curtain. To see these monsters – so fragile and beautiful. Yes, they had fangs, but they did not eat meat. They did not drink blood. They could not change people into them. Sure, they looked scary, but that was not a reason to murder them. Arius showed this author the beauty in the monsters that needed to be protected.

His employment was to write about these creatures in order to save them. To ensure their protection – to start the propaganda to turn the truth into misinformation, all invented by Arius.

The author wrote a simple story about their kind – a scary, romanticized tale. Then, following the release, Arius would control other such tales and fantasies to be told. Manufacture real-life scenarios to attribute to these fictional monsters. Thus, sowing the seeds of doubt and conspiracy into humanities subconscious, to make the fiction a reality.

Since this story was first published, their faked legend

Everyday Monsters

bled into the social consciousness and essentially saved the entire Vampire species from total extinction. Now should anyone chance upon these creatures, they would automatically presume that they were their legend, so these people would invariably run from what they thought were bloodthirsty monsters.

Arius had given this species a generous gift – this created falsehood turned those who would destroy them, to be too afraid to even approach them. Their survival was a direct effect of the story.

He had also created other histories in his time as Administrator. One of these other falsehoods had propagated to such an extent, that the complexity and variety of their condition had been totally forgotten. Anyone whose body was a betrayer of death were labeled Zombies. But in reality, there were many varying kinds. Some of them – most of them – needed living blood to rejuvenate their decaying flesh – so nowadays would buy sustenance from blood banks. Others chose to get food from the source of whatever prey they could capture. Some Zombies could not rejuvenate at all. Opposite to them, a lucky minority of their community never decayed at all. There were those who were born, riddled with rigor mortis and incapacitated until they managed to attain death. Then there were those who could run and were not burdened with such debilitating effects. The truths of these creatures were, none of them were mindless – none of them ate brains. None of them were part of a hoard. None of them randomly attacked anyone. They were people like anyone else whose bodies were not alive.

Their re-imagined history was created in the same fashion as the vampire mythos, by using the media of the age to push misinformation through entertainment. Arius knew that humanity would always be gullible – whether hearing things in a play, a book, a film or a bedtime story. They would hear the made-up tale, then about real situations, so start to believe their story was in fact real. It took a lot of work, a lot of misinformation – but it was always worth it.

Arius' lies would not be believed immediately. These seeds of lies were sewn so expertly and expounded upon over decades, that humanity eventually would propagate the lies themselves without realizing what they were doing. The perfect long con, where they took the lie and made it their own to develop.

It was ironic that the imagined reality he had created for the Zombies were his most successful, as he would eventually become one of them, and live in the shadow of their protection.

He had always seen humanity as a scared and dangerous species. A kind who vilified anything for displaying even the slightest difference –- then justified it to themselves with a fiction about an all-knowing and all-seeing sky ghost. One which they had not, nor could ever, meet. All their behaviors were baffling and cruel to him. They displayed impressive arrays of stupidity with their steely determination to destroy. He hated them – though, the reasons he hated them were also the reasons that made them fundamentally fascinating to him. They were a contradiction to themselves. They claimed to be holy, but were far from their creator. The Order on the other hand had the Elders – Deities who were real. Yet, Arius knew what most of the others did not. He knew the biggest of their propagated lies. The lie that the Elders were Gods. The lie that all the believers fed on. He knew the truth few did, that they were not the makers of any life. They were not divine. They claimed to be the makers and destroyers of all mankind -– but at best, they were protectors of their followers, and executors of the unfaithful. He saw behind the curtain, and saw them as the lesser of the evils in the world at first, though that did not last long when he saw what lay behind the many other curtains.

Raised within in the Order, he was, as a child, one of the most faithful – the most blinded. It was over decades where he began to see the cracks in the façade he himself had been promoting. Instead of rebelling, which would have resulted in his immediate execution, he decided to carry on. Not out of some morality to destroy from within – but out of cowardice. He fully admitted that he was too scared to change a thing. His hatred for humanity kept him from trying to change anything with the one family he knew in the Order. He ignored the lies as long as he could.

It was when he spoke to the real creator of the world that he knew he had to do something more than blindly follow the lies.

THE FIELDS OF BLOOD

In another realm of existence, Arius stood amongst a field of a million murdered bodies. Dressed in a dark red monk-like robe, he carried a large saddle bag over his shoulder. His head was covered by a scarf. He wore a large golden face mask, complete with two large black-glassed eye holes in it, lending him a skeletal appearance. A rough sandstorm kicked up around him.

This realm was a different world, which lay in conjunction with standard reality. It was a place called The Balance. A world of shadows and light. A realm where all balances of life had originated from. A world which was the counterpoint to the reality in which humanity existed. That reality burst with life. The Balance did not. Reality was mostly lush and habitable. The Balance was not. Reality was fundamentally good. The Balance was not. No Gods existed in reality, but one did in the Balance – and this God was the creator of all; the originator of all the balances of all lives in the known universe.

The Balance was also a realm without time. What existed there had always existed, yet at the same time would never exist. It was not a realm governed by rules or man-made

Everyday Monsters

constructs such as right and wrong, or even as time itself. It was the reason reality could exist. As order existed in that world, chaos had to exist elsewhere; here. Around these two worlds, other realms existed as offshoots from their realities. Places of darkness and light which humanity would view as heavens and hells, but were places built to allow balance to parts which these two worlds did not provide.

The Balance was not the realm where the Elders existed. Theirs was not part of the equation of reality, but stood far apart in one of the own sub-realms. Their place was not part of the natural order of creation, as they had created it themselves before they even existed. Without time, anything was possible.

Like the Chicken and the Egg, one could ponder for hours which came first. But with the Elders, the question would be How could they create themselves in the first place if they did not exist before? The answer would be After they created themselves, they existed, so were able to create themselves. In this realm without time, the Balance was a place where the Chicken and the Egg could coexist together without ever existing at all.

Many had been to the Balance. But most had not got beyond the entrance before their mind cracked open, unable to comprehend the existence they just stepped into.

It was in the Balance that Arius found his real truth. The path he was to take. It was where he met his God and rebelled against the Order.

He stepped into this world, surrounded by 20-foot-high wooden pikes. Skewered on top of each one hung an impaled human body. Upside down with their legs upwards, these bodies had been pierced by the 10-inch-wide pikes; from the front of their throats, through their bodies, and out of their groins. These corpses rested 10 feet off the sandy ground beneath. The skin from their bodies had been removed with surgical precision – all except the skin on their heads, hands and feet – the rest, a mass of exposed and dried flesh.

A million humans had been impaled here. All of their bodies flayed. All of their extremities still having their skin. The blood from each of these corpses had once fallen from their bodies and dripped onto the sand below – a million bodies' worth of spilled blood turned the ground a dark crimson color, for as far as the eye could see, in any direction one could turn.

These fields of skewered bodies littered the landscape of the Balance – a seemingly never-ending vista of death.

The sandstorm billowed around him as he walked. It created plumes of reddened sand waves, swirling around him. His mask protected him from this battering wind. The storm did not abate the intense heat of this world at all, as the bodies baked slowly. A sun not within any existence beat down its dark blood-red hue. One which scorched this desert to almost uninhabitable levels.

In the distance, through the raging sandstorm, two circling tornados danced around each other on the horizon. Two gargantuan cyclones ripping up the sand around them into a fury. They skipped across the sand with an intense rage, threatening to, but never coming towards the scores of the displayed executed. They just swirled around the distance in a perpetual dance. A dance that could and would never end, as well as never exist at all.

This was a world that did not teem with life. The Balance had no flies, no maggots -- no flesh-eating insects, – so, these impaled bodies just hung there. Never rotting, never being fed on by anything. They just hung, cooking in the heat of the sun for an eternity.

Arius, naturally, did not find this world a pleasant place to be, but was one he had to discover the truth of. He had been – as were all followers -- forbidden to ever enter or even talk about the Balance. The Elders could not allow anyone to go to the place where their creation may be unmade. The place where they had worked so hard to ensure their power.

But Arius was not one to obey this command.

He had heard one of his to-be executed prisoners, mention this realm – a place of no yet all existence. Since then, unbeknownst to the Elders, he started to include questions about the Balance in all of his interrogations. Most had no idea or just made up lies to stop the pain. But there were some with fractions of stories. None claimed to have been there – but there were occasional slivers of facts which fit in to what he had already known. It soon became his obsession. He even went as far as to ask the Elders – a brave move, though ill-advised. He had heard it was a protected place, a forbidden place, but he thought he would chance a question. He was immediately forbidden from any mention of the Balance again, then threatened with destruction if he ever broke that order. That threat, of course, did not stop him. He had to find out for himself – he needed to know.

After 42 years of searching, he finally found his answers. He learned where the doorways were, where he could traverse the two worlds.

THERE HE STOOD on this forbidden plane of existence. Amongst the impaled dead. Stood on the blood-stained sand, facing a harsh storm and blistering heat.

He had heard tales of the keepers of the faith who dwelled in the sands. Those who were followers of the one true creator. Those who acted as a bridge between any visitors and the holy word.

But he had been in this land for days now, and had not seen another living soul. No keepers, no creators, only the dead.

But this would not be for long. Soon he would have his eyes opened.

Then all would change.

After he returned to reality, the moment he stepped back into his world, he had also contracted his new condition. The undead condition. He came back from the Balance a Zombie.

When the Order found out that he had not only walked on the blood sands and witnessed their offerings, he had also spoken with the creator, they wanted him dead – but instead only banished him. Arius had written it that way. They had no choice, but to banish – despite their want for blood. They had no idea that this decision was his invention. The fact that the Sicarian could never find him, was also his will.

They did not know at that point that he had started a chain of events which would not only threaten to undo their future, but threaten to make it so they could never have created themselves in the first place.

BROUGHT BEFORE THE CREATOR

Through the scores of impaled bodies, Arius walked slowly. He looked up to each corpse as he passed them. They deserved my recognition, he thought to himself. They probably had no respect in life, so he believed that he at least owed them his – whether or not they could ever know about it. The sand blasted at him, trying to push him back, as if trying to keep him away from going forwards.

As he passed through the many slaughtered bodies, he noticed that they were of every description, Male, Female, Young, Old, Short, Tall, Thin, Fat, White, Black, Human, Inhuman. He could see that these executions were very indiscriminate – which was very usual, as most offerings to ones in power are quite exact in the lives needed.

He did not know of their purpose, yet he knew that this scale of violent sacrifice could only have been at the behest of the Elders. How did they complete this mass execution without anyone finding out? This genocide-level mass murder occurred and the Administrators knew nothing? Who were people who facilitated this?

Through moments within the sandstorm, the instances

when the wind settled for a brief moment, he could see far ahead. Far away, at least 1000 rows of bodies into the distance, and could see the start of a mountainous region. He could not see how wide the mountains were or how high they raised into the sky, but he felt that was the direction he had to go in. After the short lull, the storm soon raised again to block his view. He could only presume that this mass sacrifice went around the mountain, and that it was the center of it all. The place in which the sacrifices were aimed toward.

He did not enter this world from the desert. He had entered from within a frozen dead forest, which lay many miles behind him. A forest that the sun remained absent from. A forest where the temperature rested at freezing level. For two days, he had walked past multitudes of dead trees; all which lay lifeless from the cracked soil below. The direction he walked in was dictated by a well-trodden dirt path which ran from the entrance – the only path amongst these trees.

The woodland eventually broke and opened up on the sun-drenched, blood-soaked desert he now trekked over. As he took his first step on the sands the sun, light and heat suddenly appeared as if a light switch turned itself on at that precise moment to greet him.

A few hundred feet after he started his journey across the desert, the rows of skewered bodies came into view. It was when he walked up to the first one that the sandstorm picked up. In ebbs and flows it arrived at first, but soon became mostly continuous the further he walked. This did not dissuade him from his mission of discovery. He knew something was ahead.

For three more days, he walked through the baking sands of the impaled offerings. With no variation at all, the landscape remained the same.

He rationed his water and food the best he could, knowing

it could only last him for a week longer. Because of this, he knew that he was one day away from the point of no return. The point where if he turned back a day after, he would not survive this place.

In the forest, there had been no sun and only perpetual nighttime -- yet in this desert, there was no moon, only the sun -bleached sands. With no changing of day to night, he took the conscious decision to only stop when exhaustion kicked in. To only sleep when he needed to recharge. He slept for as long as the temperature in the desert would allow, which was very uncomfortable. But, it was the forest which he had found more difficult journeying through. He had been conditioned to excessive heat from the decades he worked in Amorfield, not the cold. The mask only worked in hot environments as it not only protected the wearer from the sand and wind, but regulated body temperature as well – something it did not do in freezing temperatures. So in the forest he just had to make do. To try and stay warm the best he could.

He gave himself a few more hours to walk – deciding that if he found nothing by then, he would rest amongst the mutilated corpses for just one more night. Then would turn back and walk toward the portal from which he had entered – back through the discomfort of the dead forest. He knew that if he did go back empty-handed, he would have to return the next time he had any opportunity. He would need to prepare better. He would bring more provisions. He had to know what the Order wanted no one else to know, and would keep coming back until he did.

As he walked past row after row of dead bodies, the storm blasted its crimson grains at him. The wooden pikes he walked beside reached up high and provided only a brief respite in their shadows from the direct searing heat of the sun. Even through this sandstorm, the bodies' exposed flesh had slowly cooked under the constant heat, lending the air a stench of roasted death and perforated bowels, a heat and roast that was eternal.

Seeing no end to this journey, Arius soon decided he should give up. He stopped and put his saddle bag onto the ground next to a wooden pike. He took out a small leather cloth from his pocket, then placed it on the ground over a small patch of dried blood. Despite this blood being dry, he felt that out of some kind of respect for the person hanging above him, that he should not sit directly on their drippings. He would rest here until his energy was (at least partly) replenished – enough to begin that hard trek back to reality.

He sat at the base of the pike and looked around. At this lower level, the sandstorm was not as thick. The desert ground was relatively flat and enabled him to see pikes in front of him for many miles. Too far to chance not making it home with his life intact.

He did not know how long these legions of the sacrificed had been dead for. It was impossible to know as there was no time in the Balance – with no time there was no rot and no decay. It also meant that they might have not been sacrificed yet, a thought which made his head hurt. They slowly cooked above him, but there was little damage to the bodies themselves. With no time, they were here and had always been here, yet just came and never were here.

Sitting on his floor rag, he propped his bag up against the pike, then leant on it. He looked up to the dead body hanging above him; it was the corpse of a small girl, who couldn't have been more than 10 years of age. Her skinless neck had been broken back, the pike entered her fragile body through her throat – just like all the rest. He tilted his head as he regarded

Everyday Monsters

her lifeless expression. One of pain and horror from her final moments of her living existence.

Pulling his scarf over his masked face, he let his head hang downward as he started his attempt to sleep. As he closed his eyes, the wind howled wildly around him.

Arius rarely slept.

When he did, he rarely dreamed.

The few times he dreamed, he awoke only knowing whether it had been a good or bad dream. He never recalled any actual details of his subconscious visions. But, in this realm, for the hour or two he managed to rest each night, each dream he had always remained crystal clear the next day – and this dream he had with perfect clarity, was always the same dream:

In a dark stone hallway, lit only by blue fire resting in torches attached to the walls, a long line of red-colored figures stood in queue. All of them nude, and in line to a door at the very end of the hallway. Their heads bald and with faces that displayed no defined features. As he walked slowly by this line of red men, he saw that not only were they not human, but appeared to be made up of the blood-stained sand from the Balance's desert. Whenever these men moved, the sand in them seemed to move and reform as it re-created their body into its new position. When one of these figures turned to look at him walk by, instead of their heads turning, the grains which they were made of would shift across the face to settle into their new positions. They had no eyes, tongue, or any definition over their entire body. Their eyes were only curved holes in the sand build heads, along with non-existent mouths.

Arius walked down this hallway with caution, past the lengthy queue of red sand people. Each one of them having taken a moment to glance at him as he passed, before looking forward again; toward the closed door they had queued in front of.

In this dream, Arius was not afraid. If this were real life, without question he would be terrified, but yet he would still continue in whatever state he found himself in. His quest for answers came from not only an unbridled curiosity, but from a desire to conquer his fear of the unknown. These figures were exactly that. Unknown. Nothing could be determined from them. If they felt emotions, he could not tell. They had no eyes to convey their feelings. No mouths to vocalize their thoughts. They were for all intents and purposes, statues. The fact they could move proved there was some magics at play.

Getting to the door at the end of the hallway, the figure at the front of the queue saw Arius approach and turned to him. The sand of his arm then disappeared into its body, then quickly reformed palm outwards to door – motioning for this guest to walk in.

Graciously accepting this offer, he pushed open the large wooden door, and it emanated a loud, ancient, creaking sound.

A shuffling noise sounded from behind him, which called his attention backward for a brief moment. He saw all of the queued figures collapsing into piles of reddish sand, then sink into the floor below – the grains disappearing until they had all vanished from view. Another noise then caught his attention – this time from in the room he was in. Turning, he saw the sand figures reforming themselves from out of the dirt floor flanking a large ancient altar at one end of the room. As they reformed, they all stared their blank stare toward him.

Behind the altar in the room, sat something which chilled Arius to the core. A familiar yet terrifying feeling which he had trouble placing.

An emaciated but gigantic figure sat amongst the shadows.

Everyday Monsters

It had a distinctly female form, but only in the loosest of sense of the word.

Its long lank hair, thin and dirty, hung the 9 feet from her flaking scalp to the small of her back, then curling in dirt onto the floor below. Her bottom half had been fused from the waist down into the sand and rocks below. Even with half of her body remaining unseen, she was towering.

Her skin bore the same color as the rock which made up the walls – a mottled gray which gave her a deathly pallor. Her arms were double the length they would normally be, in relation to her body size; both had two joints at equidistant places, which gave them a look of fleshy spider's legs. These arms bent over the altar and gripped the sides of its stone tightly.

She wore no clothes, but her nudity bore no function; her chest bore no breasts, nipples or belly button. She was a creature of stone-like skin and bone.

Most of her face was bleached out from the darkness as a bright shining light emitted from her gaping mouth This light cast the red sand figures into an eerie glow. Their shadows now loomed tall above them, appearing to dance as the light from this creature's mouth moved from side to side.

It was at this point – every single night – that he awoke in a sweat.

THE SANDSTORM still billowed hard around Arius, as he glanced upwards from his slumber and saw a figure standing closely in front of him. It was one of the red people from his dream – standing there. Staring. Motionless.

This figure must be one of the keepers he had heard about.

The wind blew off swathes of grains from its form, as other grains were slowly regenerated from deep inside. With this battering gale and the speed of this figure's regeneration, its body could never receive a proper chance to rebuild its form in its entirety – its stayed at a perpetual state of ¾ complete. When the wind eased for a brief moment, the figure managed to regenerate its body a little faster – but then, only a few moments later, the wind would resume in full force, with the sand that had built up now being blasted off, layer by layer. As it was regenerated slower. Layer by layer.

Through the eyeholes of his golden mask, Arius stared back up at this being. Unknowing of what it may have wanted or whether it was a real and present person, as opposed to a possible figment of his imagination.

As he stared, its body started to cave into itself, then reform facing towards the mountainous region which Arius had been heading toward. This figure's leg separated off from its body as another leg formed from its stump, positioned one step further away. Then the other leg followed suit; separated, then reformed into a step ahead. Then the other. Then the other. The reforming and separating happened quite fast, as the storm blasted away its top layers of sand from its body.

Arius had a choice to make. Follow this creature or go home whilst he still had provisions. The sensible choice was to leave – to get home. To regroup. To prepare better next time. But Arius was not relying on his intelligence here, as his whole being had an uncontrollable urge to follow. His brain was just a voice in the distance, screaming at him that this was a bad idea.

He followed the slow-walking red figure past multitudes of impaled corpses. As he did, the storm wailed through the pikes as strong as ever, battering both the impaled, him and his sand companion. From his periphery, he noticed other movements around him. He glanced to his right then to his left and saw other red figures, walking in the same direction

Everyday Monsters

within each row of pikes. They all moved at the same speed, as they replicated each and every motion in unison.

This procession seemed to carry on for hours – many hours. He had no way to track the time but felt like it could have lasted for a day, at least. His legs and arms struggled to carry him much further, but he knew if he headed back to the world he came from, he would have ran out of water before even reaching the forest, as well as ran out of food long before that. He no longer had a choice. He was here and had to carry on.

His steps gradually became weaker and more unsure against the power of the storm, as the mountains seemed no nearer.

It was about an hour after, that the light dimmed as he lost consciousness and collapsed onto the blood-stained ground. His energy depleted and his strength absent.

After a few paces, the sand figure's face withdrew into itself, then reformed at the back of its head – as it looked down towards Arius' collapsed body. Pausing for a moment, it looked as though it was deep in thought. The other figures in the other rows of pikes had also stopped in their tracks – and each of them stared in the direction of the unconscious Arius.

With only a fleeting moment passing, the figure standing in front of Arius fell into itself, as the sand which made its form disassembled and dissipated into the desert.

From the sand around Arius, two arms constructed themselves either side of him from the ground. His body started to lift, as the red sand built itself upwards into the eventual form of the red figure, who now carried him in its arms.

When this figure began its journey again – this time carrying Arius like a child – the hoard of other figures continued their march as well. One slow step at a time.

Arius knew of none of this, as he had been stolen away into a deep slumber – and for the first time since arriving here, his mind did not dream of the large creature in the stone room – he dreamt as he did in his world; of nothing to be remembered. All he had at that moment, was the comfort of the darkness that his dreamless sleep had brought.

IN THE PRESENCE OF DIVINITY

The wooden door to the large chamber opened wide and displayed a familiar room to Arius. This was the room from his dreams – the same in nearly every respect.

Around the circumference of the room stood dozens of sand figures, each carrying a torch of blue flame in their hand, held up high.

As in his dreams, an immense and terrifying female creature dwelled inside. Behind her altar, she was encased from the waist down in the very earth below her, the stone and sand melded to her body at the hip. Unlike the dream, there was no beaming light spewing forth from her open mouth. Instead, the blue torches held by the sand men provided the only illumination.

The sand figure who carried the now-waking Arius stepped into the center of the chamber. One of the other figures closed the wooden door behind them, a deep muted echo of this door hitting its frame sounded in the otherwise silent chamber. A chamber in which, even in his drowsy state, Arius could feel the air of reverence.

As it stopped, the sand figure holding him began to lose its cohesion, as it slowly collapsed into itself, falling to the stone and sand floor below – gently maneuvering Arius to land on his feet.

After a few moments of silence, from within his golden mask, Arius slowly regained all of his faculties. Taking in his surroundings his eyes darted around the chamber. His head pounded from dehydration.

In shock at what sat at the altar in front of him, he raised his hand and slowly removed his mask. As he did, he noticed that the sand figures around the room – in unison – turned their heads from looking forwards to looking directly at him. A wave of panic rose inside as his eyes widened. This must be a dream, he thought frantically, this MUST be a—

"Shhhhhhh" came the whisper. This creature's long, multi-joined arms moved to the front of the altar, leaning her more toward him.

"Shhhhhhh," she whispered again as she waved her finger in the air to him.

As she did this, his panic somehow subsided as his eyes narrowed. A feeling of ease and calm fell over him like a warm blanket. Like a sedative hitting him, he quickly felt none of the unease he'd felt crescendo inside him only moments before.

Despite not knowing anything of this place before that moment, as the wave of calm washed over him, his mind filled with an ancient knowledge of who he was in the presence of. A calm that did not previously happen within his dreams.

"Yer Ana," he said softly as he looked up at her, in awe. He knew her name. He knew this God's name. She was Yer Ana – The Creator. The only real God of Man who had ever existed. All knew Her to look at Her. All saw Her divinity in Her presence.

She stared back down at him with her monstrous

appearance. Her mouth stretched around from one side of Her face to the other. Instead of a nose She had two small slatted holes deep in her graying skin, which opened rhythmically as she breathed. Her eyes were bright white orbs, which sat in the large round sockets in her head.

"Welcome..." she hissed with a sickly smile, "...My sweet, sweet creation... How are you finding this existence?"

THE LIE OF LIFE AND DEATH

Arius was born in a small town called Ballymena in Ireland. Born there 262 years ago, before the very moment he stood in the presence of Yer Ana – but at the same time, he had only been brought into existence by this God a few years previous – as had many others; the vampires, the zombies, the witches, the demons, the ghouls, the Elders, The Order – all of it. Every last fantastical being. All created by this God, at the behest of the very Elders she made, requested after they were created in a land within time.

Within Her realm, Yer Ana saw the past, present and future combined as one vision. She knew what would be and how it would end – She had created it all. All in every world. She had spent an eternity creating many worlds and realms, but now She was tired of the solitary construction. She started to allow her creations to ask for more. To allow them to write any story of creation they wished to become manifest. Something, anything to entertain this now bored God. This creation came at a price, a life for a life. It was simple. If someone wanted creation, they had to sacrifice an equal amount.

Everyday Monsters

. . .

"Why do you come back?" Yer Ana asked as She raised higher on Her arms, staring down at Arius as he fell to his knees looking up at her. "Do you want to know the ending?"

"I'm...?" he started to ask as his question left his head, leading to silence.

"Do you wish to make another offering?" She motioned to the top of the altar where some folded skins lay. Skins of the impaled dead from the pikes outside. Each had many symbols written on the inside of them.

Arius looked at her, confused. "Offering? I... What do you mean?"

"You will offer again, to lay the path to return... But to what? To know more? To offer more?"

"I've been here before?" was all he could whimper.

His mind raced with thoughts of what She meant. He was physically here before? When? Did she mean the dreams he had of her?

With a slight snarl, She grabbed one of the skins from the altar, opened it up in front of Her, and stared at the symbols now facing Her.

"Without an offering of sacrifice, I will not create a question... Without your offering you are only an organism in my presence which has little meaning."

In an instant, Her eyes and mouth erupted into a bright light, as She focused on the written symbols inked on the skin she held up.

As the light touched each of the symbols, they began to burn away. Partially removed from the skin page as she read. Line by line, symbol by symbol, She scanned it – until all the symbols faded. Evaporated, leaving only the charred shadows on the skin.

When finished, the light from Her eyes and mouth subsided. With one movement She opened her enormous mouth to its fullest – and forced the used skin into Her maw, deep down into her gullet.

Somewhere in the world a baby had just been born. A baby to a woman, whom only a few seconds ago had not been pregnant. Yet as of right now, she had been pregnant for 8 months and was currently delivering her new child; a child which would not survive its 4-week premature delivery.

This God worked in mysterious ways, as people always said their Gods worked in – No one would never know the reasons behind this instant gift and death of life. None of the creations of existence were about the people it affected on a physical level, Bbut instead they were about the ripple effect their lived caused throughout the realms. A metaphysical butterfly effect added to other ripples to create and influence larger and more significant happenings.

"Were those bodies outside offerings?" Arius asked. Struggling to find any volume to his voice, or sense to this riddle.

Yer Ana swallowed the human skin and stared at him. "Your masters will not be happy you are here, will they?"

He stood in silence.

"You should leave if you wish to live?" She spoke with care. "And stay if you care to die."

"Please... I need to know..." he replied.

"You have no offering... And you have too short a life to see the end of the reality your masters made..."

Everyday Monsters

Arius had questions. He had known that the Elders hid the true power. He needed to see it.

"What if I had an offering for you?"

"You carry nothing, so I can only presume you offer your own flesh?"

"If I did... Could I know what this is?" he said, motioning around him. "How this works..."

"That would be acceptable." She smiled at him. "I enjoy desperation."

He was playing Russian roulette with this God. He had no idea what these offerings were. Was he really to die in order to get the answers? How was he here before? Was he part of the offerings outside, and somehow didn't remember? The answers at that moment, were worth more to him than his own life was.

PART VI

THE SINS OF THE FATHER

THE ETERNAL DARKNESS

Crawling in a furious rage, down through the increasing stages of decay, the Moogle fought his way deeper and deeper – through body after body which lay in his way – down and down through the mausoleum pit. His gargantuan hands reached forward as it ripped through the fused and rotten bodies, all of which got more horrific to a greater and greater degree the further down he crawled. Becoming more and more solid and more and more ancient. All until the bodies could decay no more, and they became a large collection of bones, compressed together by the sheer weight above them.

He did not know where he was going. He did not know what this was. All he knew was that he could smell the stench of the blasphemers ahead of him. Their scent sickened him, as it overtook the sweet odor of the corpses that he ripped through on this journey.

DEEP in the long dead forest within the Balance, a sect of Vampires foraged in the freezing undergrowth. Though not native to this land – as no living thing was – they had survived here for decades. After escaping the relentless persecution within their own realm, they had made this unforgiving woodland their home, where they existed in an isolated peace. They survived by living off the sustenance the ice-covered dead wood could provide and as they were cold-blooded, the freezing temperatures did not affect them.

They lived far from the predators which chased them here. Far from the terrifying violence humans had wrought upon their kind.

Being less than 4-foot-tall, and with zero fat on their graying bodies, they crawled at speed through the roots of the dead trees, and into and around their warrens. Almost identical to each other, their genitals were the only visual difference between them. They had the same faces, the same hair, the same build no matter what the sex or age.

Disrupting their foraging, a deep rumbling emanated from far beneath them, and was felt through the dirt, as the branches started to shake. An oncoming noise which forced them stop and look at each other confused and nervous.

The vibrating rumble became louder and louder quickly, as the forest started to tremble to the point of shaking like an earthquake.

Emitting squeaking sounds of fear, these Vampires scattered as this confusing disruption approached. They dropped whatever they ate, or had been collecting and scrambled across the clearing in an attempt to rush back to their warren, to bury themselves in deep and hide from this possible threat until it had passed.

From within the earth of the forest's clearing, the Moogle burst through with an almighty, cacophonous roar.

As his fist smashed upwards through the dirt of the woodland ground, chunks of dried mud exploded into the air with a terrifying force. The Moogle's other hand broke though the surface and landed with an immense thud, onto a pile of abandoned wood which one of the vampires had foraged – smashing the pile into nothing.

Like a rabid animal, he lashed out at the air as foaming drool dripped from his open mouth – he screamed a deafening and defiant scream. Dragging himself out of this hole in the ground, he scrambled to his fat-engorged feet. His large girth proving no real weight to him, as his fury carried him through. He breathed so fast and pained that he sounded as if he were close to hyperventilating. Each exhalation sounded too fast, too pained, like it was to be his dying breath – but he was far from dying. His need for vengeance was all - encompassing and fueled him. He would destroy everything in his path. No matter who or what they were. His exhausted breathing or his pounding heart would not stand in his way.

As he stood there, an eerie silence – a calm before the storm – settled in, as he glanced around the treeline like a wolf on a hunt. His breathing getting quieter and quieter. Scanning every part of where he could see.

His body dripped with sweat and filth, as he sniffed the air for his intended victims.

Almost in an instant his expression turned slightly joyous. The smell was unmistakable. THERE! THERE IT IS, he thought as he caught the waft of the familiar odor. As his grin widened, his tongue lolled out the side of his mouth like a dog when catching its breath. He took a step continue his pursuit, but in an instant, something stopped him from continuing.

He sniffed at the air some more. There was another smell here. A more immediate smell. Creatures of some kind. Nearer. Afraid. Very afraid. The stench of their fear wafted heavily upon the stale air, calling to him like the beckoning smell of cooking bacon.

In the roots of the dead trees that scattered around this clearing, some terrified vampires looked on. Seeing this horrific beast standing in their home. Silently they hoped that it would leave. They tried to remain as quiet as they possibly could, but through fear let out several small high-pitched squeaks as they exhaled.

Grinning, the Moogle turned his head toward the treeline. He had time for a distraction. He had all the time in the world, for what he was about to do.

He roared a battle cry toward the trees where he could smell the most potent fear.

FAR INTO THE wastes of the red-sanded desert, two figures – Jaden and Deacon – turned as they heard the Moogle's roar, echoing in the distance behind them. A roar which could be heard above the howling of the sandstorm whipping itself around them.

These sands still featured the same impaled bodies covering their landscape. Not being moved in the years Arius – now Deacon – had been away. The only difference was now they were blackened and solid, skewered on their pikes. Even without time existing, these sacrifices seemed to have changed impossibly over the years. Upon closer inspection, these bodies seemed to not be burned, but calcified and over them a black mold existed, unseen at first glance.

With his rucksack now mostly empty on his back, Deacon wore thick protective robes which hung over his clothes. They were heavy, leather-like and well-worn. The fabric of which was covered with carved symbols over them; a protection from the elements for him. As long as he wore these robes, he would not succumb to the heat – one of the many things he spent years planning for. He also wore the same mask that he'd worn in this place many years previously, back when his name was Arius and had all of his own body parts attached.

Jaden, meanwhile, was dressed in a dark gray beaked mask; similar to the ones a plague doctor would have worn, but this was made of metal, with long thin slats down its beak.

They heard the Moogle's battle-cry far, far behind them – but still too close for comfort. They could not outrun the Moogle on their heels. He was too fast and too relentless as a hunter.

"Let's... speed this up, shall we?" Deacon proposed nervously, his voice almost a shout to be heard over the wind.

"That's a damn good idea," Jaden said as he turned back to the direction they were headed in. "Best not wait here to die."

Deacon patted him on the arm, as in unison they began to walk faster – away from the Moogle's roars, down a row of impaled victims towards the mountain.

The sandstorm carried on its mission around them, unabated by these interlopers in its land. The twin cyclones still swirled strong in the distance. Still present, in a never-ending dance with each other.

As they hurried away at speed, the sand beneath where they had just stood began to move. At first it only slightly vibrated and was imperceivable in this storm, but it grew quickly as the grains of sand danced to a hidden tune deep within it. From the grain's growing dance, they began to swirl and dip and undulate between them. From these particles of sand, from under the surface, flies began to emerge in growing numbers. As they emerged, the sand rose forming around it into a growing column. This sand and fly mixture slowly took the form of a male figure. As if it was being lifted through the sand into the open, on an invisible elevator. With the exception of the presence of the flies, it was identical to one of the sexless red sand figures. The keepers. This figure's blank facial features changed from an unseen expression as it then grinned a lascivious and vicious smile – a smile full of malice. It stood and watched as Jaden and Deacon hurried further away into the sandstorm, towards the mountain which lay in the distance. This figure's smile was familiar. It belonged to the Sicarian – though now in a different genderless form.

Another of the Moogle's roars emanated from the forest far behind this figure, stealing its attention away from Jaden and Deacon – the furious roars were now constant and murderous. Turning toward these roars, the figure's grin slowly dropped as it lifted its hand. Within its palm, the sand began to grow and form into an object. The flies bound themselves along with the multiplying grains, as they piled out in greater numbers from within the figure. Forming itself into a long thin shape, it eventually turned into a spear-like weapon; one complete with a serrated-edged blade at one end, all made of sand. All still as deadly.

From around this figure, more sand and fly figures started to emerge from the red hued ground. Slowly they built themselves up from the grains from below. Each soon carried the same kind of sand and fly bladed spear. Each had the same expression. They were of the same mind. They were a singular but multiple force. They were all the Sicarian.

THE MOOGLE REACHED DOWN and with extreme ease, ripped up a tree with a single motion. One which made the vampires that watched on, wail to the skies in terror. As the tree and roots were torn from the earth, it exposed an entrance to their warren.

With no creatures visible within the exposed entrance, the Moogle then turned and barreled towards another tree which lay nearby – his shoulder barged his way through it.

Everyday Monsters

Shredding the trunk into many pieces, as the top of the dead tree collapsed without anything to hold it up and crashed to the ground. The trees that covered this land were so old and dead, that with little force they would break, sending a cloud of fine desiccated wood particles into the air.

A vampire which had hidden in the roots of this now destroyed tree was now fully exposed. It tried to run to the safety of a new tree – but before it could make it any more than three paces, the Moogle's stomach had opened, then bitten into the poor creature – ripping it clean in half. A few seconds after, the mouth opened again and swallowed the second half. His stomach made a dozen hurried chewing movements before it swallowed, then turned on the hunt for more potential food.

Two Vampires ran from some nearby bushes, with no option but to cross this monster's path, as they tried to make it to one of their warren's entrances. Their brave attempt left them in the open for only a handful of seconds. They had no choice, they had to find safety. But their effort was futile and their bravery wasted. The Moogle's grotesque hands descended upon them at the first chance, and ripped them both apart with his claws. He then picked up their now dead or dying bodies and cast them into his gaping stomach. Frantically eating them, then turning back for even more. The Moogle's appetite was infinite, both in capacity for murder, as well as the capacity to eat.

These vampires were not limited to being cautious and fearful, though. They were also capable of fighting back, as any threatened animal would be, when faced with death. With no other options for them, they would fight tooth and claw – literally. Though not in their nature, they were deadly when cornered. And this is exactly what they did as they watched the Moogle decimate their brothers and sisters. Three of them quickly leapt from the dead branches they had hidden in – and landed on the Moogle's sizable back. They grabbed with their clawed hands onto his lank greasy hair and with a terrified anger, bit and clawed at his skin. Their razor-sharp teeth and pointed talons cut into the Moogle with ease.

Letting out a pained yell, he reached back and managed to grab one of these attackers. Hurling them as far as he could away, he grabbed wildly for the other two on him. The thrown one flew like a rag doll and collided with a nearby tree, its body bursting open from the force of impact. Dying in an instant.

The remaining two fought him undeterred. Cuts and gouges now covered the Moogle, as he bled profusely down his large frame and onto the dirt below. Frantic and enraged, he managed to grab another one of these vampires. As he gripped, it sliced at his hand mercilessly. Lifting it up, he looked at it through its shadowed eye sockets and loosed a wild roar at it. Terrified it kept fighting as the Moogle then opened his stomach, ready to bite into this small attacking gray morsel of food – but before he could, this vampire bit deeply into his hand, forcing him to scream loudly and release his grip. The small creature fell from the Moogle's vice-like hold and down into his open belly, past the baying teeth. His stomach then closed with an aggressive hunger, swallowing the latest meal whole.

He then turned his fury toward the last attacker, who was still gripped onto his back, slicing through his flesh in a frenzy.

IN A DANK DARKNESS, the vampire which had been swallowed whole lay tightly packed amongst the other decimated parts of its brothers and sisters. This was not to last, as it felt itself moving downwards. Bit by bit, as a light emanated from the deep, up through the chunk of flesh around it. It, along with the other dead, was being pulled by an unknown force downwards to the bottom of the Moogle's stomach.

IN A HUGE DARK CAVERN, a pile of decayed and rotten body parts rested. Above this pile in the darkness lay a small circular light. The only light that existed in this cavern. Its dull glow shone its light from the top of the pile downwards but could not break the darkness beyond thirty or so feet. This cavern could have ended there or continued for an eternity – it was impossible to determine with this darkness.

Falling through this light which hung from above, body parts, along with the vampire creature, tumbled down from the Moogle's stomach and smashed into the pile of bodies below. This vampire contorted in pain as it collided with the solid pile the dead. In a panic, it scrambled to its haunches and looked upwards from where it fell. The light above was far too high for it to reach, though it didn't stop it attempting in futility to grab for the escape. Soon recognizing the impossibility, it looked around in a panic – though the light only illuminated the bodies around it, it could sense there were many, many more here. The place it was in stank of an eternity of death. As it looked at the bodies at its feet, it recognized the partial remains of some of its friends and let out a frustrated and fearful howl.

The howls continuing, it glanced around in fear, its eyes wide as it tried to see any path of escape.

From high above, from out of the same small light which it fell, more partial remains of a vampire – the one who fought alongside it – fell downwards and hit the pile of death with a heavy squelch.

With more despaired and frantic howls, this poor creature who had been swallowed whole, stood alone in the cavernous maw of the beast, amongst the bodies of its family.

The Moogle was done here.

Every creature that he could find had been murdered and eaten, though not necessarily in that order. The surrounding woodland had also been destroyed from his relentless onslaught upon the vanquished vampires. His head turned in all directions as he scanned the devastation for any more food. The smell of the dripping blood from his stomach-lips brought a sickening smile to his face. His long calloused brown tongue emerged from his mouth, as he lowered his head and licked some blood from his chest.

Realizing there was little left here for him, his mind switched back to the purpose of him crossing into this realm. He sniffed at the air – looking to catch the stench of those he was in pursuit of. There they are, he thought as he moved, with a burst of speed, away from this clearing.

His speed increased until he was in an all fours gallop, barreling along with booming footsteps in the direction that the smell led him in – leaving the now destroyed warren far behind.

As he sped through the woodland, he barged by passing trees, smashing the trunks to the ground in his wake, leaving a large trail of splintered wood and broken stumps behind him.

Dozens of sand and fly built figures stood at the edge of the desert, all of them facing the tree-line which led into the dead forest. The sand they stood on was quiet and motionless as the sandstorm lay far behind them, its wind beginning where the

Everyday Monsters

first rows of the impaled sacrifices started. The stretch of land they now stood on was the no-man's-land made of half-dirt and half-sand, the meeting place between the two extremes. The place where the heat of the desert and cold of the forest collided to form a void of both, which stretched for about a mile separating the two.

These figures all carried their bladed spears. They stood motionless, staring from their eyeless sockets toward the forest. Waiting with the same sadistic grins plastered on their crudely constructed faces.

THE MOOGLE BURST out from the tree line, onto the no-man's-land where the sand and fly figures waited expectantly.

His eyes widened as he took in the scene of the hundreds of figures in a row. All staring towards him with a cruel smile.

Emitting a loud roar, he ground to a halt – his weight and girth pushing the sand dirt upward, causing it to billow into the large plume in front of him, blocking the sight between them for a brief second before the grains fell back down to the ground.

He scanned the line of figures. All still. All staring. At him.

His breathing was loud and labored. His eyes, deep within their sockets, glared at these figures. His hair dripped onto his body, matted with sweat and blood.

As the sand fully settled to the ground, his chest slowed its heaving as he began to catch his breath.

The Moogle glanced up and down the line of the figures, who blocked his path. Considering his options. He got no scent from them, so could not be sure what they were, if anything. Normally he would not have even slowed down, as he would have discounted these things as simple statues – he would have joyously smashed his way through them. But something about this scene made him stop. Something within these statues; the flies.

Even at such a fast pace, he could hear the thousands upon thousands of flies which swarmed throughout these motionless forms.

He knew that something here was amiss. His animal instincts screamed at him to flee. Not because he needed to continue the chase. But because something here was not right.

He then cautiously considered his path. Whether to go around or through them. Before he could decide the hundreds of figures across no-mans-land -– all in perfect unison – raised their spears towards him, then lowered themselves into an attack stance.

Deep in the cavernous maw, the vampire creature sat on top of the pile of remains, crying at the above dull light, which lay too far out of reach above it.

It cried in desperation.

It cried in hopes of salvation.

It cried for the loss of its family.

It cried at this nightmarish fate.

The Moogle's claw swung through the air as he swiped at the figure who now stood in front of him. His talons ripped through its sand and fly head with great ease. But, as fast as it gouged through this attacking enemy, the sand reformed any damage within only a couple of seconds.

His other hand swung upwards, ripping through the sand of this figure's stomach. Yet again the damage caused was very short-lived. This ripped-out wound healed itself before the Moogle could even notice it had happened.

Everyday Monsters

From across the horizon, the hundreds of other figures all swarmed towards this battle, with their spears held aloft. There were no battle cries. No yells of anger. The only noise from any of them was the buzzing of the flies. The flies which surged around them with vigor.

The Moogle let out a pained roar as one of the sand spears stabbed through his tough, thick, pale skin and embedded into his side – deep through his rancid flesh.

Another sand figure hit him with the blunt side of its spear, across the back of his thick legs, the force of which sent him crashing to his knees with a thud.

All the while his arms remained slashing out at these things, as best he could. All the damage he was causing was being corrected in mere moments. He then roared as his stomach opened yelling alongside his mouth. From this kneeling position, he lunged forward launching himself – with his stomach open, ready to eat – at the figure in front of him. His stomach clamped down hard on its body.

Ripping backwards, the Moogle watched with temporary glee at the dismembered pair of legs which stood in front of him.

His gleeful expression soon dropped, as a sand and fly made hand burst out from the slit of his stomach. Then another. Both hands wrenching the stomach open with force, the pain of which seared throughout the Moogle's body.

As these sand hands opened the stomach, the severed legs stood closer and leaned their top half toward it. From within this now -open stomach the sand started to crawl out, reconnecting with its legs. Reforming into the figure it once was. All the while the Moogle screamed as the other figures took turned piercing his body with their spears.

Without any orders given, the surrounding figures then all

halted their attack, turning their intent from attacking to instead restraining the monster.

The sand and fly figure almost completely reconstructed itself, as it peered down to the now held Moogle – who roared in anger as he tried his best to break free, but these things were too numerous and too strong for even him. All he could do was scream in defiance.

Without another minute passing, the figure reached forward and yanked the Moogle's stomach mouth back open again. Its grin grew larger as it met the now-worried gaze of the Moogle.

His eyes, though deep in their shadowed sockets, for the first time since it could remember, welled with tears. Never before had he felt this level of fear or dread before, and for the first time, his mind was not filled with the need to kill, but the need to survive.

THE VAMPIRE WHIMPERED in the dark cavern of the Moogle's stomach.

Far above it, the muted sounds of the Moogle's battle could be faintly heard, though it was too muffled to discern exactly what was happening – not that the vampire wanted to know. All it wanted was to be back in its warren with its family, amongst the dead trees.

A loud piercing scream suddenly filled the chamber, as the Moogle's head – all bloodied and with rabid fury – appeared from within the light. His jaw now missing – fresh from having been ripped off from his face. His long brown tongue lolled out of this bloody wound, hanging down with blood and saliva dripping off it in a torrent. This thick plasma and spittle streamed downward and hit the vampire creature in its face – causing it to scamper backwards, terrified with a scream.

Everyday Monsters

The Moogle tried his best to roar – even despite his missing jaw. But before he could make a fraction of a sound a sharp spear made from sand and flies, came through from behind, splitting clean through his head, cleaving it open -- in half.

This fight was short, brutal and one-sided.

The mighty Moogle was bested with ease by one of the self-proclaimed Gods, the Elder who called itself the Sicarian.

This Sicarian controlled figure now stood around the dead Moogle. His head had been shoved deep within his own body, bent over double, through his stomach. His now ripped off jaw was still held in the grip of one of the figures.

The spear that was pierced through the Moogle entered from his exposed back, and sliced through and down into his stomach – deep within, where it split his head in twain.

The figures all turned away from this execution, then began their walk towards the mountain. Towards the millions of impaled dead. Towards the sandstorm, which raged as it always had and would. Each step they took sank them further and further into the sand beneath them. Bit by bit they returned to the ground. The sand and flies which built them now disappeared within the grains which made up this desert. Their bodies getting lower and lower, until the tip of their heads – the last visible part of them – vanished without a trace. The sand that built them and the flies that flew within, were no longer in this no-mans-land. All that was left, was the body of the Moogle.

The spear lodged in his head also began to fall apart. First the flies started to break free of the weapon and fly downwards -- into the sand below – then the sand of the spear started to loosen, losing any cohesion, and blew away grain by grain into nothing, on the gentle breeze which traveled past.

IN THE CAVERN deep within the Moogle, the vampire creature was on its haunches, whimpering like a puppy. It looked upward, towards the tiny amount of light that encircled the now deceased Moogle's head. The light itself had now started to fade to black. The cavern got darker and darker in seconds. Light was leaving this place and would never return. This poor creature would be trapped alive in a place of death, and now, of eternal darkness.

There was no help that could save this poor thing. There was no survival. There was no happiness left in this vampire's world. The life it had lived would now be just a memory for no one to remember. All that had known it was now also gone as would the knowledge of its very existence. The short life it had left was now sealed with a horrific fate. As the light left its last shards of decaying illumination, the darkness came to forever set in.

This creature wailed a frightened scream, and there was no one who would hear it.

THE ANGER OF THE INSECTS

Arius screamed as he lay on the floor of Yer Ana's chamber. Blood pooled out from the open wound on his back – the wound where his skin had been freshly torn from its flesh.

"Was that acceptable?" Yer Ana asked with a cackle.

In agony, with tears streaming down his face, Arius turned and watched as a sand figure held up the removed skin in his hands. Measuring a foot in width and height, this human pelt was rough along its edges where the blunt serrated knife had viciously torn it off him. The sand figure then handed the still bloody skin to Yer Ana, who reached across with her long arm, and gingerly took it -- then as she brought it closer to her, looked over to Arius.

"You amuse me, so. Pain seems to be all that people concern themselves with. They never take the time to enjoy the wonder of creation."

"Tell me... Please..." Arius pleaded with rage in his voice. "I did what you asked." He had to know the truth. He was in too deep now to back out. He had to hurry before he died. He kept thinking about the oft-repeated phrase he had told slow working employees in Amorfield, and how apt it was to him now; time to shit or get off the pot!

"You did do what I asked.," Yer Ana replied under Her breath as she reached down to Her altar and picked up a writing quill. "But what if you die before you get to write your prophecy? What if you do not have time to understand what you had asked of me before?"

Her words made him angry. She might be a God, but She was a sadist toying with him. "Just tell me!" he raged.

This made Yer Ana cackle. "The anger... So delightful when the insects of existence think they have any power to demand things from me... So amusing."

Arius clambered to his feet from the dirt floor, the blood from his back dripping down onto his trousers and trailing behind him as he walked towards this God.

"You do know that I do not have to do what you ask? I am not bound by my word like a prisoner. I do this under my own grace." Yer Ana's playful tone was now gone and replaced with sternness. "I grant those who offer to me, the power of creation itself – when it suits me. I let filth be a God for one short fleeting moment, but on my terms. So do not demand a thing."

"What else can I do?" he asked as he staggered up to the Altar and rested on it, his body weakened due to his blood loss.

She reached across towards him and placed Her large boney hand on top of his forehead. "You wish to know... I shall grant you the answers in exchange for your pain." As She spoke, Her light shone through him. The same light from inside her now beamed through his nose, his eyes, his mouth. With this, he screamed. His mind flooded with the images of the past. The images he had forgotten.

. . .

Everyday Monsters

MANY THOUSANDS of scenes raced in front of him in a single instant. The paths that were inked upon each slice of skin taken from the impaled dead outside. Each of the Catigeux symbols making a tale that was to pass with the power of this God. Each piece was part of story written by the Elders, made real by Yer Ana.

He saw his own part in this. He saw himself created by one of these skins. Created to assist in the delivering of the very offerings which he was made from. The moment he was brought into existence, then delivered to his masters to obey. They set the paths in detail upon these skins – the story of the reality they created. He saw the next hundred years play out at blinding speed. All of their requests manifested as a reality; The Order gaining power. The Order remaining a secret despite all odds – but then, the path he saw just stopped.

BACK IN THE CHAMBER, he dropped to his knees as the vision of the paths ended, the light within him cutting out as Yer Ana's touch disconnected him from her power.

Out of breath, sweating and in pain, he looked wide-eyed at the God, who now just raised Her hands up in a shrugging motion. "You all run about making lives, believing you have dominion over fate. But no matter what you do, everything ends and returns to the way it should be. All paths run out."

"Then why?" His voice cracked as he spoke, his strength almost all but gone. A darkness approached him, he could feel it nearby.

"Why do it at all?" She asked with the sickly grin returning to Her face. "Well, that is the simplest of answers. Because you always create death. No matter what. No matter the path. Death always follows. It is so fun to witness, after all – And I am so very bored."

Holding out the quill and his back skin, she dropped it in front of the altar, onto the floor in front of Arius.

"So, write your story." Her hand motioned to his torn skin as She spoke. "But you have not got a lot of space to work with... Remember though it must have balance. It must reside in both the dark and light. Most of all... Make it fun... Amuse me... Titillate your God..."

Arius had seen what had been done before for the Elders, what they had offered before. The way it had been written on each skin like a book of prose. He knew now from the visions, how the offerings worked – but he had limited time to think. He had to write. The darkness was almost here to steal away his life. He had no real time, so needed to create something for now. Something to get him out of here to consider a bigger plan.

He took the quill in his hand and moved over the skin, the open wound on his back slowly bleeding its last. His hand trembled in what he knew were his final moments.

A sand figure brought him a pot of dark red liquid in which to write with. Arius knew better than to waste time asking what this blood was. Virgin? Menstrual? It did not matter. He had to write fast.

He started his story. Each symbol written as small as it could possibly be. Improvised and panicked he steadied his resolve as best he could, to survive long enough to finish.

Deacon and Jaden stood at the foot of the large mountain in the desert. Their journey had lasted many days of walking against the wind in the boiling heat of the sandstorm. With their cooling masks and garments on, this heat did nothing to affect them, except make the journey slower.

At the base of this rock face, the wind died down to

nothing, the storm surrounding but not affecting the mountain itself. They glanced up the rock towards the clear blue sky far above.

"You're telling me a God lives here?" Jaden asked as he removed his beaked mask. The deathly decay had increased and spread over most of his face. His lack of sustenance had now taken its toll, as the zombie rot tightened his skin whilst spreading its rot over him.

Deacon soon followed by taking off his golden mask. Turning to Jaden, he noticed the effects from his lack of feeding. "We need to find you some blood," he spoke worriedly.

"Ah, I'll be fine. I'm used to it... But now... Tell me... Please... Who am I?"

YER ANA HELD the skin with the finished symbols written over it. She glanced carefully at it, reading the symbols as fast as she could. Her face lit up with the widest of smiles.

Arius was almost unconscious. He held himself up against the altar, his life nearing its completion.

She glanced down after She finished reading his offering. "This is quite a novel idea... The living dead? You just thought of this?"

Arius did not reply. She continued, "You could have made yourself anything. A God? One of their equals? But you want to be dead? And this... This path you created... It is..." She held up the skin toward him. "You offer yourself. Your own life to me? You ask for some, but offer all. This is a life of horror... So I only have only one question."

She leaned down, close to him. His strength was barely enough to keep him upright. "Why do you want to mete such torture on yourself? Not on anyone else? You will die once, then live as death, then die again, then live again... Then... Nothing... No ending that is guaranteed."

"I can't..."

"You must really despise your Elders. They create you, and you make yourself a martyr to a cause you are not sure of?"

She lifted the skin up to Her face. "At least you're clever enough to ensure you'll not feel all the pain. But that pain I take must go somewhere..."

"Somewhere?" he weakly asked.

"It is only fair... So, the deal is... This shall happen... But you must feel the pain you will not later, right... now. And that you do not feel now... You shall feel in your new reality."

His eyes widened as he heard her words. "Do I have a choice?"

"No... It is my gift to you... Feel now the lifetime of pain you were to feel..."

Her eyes and mouth burst open with Her light, drenching the skin as she held it up. Each symbol that had been intricately written now disappeared in turn as She consumed the path he requested.

As She did this, he let out a blood-curdling cry as he fell to the floor in a convulsion. His skin began ripping and reforming. On his face, the skin tore in many places. Long slivers opening up, as if invisible serrated blades ripped through it. Then the skin reformed. Healing itself. His eyes suddenly burst, then from the goo, built itself back together at speed. His heart exploded in an instant, then regenerated. His head caved in – as it was to be when the Sicarian crushed it to a pulp – then it rebuilt to what it was before. Here he experienced death after death. Cut after cut. Torture after torture. Every moment of what he was to feel later on. As much as he could take.

. . .

Everyday Monsters

DEACON AND JADEN walked into the hand-carved entrance that sat at the mountain's base. Each step they took led them further away from the madness and fury of the sandstorm, and the oncoming Sicarian

The howl of the winds still echoed down the stone corridor as they walked. This long narrow path trailed downward, laid with an uneven stone floor, with the walls carved into ever-changing Dutch angles.

Deacon glanced over his shoulder with a look of concern. The figures had not made any appearance so far. Weird, he thought. But he was not conscious last time he came here, so discounted it as just some paranoia. The Moogle though... Where did he go? He was convinced that they would die before getting here. Especially with that monster so close behind them.

Jaden was wide-eyed. Told the history of his past. A long and brutal backstory spanning many hundreds of years. Tales he could not have guessed. He was also told about Yer Ana, and Deacon's offering.

"Why did you scream when you were chopped up, then?" he asked.

Deacon stopped in his tracks for a moment as he looked at Jaden with annoyance. "After all of what you were told. That's the part you are stuck on? Not your entire history?"

"I dunno, it all seems so..." His words trailed off as he lost all cohesive thought.

"All of it doesn't matter. Only that we are on this path. You are on this path. This can be your salvation... from everything."

In this stone hallway, as the light from outside no longer reached them, the walls became adorned by sporadically placed torches carrying a blue fire.

They walked down the seemingly endless hallway, the

blue torches being their only relief from the shadows which hung between the lights, begging to escape.

Jaden was in shock. He heard his past from Deacon, as fantastical as it was. But knew it was the truth. He knew ALL of it was the truth.

A single fly then buzzed through the hallway and past Deacon's head. Noticing it, his stomach dropped. He knew that there was only one way a fly could exist here; The Sicarian.

"Quick." He grabbed Jaden's arm "We gotta move faster... She's... Here... She's fucking here!" He motioned to the fly that buzzed around.

As Jaden saw it, another flew by. Then another. He quickly came to the same realization of her arriving.

Deacon quickly picked up the pace and started into a run, with Jaden following suit. Despite him being a patchwork man made of different sized sections of body, Deacon was faster than Jaden, whose rot had slowed him down, and made his joints stiff and his muscles tighten.

The flies now swarmed around the tunnel, continuing to build in number. No matter how fast they ran, the flies seemed to keep up in a building swarm.

From within this swarm, the Sicarian had regretted being separated from his last body – the one that called herself Vix – but he had no other choice. He could not pass over to this realm within her. There would be no point – her body could not withstand the sandstorm in the condition it was in. Besides, even if it could, he could not exist within her as he crossed into the Balance. This all made him a lot slower, and significantly less powerful.

. . .

Everyday Monsters

IN AMORFIELD, Essa stood outside the room of light as the door loudly creaked open, echoing down the connecting hallways. Her arms were crossed as she looked agitated. She could see inside the room lay a mass of skin, bone and gore, which now sloughed out of the door over the stone step downwards. Behind it, a large man in black, with facial features in the wrong order swept out the remains from the room. This man's face had its mouth at the top, then nose in the middle, then eyes at the bottom. His hands were also placed left on right and right on left. With his palms facing outwards, he held a broom with his forearms crossed over themselves. This man was called Edgar. He stood as an imposing figure, nearly 7-foot-tall and barrel chested. He wore thick horn-rimmed glasses, but due to the order of his features, he had to wear them secured around the back of his head with a strap, so as to stop them falling off of him. Without a parallel set of ears to rest the glasses on, he had to make do the best he could, though, none of this stopped his positive attitude, an aspect of the man that the other workers in Amorfield loved and hated at the same time. He was the loudest guy in the room at all times, as well as the happiest – which would grate on people when it was, say, the early hours of a Wednesday morning and he would shout "Happy Hump Day!" in people's faces.

On the outside of his workroom locker, he had a small poster taped to the metal door which said You don't have to be crazy to work here, but it helps. That was the kind of person he was. Yet people still loved him despite him annoying them. He was a ridiculous light in an otherwise dark place.

"Guess this one's having a bad day?" Edgar said with a smile to Essa, as he brushed Vix's remains now fully into the hallway.

Essa just smiled back politely. Her fish features couldn't

help but looked worried at the situation – something which Edgar noticed.

"Hey, you ok?" he asked as she stared down at the guts on the floor. "If it helps, just look at this as a pile of old burger meat."

Essa heard him, but her expression did not change. She just slowly glanced from the body to Edgar – where he rubbed his stomach and licked his lips. "Yummy, yummy in my big fat tummy. I sure love burgers!" he said jokingly.

"You want to eat her?" Essa asked quietly.

Edgar's expression dropped. His lighthearted banter was not taken the way he wanted it to be. He suddenly looked panicked. "Oh Gods no. I... I was only joking... I don't eat women. I mean... Not on a Wednesday." Even in his panicked apology, as Essa stared back at him, he couldn't remain totally serious. "Shit. That's a joke as well. Doesn't matter what day it is."

Essa suddenly smirked. She knew what Edgar was like and hated thinking she'd hurt his feelings. Even through all of this, even with the anxiety her new position gave her, even with the orders the Sicarian gave her before leaving, she convinced herself to remain grounded each day – to get through everything methodically without investing too much.

"Oh." Edgar said, recognizing Essa's smile as not being mad at him. "You get it." He looked up and down the corridor. "It's ok... everyone, she gets it," he shouted.

"You okay to dispose of this?" Essa asked, changing the subject.

Edgar looked down at the mess of body remains. "This? Pfffft... This is a piece of piss. I got this."

Essa nodded with a small smile. Her arms remained folded as she turned and started to walk down the hallway.

"Uhhh Essa?" he asked.

Everyday Monsters

She glanced over her shoulder at him.

"I mean Boss... Sorry... Takes a bit of getting used to."

"What is it?"

He motioned to the body. "If you don't mind me asking. Why did this happen?"

"How d'you mean?" she responded whilst turning back to face him.

"Well... she's been... ripped apart. Why would it do that?"

"It?"

"You know... The Sicarian," he said whilst nodding toward the room of light. "Just seems a bit... cruel. He could have just left... Not done this."

Shrugging, Essa turned back to walk away. "Ours is not to question why..." she called back.

"Nope." Edgar said to himself as he looked down at the body. "Ours is but to do or die..."

He had never really understood that old adage until now. Right here, it made total sense.

The body beneath him had indeed been treated with cruelty – especially in its last moments. Her body had been ripped to tiny pieces; one last moment of sadism from the Lord of the Flies. Though Essa did not speak about it to Edgar, she knew full well what the Elder did. She had witnessed it from outside of the room. She had heard the screams as he let Vix back into her mind as he destroyed her.

"Clean up the remains after I leave," the Sicarian had said to her before stepping into the room of light.

"Can't she go where you're going?" Essa asked innocently.

"Are you questioning?" The Sicarian turned to her with a glare of annoyance.

"Of... Of course not." Essa fumbled verbally. "Clean up her body. Of course. Not a problem at all."

If the Sicarian had any time, this fish woman would have

been skinned slowly for her question. She would have then de-boned her body, with her remains eaten and passed through the bowels of the flies – all whilst keeping her alive as long as possible.

What Essa saw through the glass window on the door to the room of light, was horrific. The Sicarian's releasing the woman's consciousness which had been stuck in the prison of her own mind. Telling her that she would be let go now. Then with no pause, using her hands to rip apart her own flesh. Digging her fingers into herself and pulling out large swathes of skin and muscle without compunction. The Sicarian controlling the body, whilst her consciousness witness and then felt the pain. All of the pain.

When all that flesh that could be pulled off from her body, had been pulled off, the flies, in a quick motion, burst forth from her. Ripping her open, as she fell to the floor. Now a shell of a body, with all of her bones broken through the skin. Her skull cracked wide open, exposing her exploded brain matter. Up until the moment they broke through her, Vix had felt it all, all the immense agony forced upon her. All the panic of the oncoming darkness of death. All the fury upon her. Her last moments were helpless as she was forced like a puppet to destroy herself. Unable to control, all she could do was wait for the end. And that followed quickly.

HER EYE'S last image before the blanket of death had enveloped her, was of a fish-faced creature. One who looked through the glass door at her, mouthing the words "I am so sorry".

Essa would not let this situation affect her in front of anyone. She had to remain strong. She was in charge. She had

Everyday Monsters

to do what was asked. Even though the fate of Vix broke her heart.

Now though, walking down the hallway away from the room, she pondered her next mission. She did not know if it would end well or not. How could raising the undead army of the Order, result in anything but chaos and destruction? At least they were not to be in this world. Essa was told by the Sicarian to inform the Elders to raise them and send them immediately to the Balance. She did not know what the Balance was. And wondered why the Sicarian couldn't tell them her or himself. (Out of the female body he/she was possessing, Essa did not know what sex to refer to the Sicarian as) After all, he/she was going through the room of light, back to where the Elders were, wasn't he/she? Essa did not know that the Sicarian was not going home, but instead was going straight to the place that he/she was calling the army to. Another realm she guessed, but she did not question any more. She knew she had to be a good administrator and do what was asked.

One day she would try to find the perfect escape plan to get out of here – but today was not that day.

In the incinerator room, which doubled as his office, Edgar lifted the blue plastic sheet containing Vix's remains. Carrying them over the metal trolley in front of the furnace door. H, he thought to himself how light this body had been and how small and fragile she must have been in her lifetime. He could not fathom how she could be guilty of anything, certainly not to warrant such cruelty and violence from something that called itself a God.

Moving the blue sheet aside for a moment, he looked at Vix's mangled remains. Her face lay split in two, her chest burst open with her ribs broken outwards and her legs and arms snapped in multiple places. Placing his hand on one side of her ripped apart face, he kindly smiled. "I am so sorry," he said softly. "Sorry your journey led you to this moment. No one deserves that."

His eyes welled up with tears. "Sorry no one is here to mourn you. Sorry that no one who knew you in life is here to speak your praises."

Though the tears rolled over his chin, he kept his kind smile firmly in place, as if she could see him and he was being strong for her. "But I am here for you."

Still cradling her cheek, he sniffed – clearing his nose – and wiped away the tears with his other hand. "I will mourn you, as no one else will."

He stoked her cheek one last time, then turned and pressed the ignition button on the furnace. The fire roared to life inside. A red light illuminated above the door, as the green light next to it remained unlit: the fire on but not yet ready to consume.

"I wish I could have had the privilege to know you in life... I don't even know your name."

The green light above the furnace sparked on, as the red then faded to black. Noticing the furnace's readiness, he pulled the blue sheet back over Vix's remains. Then opening the furnace door, he pulled the trolley closer with his other hand.

"May the light lead you, my dear,." he said as he pulled her body into the flames, then shut the cast iron door behind her.

This was Edgar's way. His role in Amorfield was as the disposal operative, which in normal parlance meant body collector and destroyer. Here to remove any bodies within the complex, which were not cast into the interrogation pit – his work was to get clean up areas as if nothing had happened. He last job before this was to clean up the Moogle's latest executions, a job which took him a day to do. For each and every corpse he needed to dispose of, he would speak kind words to. He treated them, no matter who they were or what they had done, as innocents. Innocents that needed any respect and kindness before they would be turned to ashes and forever forgotten.

Edgar watched through the glass of the furnace door as Vix's body was eaten by the searing flames. The heat of the furnace was so intense that within a couple of minutes, any flesh and bone given into it would be extinguished.

Walking to the corner of the room, to where his office table was, he sat down on his chair. Leaning forward he switched on his computer's power button, then waited for it to boot up.

He glanced up to the poster on the wall; a poster which anyone could easily guess was Edgar's. It was a picture of a cat hanging from a tree branch, with the words Hang in there, written in bold lettering below. "Hang in there ol' buddy," he uttered under his breath as he read out the message.

Then, opening a squeaky metal drawer next to the table, Edgar brought out a can of cheap knock-off cola as well as an empty mug – a mug which had written on it, Edgar. He then brought out a homemade foil-wrapped sandwich. Opening the can, he poured the cola into the mug, just as his computer finished its powering on process and sprung to life.

He slowly opened the foil of the sandwich with a smile. Throughout all the horror that he endured each day, he looked forward to his lunch with glee. More than anyone normally would, but it was his sliver of normalcy in this hell.

As he took a sip of cola from his personalized mug, he then opened his emails with a single mouse click. Just as he then picked up his sandwich, the rotary telephone which sat on his desk rang loudly.

Closing his eyes, he gritted his teeth – T, trying to focus his thoughts through the constant barrage set upon him. On the third ring, he placed his mug and sandwich down, then picked up the telephone receiver.

"Hello?" he answered with his eyes remaining tightly closed. "Sure.... 2 bodies?" He then mouthed the word "fuck" silently to himself before continuing, "Of course, I'll be right there."

Hanging up the phone, he rewrapped his sandwich in its foil, then placed it back into his drawer. Moving his mouse, he then selected the power off function.

Standing up from his desk as his screen turned black, he walked slowly over to the furnace and with a forlorn look, reached up and turned the switch off – killing the roaring fire inside in an instant. Looking into the glass, he could see that the body of Vix was now gone. Disposed of by the flames.

Walking over to the door, he bent down and picked up his mop and bucket which rested beside it. Then with his free hand, opened the door and exited.

"Hang in there," he muttered to himself again. He then walked further down the hallway – slow step by slow step – away from the peace of his office, to collect more bodies for him to mourn.

Essa looked over the ledger which rested on her office desk. She held a pen lightly in her webbed hand, hovering over the blank page in deep thought. She had not written a single symbol. Not one word written to the Elders.

Her office was now a lot brighter than it was before. The executed human remains which were previously sat at the end of the room, had been cleaned up. A small sofa now sat in their place. A large fake plant sat next to it, with a floor lamp on the other side shining brightly. A white rug lay, covering the dark stone floor. Her desk had new lamps which now sat either side of its stone top. She had to make this place her own if she was to spend time here.

She glanced up, considering what she needed to write, her mind though, blank. Then looking around her office, she felt at home. Mainly as all the furnishings here were from her house. She would never have dreamed of asking for money to be spent on her – mainly as she knew that the Order would never spend money on such frivolities. They viewed comfort as a luxury rewarded, not acquired. But she knew she had to remove the nightmarish air of this office if she was to remain. She had not felt comfortable in here since the moment she was given the job. Getting Edgar to clean up this "kill room"', then requisitioning workers to leave their posts, in order to move some furniture – could have technically been looked at as an abuse of power, but it was a necessity done for the good of the company. That's what she told herself. That's what she had to tell herself.

Now despite liking this office, Her office, she could not write a word. Not one. The Army was to be raised – not that she really knew what that meant – but how was she supposed to say it?. No one had told her the proper way to inform the Elders of anything. formal? informal? Who knows?

Their Army was normally just a threat. Essa never dreamed that they were actually real. She thought that they were just something used to scare enemies and keep children obedient. She had never seen any trace of this army, though had heard the tales growing up of when, many years ago, this legion of the dead were created by the Elders to protect their realm. The stories were that the armies were to protect the Order from any human abuse. To protect them from any powers who wished to grab their powers. From the Nazis to the Mongols, the stories told that all had attacked. Yet – because of the army – none were successful. To which their defeat signaled their whole regime's collapse. The truth of the matter was then rewritten by human victors, not for any nefarious use, but as the Elders had written it to happen that way. No human could know the full truth of their existence. So they didn't and had no recourse but to rewrite the reality with stories they could fathom and understand.

According to the legend, the Order's army, made up from the bodies of the dead, lay in the wastelands of the Elder's realm. Waiting for their command. Willing to follow any orders until the moment they could return to the quiet death they had awoken from. Each of them mindless with the single focus of their mission as their only guide. There were no personal identities. No personalities. No dissention. They were just a force and a force alone. They would never have the need to rest. This is what Essa had been told, anyway. She had still never seen any evidence.

With her pen on the ledger, she decided to bite the bullet and just write what she could in the only way she could think of to do it. To follow the Sicarian's command. If the army did exist, she would soon know it.

She didn't know what to expect after she wrote the symbols. She didn't know if there would be a reply at all. She didn't even know if her request would be read. She had no choice but to ask, she was ordered to after all.

On the opposing column in the ledger, symbols slowly started to materialize. Bleeding onto the page from nowhere, like tissues soaking up blood.

These symbols simply translated as – They will rise.

AND WITH THE FLIES CAME DEATH

Jaden and Deacon moved at speed as they ran further down the large stone corridor. The flies that followed them had now fallen behind as they formed into a sand figure, which now walked slowly behind them. The Sicarian slowed in his step – not out of choice – but needed to, as the amount of sand in this corridor was limited and caused the process to take a lot longer.

Deacon knew that despite currently outrunning the flies, they were running deeper into a mountain which would have to invariably come to an end. To the place where the doorway to Yer Ana's chamber stood – he hoped. He could only guess it was here. He was only conscious in this hallway in his dreams after all.

"Thank fuck!" he rasped in relief, as he pointed to the door at the end of the hallway in front of him and Jaden. "There! We gotta go in there."

THE TREE -LINE at the end of the forest had seen very little activity for decades. The sand and fly figures annihilation of the Moogle was probably the most excitement it had witnessed since the million-people were led to be sacrificed here as offerings.

In this no-man's-land the silence hung deep. Only a slight breeze travelled though. It brushed over the Moogle's corpse. Sweeping by, lifting a couple of hairs from his blood-stained head, making them flutter with the wind. The stench emitted from his corpse being carried off into the distance with it.

When the wind chose to lull and if someone had been there to listen closely, they would have heard the faint dying whimper from the vampire, as it lay trapped deep within the Moogle.

The leaves on the trees soon began to vibrate as a rhythmical booming sound started to be heard from the distance. Something big was coming.

The trees then started to move to a strong shake as dozens upon dozens of figures sped outwards in unison. Skeletal figures – their bones all adorned with intricate carvings. Symbols of many dead languages. Symbols which spread over every single inch of every single bone in their bodies. These soldiers were only bodies though, as they all were missing any skulls. Existing as torso and limbs only, they carried ornate double-ended swords, each with two curved razor-sharp blades on both ends. These soldiers moved at an incredible speed, and in a perfect unison that they resembled a hurtling machine of many exposed parts. Each body like a piston in the makeup of this goliath.

At first there were hundreds of them, which soon gave way to thousands – many thousands. All racing through the tree-line as far as the eye could see. All in the direction of the sandstorm-filled desert.

. . .

Everyday Monsters

PANICKED, Deacon was about to open the door, but first looked behind him, then back to Jaden. FUCK! We haven't got time! his mind screamed silently. He may not have said it, but his face did.

This was supposed to be the easy part, he thought to himself.

"Your purpose... it's here. This is the end," he said as he let go of the door handle and grabbed the rucksack off his back. Opening it, he pulled out the symbol-adorned skins and looked through them. Finding the one he wanted. He placed it on top then handed the pile to Jaden.

"Get her to read this first. Before anything else. Understand?"

Jaden took the skin but did not answer. No, he didn't understand. His whole life had been unraveled. He had nothing but confusion.

"Just tell her this is the first offering, but it needs to be done NOW. At any cost. To save it all."

The flies' buzzing got louder and louder as the swarm got thicker and thicker, as it advanced on them.

"GET IN! NOW!" Deacon screamed as he opened the door behind him, then pushed Jaden inside. "PROMISE HER, HER REVENGE!!!"

Without even looking in, he slammed the door after Jaden was safely inside, then reached back into the rucksack and pulled out a machete. He knew this weapon was mostly useless against the oncoming foe, but it made him feel at least like he was taking a stand.

He waited.

Ready.

The Sicarian smirked from within the swarm, as Deacon came into view and he noticed the foolish choice of weapon.

. . .

JADEN STOOD in the chamber of Yer Ana with his expression dropped. Though Deacon had told him of what dwelled in this room, he did not really know what to expect. He knew he was to see a God. He knew they had to make the offerings of the skins to it. But when told that, he had visions of a man sitting on a cloud. Dressed all in white. With a huge long white beard – basically, he thought, this God was supposed to look like Santa Claus dressed in a robe. This reality was far, far different.

Despite Yer Ana being a terrifying creature in the past, what She had become was worse. Years of decay had set in over her. The stone floor was now blackened with mold, which carried itself up her midriff, and over her body. Her long hair was now sporadic and exposed multiple patches of a balding decaying scalp. Her complexion had been turned from a gray into a yellowing green. The light from Her eyes now much paler than before. Still shining with a light, yet now more subdued. She slumped behind the altar masked in the darkness, Her face mostly shrouded. The only other illumination in the room, came from the two blue-flamed lanterns sat on her altar.

Her long arms had been shackled by big golden handcuffs, complete with chains which ran off into large holes within the walls. These cuffs looked ancient in origin, yet despite their age were pristine– standing out in their golden splendor from the decay and mold which took over the rest of the chamber.

Is She dead? Jaden thought to himself.

As he thought, She leaned to one side, still hidden within the shadows, letting out a low moan. Her dull-lit eyes sat half-open as she sat, stolen of her previous energy.

"Who are you?" She whispered from the shadows in a weak and serpentine voice. Slow and pained, she leaned forward, into the illumination of the blue light.

Everyday Monsters

"Who... Are... You?" She spoke again weakly, yet fiercer.

"Deacon sent me... He said you have to read this immediately..."

"Who is this Deacon? Who is he to make demands of me?" She coughed at the end of this sentence. A hacking, gurgling, deathly cough. Her whole body arched up with each wet and guttural sound. Blackened drool dripped from her lungs and out onto her lips. As she wiped away the spittle with the back of her arm, the large cuffs made a clanking sound with each movement.

She reached forward, motioning for Jaden to hand Her the skins. Her fingers, each at least 12 inches long, resembled dinosaur talons. The skin over them now so old, rotting and paper-thin that she looked like the corpse. Her nails were clawed and pointed outwards. Each caked with dirt and cracked in many places.

"Hand over what you are so arrogant as to demand!" Her tone remained angry. More so with each word that was uttered. Jaden handed her the top skin, keeping the others with him. "This is the important one," he tried to say loudly, yet only managed a whimper.

She grasped it, brought it up to Her face and like a lion over its prey, smelled it with a long inhalation. The two tiny slats of nostrils on Her face opened for a brief moment as she took in the skin's scent.

"Him!" She smiled. "I have been waiting for him. Where is he? Is this all that is left?"

"We don't have much time. It's out there. The Sicarian is—"

"That!? THAT is HERE? IN MY KINGDOM?" She screamed as She roared, Her shackles clanking loudly with rage.

"You brought that THING here!" She lunged forward to Jaden.

"No!" Jaden tried to protest. "He's chasing us. Trying to stop you reading this!"

She glanced down at the skin in her hand, then to Jaden. "I have waited for years for him to complete his offering. And he brings back..." She held up the skin by the tip of her fingertips – like it was a soiled rag. "This morsel..."

Realizing he still had the other skins in his hand, he took a step forwards and placed them on the altar. "And these... He has these for you as well. But after..."

"Your God's castrated my purpose... Starved me as punishment for his first offering... Soiled then usurped my acolytes. Then you think I am so unworthy of your faith, that you insult me with a meagre handful of these offerings?"

Her long-rotted arm, reached forward to Jaden and pointed at him. "You ... You must be the one he wrote. His avatar."

With her other hand, She flicked through the skins on the altar with the back of her fingertips. She scanned them. Taking in the story written to her as quick as she could. She glanced at him a few times as she read.

The She reared up, Her two hands clasping the sides of the altar. "You were made to lead this. Like a hatchling in a wasteland, you are to face that world alone. He re-wrote your existence to this..." She spat with glee. Her show of strength though was short-lived, as Her body crumpled down and She expelled another vile and guttural cough.

OUTSIDE THE CHAMBER, Deacon was panicked. What was taking so long? he thought, as he swung his machete to the swarm of flies that advanced on him.

"Did you think you could hide from me?" the Sicarian shouted from within, as a fly-built hand lunged at Deacon from within the swarm. Unlike the sand and fly figures it used as its before, this form was now solely made of flies.

YER ANA COCKED Her head to one side with a half-grin "When he was here before, He offered me the very skin from his back. That offering was worth more than the million sacrificed innocents..."

Jaden glanced at the skin in Her hand then to the door.

"...The selfless offerings are the most beautiful... The most selfish offerings are the most tainted. But all are beautiful to taste."

"Please... I don't know what I can do... I don't know about any of this..."

Yer Ana's eyes widened, almost caring. "My sweet creation... You are lost... He created you from another's life in order to save everything. All because of who you were and what you had done..."

From outside, Deacon screamed in a rage. Yer Ana looked up towards the door with a snarl, then lifted the skin to Jaden and asked, "If I do your bidding... What do I get in return?"

Jaden remembered Deacon's parting words... "He said you'll get your revenge..."

Yer Ana glanced at the first skin more thoroughly, taking it all in. Each symbol. Seeing what was meant to be She then looked toward the door with a growing smile. "Then... He knows my needs. He knows what I will do to address the balance. We have a bargain... But you must agree to something as well..."

. . .

Deacon screamed with every swing of his blade at the forming fly figure. He could only hope that Yer Ana had not killed Jaden, but he could not predict anything.

"HURRY THE FUCK UP!!" He screamed to Jaden in the chamber behind him.

"What are you planning, filth?" The Sicarian sneered in a fury with its form now fully constructed from its insectoid minions.

"You must also do something for me... Do what I ask when I am done..." Yer Ana held out Her hand. "Accept these terms..."

Deacon screamed from outside as he battled with the Sicarian.

Jaden had no choice. He couldn't think straight. He just grabbed Her hand and shook in agreement.

"Stand aside!" the voice of the Sicarian screamed from outside.

Yer Ana released Jaden's hand, then looked at the skin as She held it up. She sneered a sickly as her eyes lit up brighter. "Very clever," she mused to herself.

The Sicarian marched forward and with a terrifying might, smashed Deacon into the wall with one of its arms, cracking his spine upon impact. His mouth erupted with blood as he collided with the stone, his patchwork stitching breaking apart in many places.

Yer Ana's eyes and mouth illuminated with light brighter and brighter as She began to consume the symbols.

Everyday Monsters

The door to the chamber then burst open – splintering off its hinges. The Sicarian's stood in its place, its fly-built body grimaced at Jaden and this God. Before it could take a step further, before it could unleash any anger upon them., Yer Ana's illuminated consumption of the skin concluded.

Going to take a step in, a shock of blue electricity erupted from the floor and blocked the doorframe, coursing through the figure's form. This shock caused it to burst apart for a quick moment in defense – the swarm breaking apart this figure, before it could reconstitute mere moments later.

"WHAT IS THIS?!" it screamed at the chained God.

She glanced at him with a grin, then lifted the skin up and put it in her mouth.

"NOOOO!!!" the Sicarian screamed.

From the floor outside, Deacon -- laying broken and bleeding – saw as Yer Ana made this offering permanent with her ingesting of the skin. As painful as it was to do, he couldn't help but laugh. He knew his time was almost up and that even though he would not witness the new world as himself, the Sicarian would not be able to stop it.

The Sicarian then turned with a renewed fury, reached down with a terrifying ease, and lifted Deacon up by his hair.

"What is this?!" he sneered at Deacon's still grinning face.

"You can never go in there... ever. None of you can... It's done," he said as blood torrented out of his mouth

The Sicarian growled as Deacon continued in a gurgle, "Send your infinite armies. Fire your universe ending weapons. Pray to every fucking God you want to make up... You will never, ever stop this... You can only sit back and watch."

The growl from the Sicarian turned into a scream.

"Fuck you, you shit-eating bastard!" Deacon yelled with glee.

The Sicarian then punched Deacon's face with such force that it crushed in on itself with ease, the bones splitting inwards and sending his brains and eyes spewing forward. Killing him instantly – a death given to him a second time by this Elder – but the Lord of the Flies was not yet finished, not by a long shot, as he ripped and gouged at the now- dead body. He tore at Deacon's arms and legs, ripping them off one by one from his torso – all as the flies swarmed around his remains, landing and feasting on them. S, slowly ingesting and breaking them down to nothing.

Jaden looked at into the hallway in terror – Whereas Yer Ana smiled at the Sicarian's fury. It had been the one to imprison Her. It had been the one to deny Her offerings. It had been the one to pervert Her acolytes. It was the one who chained and neutered Her; the God of all creation.

Bursting into the swarm of flies again, the Sicarian hurled itself at the open door to the chamber. The blue lighting appeared again and on each attack the Sicarian tried, with each attempt failing.

"We are at your beginning," Yer Ana looked down to Jaden. "The offeror is no more..." she said as she motioned outside to Deacon's corpse. "Yet his life is within the offering... He cannot rise even in the new world... Those who have passed in one realm, cannot rise in another. Their life-force already bled into the fabric of creation. Their balance addressed."

"I don't understand..."

"Your path is his path now. You are his vessel. And he has

created his life for you. In payment for taking your last life. He has gifted you rebirth. And one where your answers await. Your past and future awaits."

Jaden closed his eyes.

"You have your price to pay first. Our bargain must be paid," she said, then without hesitation moved her clawed hand up to her arm and began to cut into her skin. No blood came from these incisions, only a fine dust which crept out from her insides. She exhibited no pain as She gouged out a 6-inch square patch of skin, then peeled it off from her flesh with ease.

Laying it on the altar in front of her, she looked to Jaden.

"Here..." She said as She pushed it near to him. "You shall write my offering..."

From the back of the room. From the flies trapped outside of the doorway the Sicarian spoke. "I shall give you your own kingdom, dead man." Its rage had subsided, replaced with a fake sincerity. "I shall reward you unlike any other being in existence."

Ignoring his words, Yer Ana leaned down to Jaden. "It brought this onto me. It made me a slave, so with this this last offering – you need to redress his actions. You will write what I ask of you..."

She motioned to the quill and the inkwell which sat -- dusty and unused – on the altar next to him.

"You will write of my death. You... will save me from this living prison. Then you shall make me live forever... Then you... You can face your new existence as is written."

The Order had created a world of impossibilities and loose ends. An existence with little cohesion, where only self-gratification of their own selves was prioritized. A place where from within, you would see the world as a whirlwind of chaos.

Where the threads of journeys run and end with no meaning. For their existence was chaos. So their created reality was too.

What Deacon had written in his offering, though, was his utopia.

But any paradise has the snake hidden within.

Waiting to strike.

THE COMING DAWN

The alarm rang with a shocking volume. The repeating tones echoed throughout the brownstone townhouse, which sat in the heart of New York City.

From inside the master bedroom, the sheets covered a sleeping figure. A man who needed this alarm set at maximum volume in order for it to wake him – not that it did here.

A woman walked into this room. Essa. Dressed in an expensive and fitted black suit – a Bluetooth headset sat in her ear, as she busily talked on a call. She carried an iPad in one hand and a steaming cup of coffee in the other.

"He'll be on time. Yes... I promise!" she said as she placed the coffee on the bedside. "11a.m. Yup. I assure you. What else do you want me to say?" She then hung up the call by tapping one side of the headset.

"Wakey, wakey. Time to greet the morning," she said loudly to the slumbering figure. "Don't make me a liar, you lazy bastard."

Walking over to the large curtains, she opened as them noisily as she could. The metal hooks creating a piercing screech as they were pulled across the rail which they hung on.

The man in the bed still did not stir, he was too busy dreaming the same dream that he dreamt every night. He stood in front of a God, then struck a bargain with it. Soon after – reality changed. Then he lived someone else's life in the same body. Without a memory of his old life.

"Get up!" She kicked the side on the bed hard.

Waking with a start, the man stared wide-eyed at her in shock. The memories of the dream slipped away from his mind and lay in wait, ready to reappear the next night.

"The fuck?!" he asked loudly in rhetorical complaint to her. These were the only words he could form this soon after waking.

"Breakfast will be downstairs," she said, motioning to his cheek. "You need it…"

He moved his hand up to his face. He felt some patches of rot setting in.

"You skipped eating again, didn't you?" she asked as she then grabbed the cup of coffee from the bed-side table, and handed it to him.

"You've got 30 minutes," she said as she turned and walked out of the room.

Taking a sip of his coffee, he pressed the power button on the remote control from the sideboard. The TV sprung to life as two newscasters talked about the latest tragedy; a school shooting. A terrible, but seemingly increasingly common occurrence. The human male newscaster spoke softly as he detailed the tragedy surrounding those who had died. The female newscast sat next to him – with her green scaled skin, pointed ears and wide razor-toothed mouth – trying to fight back the tears as she spoke. Trying her best to remain professional.

He turned off the TV with a sigh.

The clock tower in the city square rang 11:45a.m. Essa opened the door to the limo parked in front of the bookstore. A baying crowd of fans waited patiently outside, all of whom clutched various books as they waited for the man in the car to make his appearance.

"Mr. Sorbic? Can I have your autograph?" pleaded one fan, holding a book and a pen towards the man as he stepped out of his car.

"Of course," he replied, smiling at her, taking her offered items. "What's your name?" he asked, getting the pen ready over the title page.

"Dawn..." she said meekly.

"Deacon, we've gotta go," Essa interrupted, as she saw the book owner in the store window, beckoning them inside.

"Once second..." Deacon said as he wrote "To Dawn, you are my kind of monster, best wishes, Deacon Sorbic."

The small fan looked at him in awe. Her eyelids blinked rapidly from left to right like a lizard's.

The other fans then moved in, all shouting requests at him.

"Deacon!" Essa demanded sternly.

Deacon then turned to her with a grin. "Fine! Let's go." He motioned for her to walk in before him.

"I'll see you all inside!" he said aloud to his fans.

A large poster adorned the inside window display. It featured Jaden, looking very healthy, without any of the decay he previously was a frequent victim of. It said

TODAY ONLY

THE BESTSELLING AUTHOR OF

"THE FALL OF THE ORDER" AND "THE CHANGELING"
DEACON SORBIC
SIGNING HIS NEW NOVEL
"EVERYDAY MONSTERS"

The owner walked up to Essa and Deacon as they entered the store. "By the grace of Yer Ana, you're here, finally!"

"By the grace of morning coffee, you mean?" Deacon replied with a grin.

FOR THE FEW fleeting moments within his recurring dreams, he saw his past life. His past self as Jaden, and before that. His unknowing of who he was before. But that reality quickly disappeared each and every morning – leaving him with vague ideas, flashes of events, slight recollections. It was these vagaries which he chalked down to his own imagination; things he would then put into his writing. It was these dreams of his last reality which made him the successful author he was today.

In his books, he wrote about the past life he dreamt of – He never knew that everything written down was, in fact, true. It all happened.

He would never remember that he granted Yer Ana Her request to live forever. That he gave her an eternal existence within the hearts and minds of humanity and monsters alike.

But he did not know of what was to come. He was blissfully unaware...

He only knew that he was Deacon Sorbic. Successful novelist. Part of humanity...

A normal zombie.

An everyday monster...

Printed in Great Britain
by Amazon